Bonded in the Dark

Samuel Niland

Contents

Chapter 1

J za covered herself in glass fragments as another window burst. Once more raising her head, she was horrified to discover her priceless library in ruins. Glass and parchment were all over the place, and some bookcases had been torn apart by the force of the explosion outside. Jza was shocked to see that one of the page boys she had been using to assist her gather books was now pinned beneath a damaged bookshelf.

She swiftly hurried to assist him after gathering her skirts.

She reassured the terrified youngster, who was fighting back tears, "Don't worry, I'll get you out." Lifting such a big object would have been agonising for a typical princess, but Jza wasn't your typical princess. She had endured a hard life as a farm worker for the first thirteen years of her life, not even knowing that she was a princess. Her tolerance for manual labour was still far higher than that of her half sisters even after so many years.

Jza picked up the black wood, unconcerned that the splinters would stab her hands. With each motion of his body, the child drew himself out of the hole. Jza let the broken shelf fall in a heap as soon as he was out of the way. Paper fragments and dust were scattered around.

Jza heard someone running into the library as she was assisting the boy up while hearing their loud footsteps. When she turned around, she was relieved to see that it was one of her father's men rather than an adversary. Nowadays, every shadow was to be seen as a serious menace. Who knew when someone would break into the fortress.

The dusty footman cried, "Princess Jza, Thank God you're safe. Your father has been hurt, and we're planning to move him to Goridon castle."

Jza couldn't help but ask the first thing that came to her mind, "Is he expected to live?" She was utterly terrified to even consider having to lead the fight without her father. All hope would be lost if he were to disappear.

The footman calmed her with a weary grin, but it was still a smile. We must leave this castle because the enemy has broken through the first line of defence and the second is also teetering. We cannot take the chance of the Royal family being taken prisoner.

She said, "Good Lord," and thought of the boy she was supporting. "Please take care of him; I have to attend to my father right away," she said, holding the boy forward in front of the man. "His leg has been injured."

She hurried towards the hospital, relieved to see that it had not yet sustained serious damage. Every nook and cranny was occupied by wounded soldiers. While some were unconscious, others were screaming in pain. She quickly made her way through the mob and went inside the royal hospital. She was profoundly troubled by the sight of her father, who appeared terribly silent and pale. Jza's half sisters and step mothers were also in the room, and she noticed that they were all the quietest she had ever seen them. Jza stood motionless in a corner of the room in an effort to obtain a good view at the King because she had enough sisters to occupy the entire space. His chest and head were both wrapped in bandages, and she could tell by his paleness that he had lost a lot of blood.

Samuel is trying to say something, so please be quiet, said one of her stepmothers.

Then, as everyone drew closer, one of the women gasped, "He's calling for Jza."

Jza was startled by the intensity of the looks all the females in the room were giving her. While some of them were genuinely nasty, others were just interested. She had never truly fit in with the women of the King's family, even after five years of living with them. Only two of her twelve sisters thought she was important enough to talk to, while the others either ignored her or resented her. Even though her life in the Royal family wasn't perfect, Jza wouldn't trade her new family for everything.

One of her stepmothers sternly beckoned her forward, "Come on girl, what are you waiting for," and Jza hurried to her father's bedside.

She tenderly replied, "Yes, father," as she clung to his hand. He turned out to be considerably more active than he had appeared to be from across the room, which gave her considerable relief.

The King spoke as loudly as he could, "I wish to be alone with Jza," and Jza could imagine the immense humiliation and dread the other women in the room were experiencing.

The eldest half-sister urged her father, "Surely, we can hear whatever you want to tell Jza. After all, we too are your flesh and blood."

I hope you will heed my plea. "No, darling, what I have to say is for Jza's ears only."

Jza raised an eyebrow as soon as the women left the room, nursing their bruised egos. They don't really think much of me anyway, so why must you continuously persist on favouring me in front of them like that?

The King smiled at his favourite daughter but wheezed, "There are far greater things in store for you. What my other twelve daughters think of you is not that important anymore."

Jza teased, "Far greater than being a Princess."

The King attempted to stand up while nodding, but he didn't seem to be able to. Jza offered to assist him in getting up, but he waved his hand in rejection.

The King explained weary, "As you know, Lord Tarquin's soldiers are upon us. My men, though courageous, cannot hold them off any longer, therefore I've given orders to evacuate the castle.

Jza smiled melancholy and nodded, "I've heard." Their predicament was quite bad because evacuation had always been their final resort.

The King said, "We shall use the southern tunnels to leave quietly in the dead of night," and Jza realised what he wanted from her.

She quickly added, "And I'm supposed to organise my sisters for the trip and be in charge of them. King gave a nod.

"My thirteenth daughter, you are the only one who has the mindset to accomplish this, but it is with a heavy heart that I must tell you that my daughters are not going with me."

Jza asked, his eyes wide with confusion, "But where shall we go if not with you, Father?"

The King paused and looked adamant, "To a far safer place, Jza. Goridon too shall fall once Tarquin lays his eyes upon it and I cannot let him get to my daughters. Fortunately or unfortunately, all of my other daughters have made a name for themselves in the country. They are so renowned for their beauty and talent that my sources tell me even a man like Tarquin, so isolated from society, knows about their existence. They are naive and too ignorant to understand what it is to be the spoils of war. I neither want my daughters to be slave to such a man nor to be used as a bargaining chip.

"While twelve of my daughters chose to become so renowned in whatever talent they chose to pursue, I did always wonder why my thirteenth chose to stay away from the limelight. Even now, people refer to the twelve princesses as the ideals of beauty and don't even remember the thirteenth. You certainly aren't lagging behind your sisters. After all, you do have my face and eyes."

Jza laughed at her father's arrogance. He had always been aware of his attractiveness.

Jza looked down at her filthy, bloody hands and said, "You very well know I never grew accustomed to being treated like a Princess. People offer me regard and respect that I never deserved.

The King gave her a tender stroke on the head and said, "But you have earned it. Out of all my daughters you are the one who has earned it the most. My warriors are a dirty bunch when it comes to talking about women, yet you are the only one they talk about with genuine respect.

Perhaps it's because I was the only archer to beat the Major in that competition, and it happened to be a woman. That got people's attention, even if the Major was only preoccupied with himself and his own self-worth at the time, Jza said. Her wistful grin abruptly vanished.

We were talking about how you were going to get away from Lord Tarquin, Father, so stop attempting to dodge my inquiries. You are a master of diversion.

The King groaned, "I could never trick you, Jza. "I damn Tarquin to the seventh depth of hell for the great injustices he is doing to my country. He knows I have no direct male heir to the throne. He could have asked one of my daughters for marriage and he would have had much easier access to the throne. I would have probably said yes since he is rumoured to be quite rich and handsome. Now, my only prayer is that they don't see him.

Jza, shocked at the news, questioned, "Have you met him?"

The King shook his head angrily. "I was invited to his coronation. A devilishly fine young man he was even at seventeen. I knew his country would prosper under his iron fist. What I didn't know was that the small princely kingdom would grow so well that it would threaten our very existence in less than ten years. I would admire the man if he weren't such a blood thirsty fiend.

Where else must we go, according to Jza, who was anxious.

The King didn't respond to her; instead, he removed a gold locket from his neck and gave it to Jza.

The King murmured cryptically, "In your hand lies the key to your safety."

Jza asked while looking at the locket.

The King murmured, "You recall me telling you about meeting a gateway maker once?

"Yes, and I distinctly remember telling to not dabble in such nonsense," Jza murmured sternly. Although magic and mysticism were not the province of her country, her father was still entranced by the charms that the various touring parties carried with them. Although it was a waste of time for a realistic girl like Jza, she could not ignore the strength of the belief.

The King said sheepishly, "Well, yes; I decided it was highly worthwhile to invest in one."

"So this key opens a portal that will take you to a place in another realm," you say.

The only way to link two different realms is through the key in your hands. Give it to Raymond; he is the only man I trust to take care of my daughters. Remind him to tell him that he must not enter the portal at all costs; the key will be lost to us if he does.

Jza exclaimed in a flash of clarity, "If it is big enough for all of us then why aren't you coming with us, Father, we could get away from this wretched war."

I am the King of this land, and I cannot abandon my people in their hour of need. I have sworn it and I am bound to this pledge. Even if I hadn't, I still couldn't go. I shall lead my people through this conflict until the day I die.

Jza was in a bad mood. Though she secretly resented her father's arrogance, she understood deep down that doing the right thing was the right thing to do whether or not he was bound by his pledge. A person who was bound to a pledge was unable to violate it at any time. Most rituals, including weddings, coronations, and apprentice graduations, featured vows that included the promises. Although it was becoming archaic, many people still had a hard time believing in someone who hadn't linked to a commitment.

A blood-splattered guard sprinting inside the Royal hospital broke her solitary agony.

The guy trembled nervously, "Your Highness, The second line of defence has broken. We must act now or we shall have to bear the brunt of the enemy forces."

Jza got up, yelling at the man, "Guard, start clearing the infirmary now; these men are the most vulnerable." She didn't stop until she noticed that both of the men in the room were looking at her. Giving instructions in the presence of her father, the King of this realm, who was still somewhat healthy and sane, was rather inappropriate.

Jza remained mute till she realised her father wasn't joking, "Oh, why did I even think I needed a son to rule this country when my daughter is enough," The King laughed, "Go on, guard; listen to her.

The Princess is now the second in command." She soon completely forgot about the man and began to plan her escape. Halfway in the tunnel, the numerous nobles who had gathered at the castle were already there. She planned a more secure path for the staff and the wounded soldiers to take through the fortress.

The guard pleaded, "And what about the Princesses; they still aren't ready to move, and they intend to take so much luggage through the tunnel that it shall be harder to move for the other survivors."

We need to carry the King, so leave them to me and send 10 of your best and strongest soldiers my way.

The King laughed as the guard walked away, "Yes, yes, talk about me like I'm just luggage." Jza gave him a cheek kiss while stooping. The King gripped her hands tightly as tears brimmed his eyes.

The King pleaded with Jza, "Promise me, Jza, that you will take care of yourself and your sisters, Promise me."

Jza wanted to cry when she saw her father's pathetic state. "I promise, Father," she pleaded.

They learned that their soldiers were here when they heard a knock on the door. Quickly entering the room, the men assisted their King in transferring to a wheelchair. She gripped her father's hand tightly.

She said goodbye, "Be safe, Father," not knowing if she would see him again. He returned her smile before leaving. In the room by herself, she wondered what the castle would look like if the residents were gone.

Jza left the hospital but was unable to spot anyone. Without the vitality that the numerous nobility, servants, and warriors brought to the castle, it would have been a terrifying place. As she ascended to her sisters' bedrooms, her steps reverberated. Major Raymond appeared to have disbanded his station as she scanned the area for any traces of him.

She heard voices as she rounded a corner. She ducked low as a protective reaction to see who the people were. Possibly, the enemy was already inside the fortress. She was relieved to see Major Raymond, but the man who was with him was unknown.

The unidentified male said in a clipped accent, "And you say that the castle has been evacuated."

Yes, regrettably, though I am positive that the Princesses never entered the tunnel, Raymond answered with a crooked grin.

The unidentified man mumbled in a slimy manner, "You mean to tell me the twelve famous beauties are still in this castle; did their father mean to appease us by offering his daughters?"

Do you want to check on the Princesses in their rooms? 'I doubt so; the old coot usually has a card up his sleeve and he didn't care to inform me of his latest games', Raymond growled.

It would be wonderful to find such diamonds among the treasure. I suppose Lord Tarquin will arrive in a few minutes. Once he is sufficiently situated, we can begin the search for the missing Princesses.

Jza gaped at the two men's retreiving backs. She never in a million years thought Raymond would end up being a traitor. She instantly rose from her hiding place and dashed towards her sisters' apartment on the second level, disregarding everything that was appropriate for a Princess like her.

She was surrounded by her sisters and barraged with inquiries the moment she opened the doors to their rooms.

Why do you appear even worse than usual? "I can't find my hair brush," you're asked.

I need you to obey commands just once, so be quiet; there is no time for inquiries.

The oldest half-sister said indignantly, her feathery hair for once in her life in total disarray, "Who are you to order us around like this?"

Jza paused again, unable to speak further due to the ferocity of her sisters' cries of panic. "Our father left me as the second in command and that gives me complete command of this castle. I shall ask you to honour his wishes for once," she said, running a hand through her brown hair that was blown in the wind. Jza inhaled once more before taking a look inside the locket her father had given her. It actually did have the literal key to the gateway.

The key had complex swirls all around it and was made of solid gold. As she struggled to find out how to operate it, she glared at it and muttered an expletive. Her keen eyes saw a text hidden within the swirls. When she realised these were directions, her eyes widened.

She gave them another read and felt they were reliable. Her sisters were frantically circling, snatching their most priceless possessions, and shouting uncontrollably while yet being fully unaware of what Jza was doing. Jza would have chuckled at the chaos if things weren't so bad. She had no idea when the opposing forces may burst through the doors.

Jza wished fervently that the promised door would materialise in front of her as she waved the key anticlockwise and quietly breathed phrases from a long-forgotten tongue.

An actual wooden door was present in the room's centre when she opened her eyes. Her sisters all let out a collective gasp at the bright brightness around it. The gold lock unlocked without difficulty as the key slid in. She opened the door and brilliant light poured out. Jza attempted to look inside, but all she could see was the enigmatic light.

Jza turned back and tried to explain, "Father built this portal for us so we can get to safety in times like these."

One of the girls shouted up, "Does it lead to somewhere safe?"

There is no time to argue about this, so act quickly, sisters. The adversary might be at the door as we speak. Father says so; I believe we should trust his judgement.

The sisters decided to enter the portal out of fear of being taken by the enemy. The sisters ascended the doorway into the light one at a time. They clung to each other's shoulders in an attempt to appear unfrightened, but they failed horribly. The final person to approach the doorway was Gabrielle, who was the second youngest of her half sisters. She turned to face Jza, who was observing the horrific battleground outside from the window. Even though the fires were still raging, the air felt strangely silent. It appeared that the adversary had triumphed.

The sister pondered, "What's going to happen to us in there?"

Jza walked over to Gabrielle, who was starting to appear foggy in the soft light coming through her hair. Jza murmured, "I don't know." She grabbed the blonde's hand and gave it a final squeeze as a sign of goodbye. When Gabrielle realised what was going to happen, her eyes widened.

She exclaimed, covering her face with her hands, "You aren't coming with us."

Jza closed the door after shaking her head. When she bolted the door, it disappeared by itself. She pulled the chain down her long brown hair until it rested on her breast and put the key back in her locket, saying, "I can't."

Jza collapsed to the ground, exhausted beyond belief. The notion of the enormous responsibility resting on her shoulders made her quake. If she was ever taken prisoner, how could she defend her sisters? What if she failed to perform as required? If something happened to them, she'd never have to look her father in the eye again. If her attempts failed, she didn't even want to live.

Jza was aware that she had a chance to stay undiscovered inside the castle. She was familiar with it and it was big and complicated like a maze, but she could not undervalue Lord Tarquin. What if they succeeded to kidnap her and torture the information from her? Jza was more concerned about stumbling in the face of difficulty than she was about being persecuted.

Jza considered suicide but dismissed the idea after glancing at the knife on the fruit basket that was center-placed on one side table. Her passing would result in the loss of her sisters for all time. She did stand up to remove the knife out of the red apple, but it wasn't for self-immolation; it was for defence.

She suddenly recalled what her father had said about vows binding people together as she experienced a flashback. Jza paced as she made an effort to remember details she had learned over the years. She was aware that the bound could never break their commitment but wondered if this was due to physical impossibility or fear of suffering unknowable, severe consequences. Jza was unable to recall any evidence supporting such a theory.

Jza slid her eyes shut. She made her decision in a flash of startling clarity, and immediately some well-known words sprang from her mouth. "Give me strength," he said, "and I will keep my sisters safe at all costs, just as I have promised heaven above, that I will fulfil my duty as thou hast prescribed until I lay at thy altar of death."

She could feel the light bursting into the room even with her eyes closed.

Jza was awakened at that very moment by the sound of numerous footsteps entering the room next to hers. Jza immediately crouched down behind one of the sofas, cursing herself for staying in the Princesses' chambers when she knew full well that this was the first area the enemy intended to check. The enemy soldiers had finally come.

She was surrounded on all sides by the sofa, which was shoved up against the wall. As the men explored the room, she overheard obnoxious groans and noises of things shattering. One man got close enough, but he decided to kick the sofa in the direction of the wall. She was struck in the forehead by a sticking piece of wood that was concealed in the upholstery, but she refrained from screaming in agony.

Jza carefully waited for the action to quiet down while holding her head up. She snuck out of her hiding position as she realised there was no longer any presence in the room. Due to the hour, the living room was darker, but she was still able to move around in it in the dim light. Despite almost falling over a vase that had fallen on the floor, she made it to the Princess' chambers' central, tiny passage. A powerful hand clutching her own pulled her hard backward just as her hand was about to grasp the handle of the main entrance that led out to the rest of the castle.

Before she could utter a cry, the attacker forced his other hand over her mouth and used his whole weight to push her against a wall. He was too powerful for her to escape, despite her best efforts. She finally gave up after seeing that her efforts had been completely ineffective. She became aware that she was staring into a man's amber eyes who was standing close by as her vision sharpened.

Chapter 2

J za rolled her eyes as the energy of the battle left her. It's over, she believed.

Although she was aware that her prospects of surviving in a castle that the enemy had taken over were minimal, being apprehended so quickly and with such ease was upsetting.

The man asked in a plainly foreign accent, "Who are you?" They lost the meagre chance that he might be one of their own men.

Jza blinked open her eyes to look at the man. He had leaned in so closely that she was only able to feel his breath on her face and could hardly see anything past his eyes. It was absurd that he expected her to speak with such an obstruction while holding a firm hand over her mouth. Jza understood that even if she had complete mouth freedom, she would still remain silent since too many people depended on her.

The man tightened his hold even further. Her mouth began to hurt beneath the pressure as her wrist was brutally pinched. The fruit knife she had tucked away in her free hand was her only hope. Small in size, the knife had a gold-gilded handle. It was so little that it could easily fit inside a person's palm when it was closed into the handle. Although the knife's supposedly sharp edge was dull and small enough to simply cut fruit, this feature made it simple to conceal. Jza was concerned that any offensive it launched might be totally ineffectual.

Though Jza attempted to free it, the man and her body prevented her from doing so.

The man asked slowly, as if she could not understand, "I repeat, who are you?" Jza sensed that his menacing eyes were enveloping her as he drew in even closer.

Jza decided that enough was enough and chose the only option open to her. He got her hand bit.

When the man hissed and immediately drew away, Jza seized the chance to liberate herself. She pulled on her imprisoned hand so ferociously that it appeared as though she was prepared to abandon her arm if it enabled her to flee. After successfully escaping, she fled out the door in a flurry of skirts.

With all the energy she could manage, she raced without so much as glancing behind her to see if her abductor was still pursuing her. She felt herself slowed down by her soft slippers and cursed them, wishing she was wearing her more sturdy boots.

Jza mentally weighed her options as she ran in the direction of the east. The guest rooms and the entertainment spaces were located to the east. She instantly recalled the ballroom and how the cooks were accessible from there. The stairway that the servants used was on one side of the ballroom. If she descended the stairs, she could access the kitchens and even leave the castle, but if the enemy was already in the kitchens, she may head for the attics. They were huge spaces stuffed to the gills with royal junk. Most likely, the enemy would be discouraged from examining them simply by looking at their dusty, cobwebbed countenance.

As Jza approached the hallway with the door to the ball room, she paused and peered around. In an effort to blend into the background, she knelt down against the wall and shuffled gently in the direction of the door. She sighed in relief as she reached the big space. There was still a chance that she would discover her sanctuary.

One of the bigger chambers in the castle was the Ball Room. The walls featured grooves in the panelling that were gold plated, and the floors were white marble, in contrast to the rest of the castle. The priceless stone hanging from the chandeliers accentuated the room's opulence. When the torches were lit, the stones' reflections caused the chamber to shimmer throughout. She was happy to recall her own debut Ball in this space.

The space at that time was a mere shadow of what it once was. There were pieces of furniture scattered throughout, the enormous windows were broken, the drapes were torn, two of the chandeliers were broken and laying on the floor. Jza crossed the room gently as she sobbed at the harm done to her house.

She was so preoccupied with her thoughts that she was unaware of anyone else's presence until a hand came down hard on her shoulder.

A voice teased her from behind, saying, "Look, what we've got here, a lost lamb in the middle of so many wolves."

Quickly pulling back, the hand essentially ended her chances of fleeing by whirling her around. The man was too powerful to let go of the hands that were holding her shoulders.

Just one glance at her new captive made it clear why. Jza was half as wide as the man, and she was just slightly taller than him. Even though he was dressed in conventional military garb, the man's powerful muscles were clearly visible. Jza was held for the second time, and this time she felt even more useless.

She glanced away in disgust at what her captor's smile suggested as he peered down at her with a wolf-like smirk.

Her face was pulled up and back towards him as he gripped her chin.

"What are you doing over here, little lamb? Have we lost our shepherd?"

Jza attempted to wrench her face away from the man's hands, but she felt that doing so would be like attempting to push against a wall. He had one hand on her face and the other on her shoulder, leaving her hands free, and she attempted to shove him away with her fists.

The soldier merely grinned.

You won't be able to escape this wolf's clutches, feisty little lamb.

He caught hold of her hair and jerked her back as she kicked him on one of his legs. He nearly lifted her off her feet by pulling her head backward, which caused her to arch her back.

His blue eyes flashed as he hissed, "Not the best of ideas, lamb."

Jza stared back, "Let go of me," but instead of infuriating the man more, she brought back his giggle. Jza's focus was once again on the knife she had her fingers clasped. A small cough from behind interrupted her as she was about to raise her fist.

Vladimir, have you caught my prey?

Her captor immediately released her, and she immediately fell to the ground with a flare of her skirts. She ignored the pain in her ankle from the fall and sat back up, bracing herself for the possibility that she would have another opportunity to go. Jza was not the type of girl to trust fate with her life. She was going to find freedom if there was any possibility at all.

The enormous man bowed gravely and said, "My Lord," which attracted her attention because of the respect he showed the newcomer. Although Jza understood the majority of the population would have been smaller than the man she now knew as Vladimir, the man was smaller than her current captor. She thought it strange that Vladimir's supervisor was a man who was considerably younger than him.

The Lord had light brown hair that was tangled with various tones of light and dark. He had pronounced cheekbones and a pale, slender face. His most remarkable trait was his eyes. They were brown with swirls of various hues that, in the fading sunshine, reflected as amber. They had a very little unique slant to them that was unusual in Jza's region of the country. Jza noticed the other man via his eyes, and her eyes widened.

Her garment was caught by the back, but her feet refused to obey as a hand pulled her up.

As he tried to make her bow like a mannequin, Vladimir repeated, "Bow, to your new King; Lord Tarquin," but she resisted. She was placed back on the ground after he eventually gave up.

Despite having a low voice, Jza muttered, "I will never bow in front of your false king." She felt as though the crumbling Ballroom echoed her words. She screamed when she felt a solid thump kick her in the stomach. Jza slid over, gripping herself in agony.

The voice of the Lord reached Jza through the agony, "Vladimir, is this how you treat a young lady?" The words don't give the impression that the tone was stern. The speaker couldn't have given a damn about Vladimir's treatment of young women; it was callous and passive.

Jza was still lying on the ground, trying to get her stomach to stop hurting so much. In an effort to mask how weak she felt, she gulped her watery eyes.

The Lord pulled her face up by her hair, "If I remember correctly, we still have a conversation to finish." The question "Who are you?"

Jza was unable to physically turn away, but her refusal to respond to the man's query was evident in her eyes. She was raised higher by the man before being seated once more.

With his blue eyes gleaming, Vladimir questioned, "Is she one of the Princesses?"

The Lord said, "No," after continuing to examine Jza's face. The man lifted Jza's hand and looked at it, "She looks nothing like how they're described; No blue eyes; fair hair; not 'breathtaking to behold' as the bard's song goes." She also has hands that are not as smooth as those of a lazy princess.

Jza considered it a minor accomplishment that she had kept her identity a secret. It would be just as terrible if she was thought to be a princess as if all her sisters had been taken prisoner. One Princess alone was valuable enough to be used as a negotiating tool.

Although Vladimir appeared dejected, the subsequent few words significantly improved his mood.

The Lord turned away to look around the room, entirely uninterested in what was going on. "Take her, Vladimir. Get more information out of her," he said.

Vladimir smiled at her and drew her up again, saying, "With pleasure, Lord Tarquin."

Jza fought, "Let go of me, I demand it."

Again saying, "Wait," was the man behind them. Vladimir whirled around, spinning Jza with him while her skirts moved naturally in sync.

You are not a member of the Royal family, but I don't believe you are a commoner; possibly you are a nobleman's daughter.

Jza turned her head away, embarrassed that she may have given the man a better idea of who she is.

Vladimir muttered, "Speak when the Lord bids you to speak," but there was no response.

The younger man moaned, "Take her away, Vladimir," upon observing Jza's steadfast attitude.

Jza was once more compelled to retreat towards the Ball room's exit. Jza attempted to kick Vladimir once more, but she was suspended in the air and resting like a sack of potatoes on his shoulder. She pounded the man's back with her hands and tried to rip off the collar of his shirt, but it didn't appear that her attempts had any effect on his pace.

When they arrived at the entrance to what Jza recognised as the dungeons, he just laid her down. Nearby, two men in strange clothing were seated on a bench.

One of them smiled and said, "What do we have here, Commander Vladimir?" as they all laughed at her.

She shrugged off Vladimir's arm as he said, "The spoils of war; I told you the end of this war would be fruitful for us. Well, here is my fruit for the day."

Jza tried to turn aside when one of them wolf whistled in order to restrain herself from lunging at the man with her knife. She still held the weapon in her hand, waiting for the appropriate moment to draw it. She didn't have the best chances with four men and a knife. She resolved to control her rage as long as no one put bodily harm on her, and she prayed to the gods that she would manage to escape unharmed.

She was carried by Vladimir into a dungeon chamber. After almost tripping over something, she turned around to see what it was. She saw that it was Raymond's body, and her eyes widened. It had a cut in his throat and was lying face up with its wings spread. Jza was shocked to see how much blood had spilled from it, covering the ends of the gown that swept the ground. Jza noticed her feet swaying.

Vladimir scoffed at the corpse, "We don't trust em traitors. Once a traitor always a traitor.

Jza bit her lip and turned her head away from the pale, bloody face of the deceased. It was clear that he had not anticipated being attacked. Jza was aware that his visage would persist in her recurring nightmares.

Once more holding her by the waist, Vladimir pulled her up and placed her properly on a nearby desk. Jza observed him weary and waited for him to act as he pulled up a chair for himself. She was on the verge of cringing at the following strike as she waited on edge. Her body had become accustomed to taking a battering whenever she made a mistake.

Never in her life had she had a touching moment like this. She was treated with the appropriate respect even in the early years when she resided at the farm because she was still the farm owner's niece. She was periodically spanked for being mischievous, but those beatings were mild in comparison to the fury she was currently experiencing.

Jza's comfort level with boys was much greater than that of other aristocratic women because she had spent some years as a youngster playing and wrestling with boys her age before being rigorously forbidden by her nanny because she was too old for such antics. But since she had been living in the palace for some time, her only interactions with men had been her father's pat on the head and a kiss on a gloved hand. She was now disgusted by the unwanted physical contact she was having with her kidnappers. Jza's insides were about to collapse from the innuendos being flung at her, but she was determined to maintain her composure. Never would they succeed.

Tell me, are you a noble's daughter. "Princess or a Pauper; I don't think I could care less but the Lord gets what he wants."

Jza turned her head aside as she gripped her knife tightly.

When the man pounded his fist against his desk, she backed away.

She was bombarded with inquiries, such as "Tell me, where are you from, have you always lived in this castle, and where are the twelve princesses," and she bit her lip in an effort to hold back her speech.

Vladimir quickly got out of his chair, grabbed Jza by the shoulders, and stood up. Spit hit her face as she yelled "SPEAK!"

Jza was indignant, glaring back at the man whose face was inches from hers, "Never," she said. She hoped he wasn't able to sense her shaking.

Vladimir grinned at her and said, "Fine, then we'll have to do this the difficult way." When his hand reached one of her sleeves, it tore the translucent, plum-colored material. Jza attempted to escape from where she was, but Vladimir's arms appeared to be made of stone.

He moved further closer before inhaling into her hair. Jza wrinkled her nose at the smell of burning and blood coming from him, "Sweet as a rose."

Jza screamed, "Stop," in a voice that was both an order and a sob. It was heartbreakingly clear how frail she was. Despite the fact that his presence fully engulfed her, she still managed to kick despite a tear running down her cheek.

You think you can stop me, or what?

The knife unfolded with a click of a little trigger as the Princess was reminded once more of its cold presence in her grasp.

He was stabbed in the neck by Jza.

She heard the enormous guy cry out in agony as he fell to the ground. He attempted to remove the knife, but Jza jammed it deeper into the pocket with her foot before he could. He growled again in anguish at this action. Jza hurriedly searched the area, fearing the man would overcome his discomfort and stand up.

She turned around in search of a different weapon and was delighted to spot a sword hanging on the wall. The sword served as a remembrance of her great grandfather's victory over the brutal barbarians a century earlier. They had this castle taken from them, and the dungeons were where the former owner of the castle had been put to death by the ruling monarch of the time. Jza was shocked by the sword's weight as he removed it from the wall mounting. She found it difficult to lift, and ultimately concluded that dragging it to Vladimir would be a much better choice.

As soon as she was close to the lying man, she mustered up the effort to lift the tip and lay it on his stomach. Vladimir expanded his eyes.

Jza snorted, "Yes, I can stop you."

He croaked again, this time with wonder in his voice, "Who are you?" A man like him, in her imagination, would never have dreamed that he would be at the other person's sword with a woman holding it.

As the door squeaked open, Jza raised his head. I was expecting the damsel to be in trouble, but instead I appear to have discovered one of my best men at her mercy.

Lord Tarquin appeared just as composed as when he left them earlier as he leaned against the door frame. Even now, he seemed less concerned and more amused.

Jza said as she raised the sword and pointed it at the lying man, her adrenaline finally allowing her to do so because of the increased risk. "Do not come any closer or I shall drive this through your heart," she commanded.

The Lord raised an eyebrow and said, "Oh, and what makes you think you can stop me?"

"The very same thing was said to me by the fact that this man had a knife in his neck."

Chapter 3

L ord Tarquin smiled widely.

"Did he?" The man sauntered into the room unconcerned about the girl wielding a sword in front of him.

Jza was straining under the weight of the sword. She tried to look unconcerned by the excessive force on her arms but it was getting harder to keep the effort from her face. A lone bead of sweat darted down her forehead.

"Yes, do not underestimate me." Jza threatened as she subtly brought her other hand up to help her keep the sword up. The muscles in her right arm were already burning from the endeavour of keeping it up with one arm.

Her foe ignored her for his twitching commander.

"My Lord," Vladimir slurred as his King examined him from above.

"You will live, Vladimir, but I wonder if you shall live down the fact that a mere girl defeated you. And I thought you were really my best," The Lord shook his head though his disappointment seemed superficial as amusement flooded back in his eyes.

Jza squeezed her eyes shut and turned her face away as Vladimir tried to speak but gurgled blood instead. Blood was still sprouting forth from the man's wound which still had the fruit knife sticking out from it. The cobbled floor was beginning to grow dark from the congealing liquid.

Jza still had her eyes closed when she felt a presence approach her. She lifted her sword back at the Lord who still looked unconcerned.

"A-another step and I'll-," Jza cursed herself when she took a step back instinctively as the man moved towards her.

"Go ahead, I am unarmed. You can do whatever you like with me," Lord Tarquin lowered his face so he could look her in the eyes. He took another deliberate step forward.

Jza blinked trying to understand the man. Most men she knew, including her father, were easily readable. They raged and ranted when things didn't go their way; their egos easily playable but this man was unpredictable to the nth order. It seemed like he just wasn't perturbed by anything she did.

Jza took another step back, her sword still facing her adversary, though it was shaking along with her hands.

"What are you waiting for?" The Lord goaded with another step, the sound of his foot step echoed in the empty dungeon.

Jza flinched when her back collided against the cold dungeon wall. The chill of the stone walls easily seeped through her satin dress. Even though the dungeon was supposed to be quiet Jza's senses were enveloped in the sounds of her heartbeat drumming in her ears.

"You can't do this, can you? Just a foolish little girl accidentally left behind in this draughty castle," The man cornered her with this taunt.

Jza closed her eyes trying to summon the courage to use the sword in her hands. Her previous use of her knife on Vladimir was an action she performed in the heat of the moment. His presence threatened her on an instinctive level and she lashed out without even thinking. Right now even though the situation wasn't any less dangerous the quietness of moment took away a lot of her instinctive courage.

"Your stance is all wrong; your grip is too weak; you put weight on your heels leaving you with little grip for with the rest of your foot. You are more liable to do yourself more harm than good so I would suggest you give me the sword immediately," The man spoke critically as he held out his hand.

"No!" Jza shook her head vehemently, not ready to give up.

"Give it to me," The man spoke quietly though his voice contained more force than Jza's shout. The distance between them closed and his actions gave Jza the motivation she needed. She crudely swung the sword at the man. Even with little strength behind the movement it still managed to slash through Lord Tarquin's shirt. A dark red line emerged from the thin streak Jza had carved in the man's fawn shirt. He looked down and for the briefest of moments surprise flooded his eyes.

"Stay back," Jza cried out. She swung again but this time Lord Tarquin caught her blow in his hand. He looked into her eyes fiercely, undisturbed that a fairly large sword was cutting him in the hand. In seconds blood welled up around the blade and started dripping down on the floor. Jza was so stunned by his actions that she let go of the sword. It fell down with an echoing clang.

Her heart fell when the man bent down to pick it up. He ignored his bleeding hand and seemed untroubled by the weight.

"The carving on it is masterful. I did not know Goridians were so adept at sword making," He murmured to himself as he examined the sword. The sword's hilt was a striking mixture silver and gold. Small emerald stones were inlayed on the circular pommel.

"This is the sword of Galios, it carries the blood of the barbarians. Did you expect it to be anything but beautiful?" Jza spoke unable to stop herself. The sword in hands of the enemy was a source of national pride. It was a national treasure handed down from one king to the other. Even the commonest of peasants knew of its bloody history and how significant its role was in the making of their kingdom.

Lord Tarquin looked up sharply. "The sword of Galios," He stated, "Ironic that my people win and yet my barbarian blood still ends up on this damn thing."

Jza spoke again without thinking, "Barbarian? But you are not-"

"Enough chatter," The Lord snapped at her finally showing a hint of true emotion, "Come with me."

His hand firmly clamped down on Jza's arm that was bare because of the ripped sleeve. Since he was holding the sword in his uninjured hand it was bloody one that held onto her. She felt the coolness of her captor's blood slide against her warm skin.

"Leave me this very instant," Jza whispered harshly finally losing a good portion of her voice from the all the shouting she had done. The man holding her smirked as he easily led her away from the wall and towards the door. Before he could pull her out of the door way Jza desperately grappled for the door.

"Stop being so vexing, girl, would you rather I carry you?" Lord Tarquin threatened though from his strength it did not look like he needed to do anything quite as drastic.

Jza's weak grip on the door diminished completely as the man managed to pull her away with sheer brute force. Jza knew her arm was probably a mess of bruises but vanity was not a good reason to stop fighting. Lord Tarquin yanked her outside into the hallway. Jza looked away from Raymond's stiff body.

"My Lord," One of the men Jza had seen earlier bowed down, confused. He was the only one left guarding the door. The soldier's eyes widened to see blood on his King's shirt.

"Commander Vladimir needs your assistance inside so I suggest you help him immediately," Lord Tarquin ordered. He rebuffed his soldier's attempt to assist his King instead.

"Tis only a flesh wound. I don't require any aid."

Lord Tarquin forged ahead when another soldier accosted him. The soldier eyed the odd couple his King and the enemy prisoner made, curiously.

"My Lord, are the rumours true?" He spoke in a hushed voice.

"If you wish to question me about Commander Vladimir then I suggest keeping vigil at the infirmary would give you more concrete answers."

"What about the girl? If the commander is in no position to keep her maybe I-"

"She shall remain under my care. It is apparent none of my men are capable of looking after themselves much less a young girl," Lord Tarquin replied calmly. He continued walking at his own pace with both Jza and his soldier both hurrying to keep up.

"But-" The soldier tried to reason with his King but was cut off.

"Are you arguing with me, Mikhail?" Lord Tarquin's voice was deathly quiet as he paused to stare at the man.

"N-no, my Lord, never," Mikhail stuttered.

"Good, now tell me which rooms have been cleared out and made ready for inhabitation."

"We, uh, tried to open the Royal chambers but the seal they used to close the room is still being worked upon by my men so we found alternative lodgings nearby."

The King muttered something about the incompetence of his men but followed Mikhail who took him to the rooms in question. Jza snorted at the irony as she realized which rooms they were being led to. The chambers were always supposed to be for the heir to the throne. Her father, like his father before him, resided in this room before his coronation. It was only after the new King was crowned would his place of residence change to the Royal chambers. Her father was never able to provide a male heir so this room had been empty for more than thirty years.

The door to the rooms opened in a large wallpapered parlour with ceiling high windows. The torches were lit and they cast ominous shadows on the green walls.

"Everything is ready for your comfort, My Lord. The rooms have been dusted, new linen found and hot bath water is ready in the adjoining bathing room," Mikhail announced proudly.

"Leave," Lord Tarquin uttered completely uninterested in what his soldier had to say. He was busy observing the room.

Mikhail fumbled for a moment but decided against opening his mouth and left the room, shutting the door behind him. As the door closed with a resounding thud Lord Tarquin finally let go of his tourniquet like grip on her arm.

"Don't even think about it," Lord Tarquin muttered. Jza stopped in her tracks stunned her captor knew what she was planning to do even though his back was turned towards her, "My guards are right outside so running away will be utterly futile."

Jza sighed morosely as she watched Lord Tarquin open a door. "Come on," He raised an eyebrow at her but Jza was not ready to comply. She raised her eyebrow back at him.

"This time around I am the one with the sword in my hand and fortunately I know how to use it. I would suggest you move or the consequence will be unpleasant," Lord Tarquin spoke blandly.

"I-I," Jza wanted to argue but before she could formulate any words the Lord continued.

"Keep your false bravado to yourself. You are alive because I am feeling generous today."

He grabbed her hand and tugged her towards him.

"After you, my Lady," Lord Tarquin mocked as he helped her inside the room which to Jza's horror turned out to be the sleeping chambers.

"No, no, no," Jza whispered. Old lessons by her governesses flitted through her head. Some of her first lessons contained talk of propriety and the appropriate behaviour for a lady. A woman walking into sleeping chambers with a strange man were the height of impropriety.

"I cannot be in this room with you," Jza muttered frantically trying to steal past the presence behind her.

"Why not," The Lord murmured in her ear and Jza flinched when she realized how close her captor was standing behind her. Ignoring her discomfort at the close proximity she stretched her neck slightly to the left and looked up.

"I refuse to go anywhere with you especially in your chambers you vile, odious man and, and-," Jza spoke harshly hoping the real reason of her panic never surfaced. After the ease with which Vladimir tried to take advantage of her she could not let herself be in a position of such vulnerability again.

"And it's highly improper," Lord Tarquin finished her incomplete sentence. He sighed as she gaped at him. Her cheeks burned with humiliation and she looked away.

"Your hair is a mess, you are covered in blood and you smell like you haven't bathed in days. I assure you, you are safe with me," Lord Tarquin muttered as he shoved her inside the room.

"Why would you keep me safe?" Jza thought out aloud as she swirled around to face the man accusingly.

"Because I know you are more than you look. You are no peasant, of that I am perfectly sure of but what you are exactly I have not surmised as yet. Keeping you intact to a certain degree seems like a good gamble for the future."

Jza wanted to speak but she clamped down on her tongue. Her captor was already plotting something and she did not want to give him more food for thought.

Lord Tarquin threw the sword in his hand on the floor and Jza was offended by his lack of respect for a revered national treasure.

"Go clean yourself, you are filthy," Lord Tarquin spoke to her as he took off his large belt and the scabbard containing his own lighter, slimmer sword.

"Let me be," Jza growled.

"I do not tolerate disobedience when I give a command so I would do as I wish," Lord Tarquin spoke calmly as he fumbled with his armour.

"I don't take orders from a King not my own," Jza replied hotly as she inched towards the exit.

"You are under my care; at least go and wash your face."

Jza was almost at the door when she noticed Lord Tarquin pulling at the knots of his white, blood splattered shirt.

"What are you doing?!" She asked horrified all thoughts of escape forgotten.

"Changing my clothes," Lord Tarquin shrugged. He looked back at her and arched an eyebrow when he saw she was less than a stride away from escape.

"Why?" Jza squeaked as she looked away. The man continued to tug at the knots in his shirt ignoring that fact that Jza was too embarrassed to look up again.

"The mind is a great gift, my lady, use it and the answer shall come to you instantly."

"I use my mind a great deal more than some of your soldiers," Jza growled though she still did not have the courage to look up.

"I told you to leave this room but since you did not comply I shall have to pretend you are not here."

Jza looked up so she could reply scathingly but glimpses of more skin made her blood boil.

"You win; I shall leave this room. Keep your naked flesh to yourself," Jza spat as she charged out of the room and into the bathing chambers. It was much larger than the ones she and three of her other sisters shared. The cast iron claw foot bath was full to the brim with steaming hot water. Jza was tempted to dive in fully clothed but she decided against it.

Jza looked at herself in the large mirror leaning against the wall. she could scarcely recognize herself. Most of her hair was standing on edge in large clumps. Since the war had started she had barely any time to groom herself and the last few days of the siege had been eventful enough to make her disregard any need to change her clothing.

Her torn sleeve revealed a blood covered arm but even the blood could not hide the finger marked bruises forming on her skin.

Jza's eyes landed on the locket still safely adorning her neck. She wondered what her sisters were up to. Jza snorted as she imagined them bickering with each other and cursing her for their predicament.

Jza tried to imagine her father was safe in Goridon but she knew the Royal party was being hunted down by Tarquin's men. A solitary tear fled her eye as she imagined the beautiful castle under siege. Her legs gave way from under her and she huddled on the marble against the wall.

"Damn you, Raymond," Jza swallowed as she pressed the back of her hands against her watering eyes. She imagined how easier it would have been for her if her father's man had kept his loyalty. The castle wouldn't have been infiltrated and there would have been no need for her sisters to hide. She wouldn't have to feel like she needed to fight all the time. She felt so tired and each and every part of her body ached.

Jza let a hiccup of a sob and finally succumbed to her emotions.

Chapter 4

"Milk the cows, you miserable cretin," Hyacinth shook Jza viciously, "It's already sun up and you're lazing about like prissy little princess."

"But I am a princess, how can I milk cows?" Jza protested, feeling disoriented.

"You are no princess. You are only the bastard child of the master's sister. You should be lucky he keeps you fed and gives you shelter."

"But father swore he married my mother," Jza sobbed miserably.

"You don't even know who your father is," The elderly farm worker sneered, "Now, get up."

Jza woke up with a start. She took in great gasps of breath heavily for a few moments before realizing she hadn't ended up back at the farm. The memories of living as a lowly milkmaid before her father discovered her existence still tormented her. They would flit about her subconscious and when she would wake up she would always say a prayer for her father for taking her away from the wretched existence.

Jza felt an ache rise in her body and cringed as the pain brutality hit her. It felt like she had fought of a whole squadron of men all by herself. Her head throbbed while her arms and legs felt like they pinned down by a heavy weight.

The princess lifted her sore head and noticed she wasn't in a bed but on the floor, curled up against a mirror. Jza blinked to get a better bearing of where she was at.

"I thought you would never wake up," A male voice startled her. She turned her head to her right to find a man standing at the window staring out from it. The morning light made the figure's silhouette hazy and ethereal.

Jza tried to remember who he was but he turned around before she could fully recognize him.

"You," She hissed instantly alert when he revealed his face.

Lord Tarquin raised his eyebrows unimpressed by her level of deduction.

"Who did you expect, your great King Galios?"

Jza did not reply to his mocking words but continued to glare at him from the floor.

"This castle is now mine and you should get used to my authority and presence," He sneered.

"Never! This is King Samuel's domain and I shall not allow a foreign nobody to claim his throne."

"A nobody," Tarquin laughed bitterly, "Then tell your historians that it was a foreign nobody who defeated your illustrious King, the grandson of King Galios."

Jza looked away sullenly, having no answer for the Lord's proclamation. It was true their armies had fallen too easily to the enemy although the defeat could also be attributed to the betrayal of a key member of the army. Richmond was heading most of the war efforts and if he had turned traitor then he was the one who led his men to their deaths deliberately.

The man walked towards the bathing tub and gently led his hand through the now visibly tepid water.

"What a waste of splendid hot water," He commented causally.

Jza watched him carefully as he picked up a gold gilded pail and smoothly swooped some water in it. Without any notice he threw it all over her. The girl cried out in horror as she was soaked to the bone. Her tangled hair flailed across her face sloppily.

"I gave you the opportunity to use the facilities in this room but you chose not to. I cannot stand the sight of you so I decided to take matters into my own hands," Tarquin explained blandly unfazed by Jza's spluttering.

The princess pulled her hair back so she could give him a piece of her mind but Tarquin swiftly cut her off before she could even start.

"Now, leave. I had my men bring a dress from a wardrobe from somewhere so you may change."

Jza opened her mouth to argue but he raised a hand silencing her. Tarquin turned around and pulled his new shirt from one of his shoulder, baring it. He looked back at her from his shoulder and smirked knowing his actions would clear the room out. Jza quite predictably gathered her walked out in huff.

She dripped all over the decorative carpet but Jza felt like she did not care. She wished she had pulled a towel with her the Lord's antics did not leave any room to think. He was already aggravating her enough that she worried she might lose her temper and reveal who she really was.

In the middle of the bed was a gown as the Lord had said. It was a peach lace dress with large puffed sleeves and baby pink trimmings and slip.

She recognized the dress immediately, having been a sister's favourite. While she had nothing against peach or pink, the way the dress was designed made the wearer look like a sparkly, fluffed up cupcake.

Jza sat down on the bed feeling the soft gauzy material. There were multiple laces that needed to be tied and an inbuilt corset that required at least three maids to help pull the dress on. It was ridiculous to expect her to wear something so complex and something so wretched a colour. Jza stonily waited for the man to come out.

"Are you decent?" Lord Tarquin asked from the entrance.

"I am always decent," Jza replied, wearily. She had refused to follow his orders and imagined he would try to force her into it himself. But she still took the chance.

Tarquin stepped out from the behind the hanging curtain, rubbing a towel against his hair and tutted with amusement seeing the unworn garment.

"Why am I surprised? I should have been prepared for your disobedience," He stated with a roll of his eyes, "But I thought a girl would show more enthusiasm about new clothing."

"I- I do not dress myself," Jza replied feeling uncharacteristically hesitant, "I require a servant with this heavy dress and complicated lacing and..."

"And," Tarquin asked curiously.

"It is not the colour I would prefer to wear," Jza coughed out. Her body tensed waiting for the next blow to her. Would her hit She eyed the nearest candle stand wearily.

"My, my, I am really behind modern fashion. I thought pink was a girl's best friend. Pardon me for not keeping up since I had a war to plot."

Tarquin opened a gilded closet and pulled out a purple effervescent dress with a sprawling black train. The man took one look his prisoner and threw it on the floor with an exaggerated sigh. He then went through a number of dresses swiftly until he found a green simple empire cut number and Jza eyed it curiously trying to remember which sister had owned it. Tarquin noticed her interest and threw the gown at her.

"I hope you can manage this on your own because in about half an hour dinner will be served and I don't want our guest of honour to be late."

"Guest of honour! That's absurd. You shall trot me out in front of your soldiers only to humiliate me," Jza snapped at him.

"If I wanted to humiliate you I would have left you with them and not brought you in these room under my protection," Tarquin spoke slowly and dangerously, with his eyes fixed on Jza's face, "Then you would have truly found out what humiliation means."

The girl closed her eyes understanding the threat in his words. The option of leaving her, fending for herself was still there.

"Now, clean yourself and wear that dress. I shall be back in fifteen minutes whether you are ready or not," Tarquin ordered and walked out the room.

Jza for a few moments pondered whether climbing out of the window was a good option but let the idea slide. She had nowhere to go to even if she broke out. There were enemy soldiers teeming in every inch of the castle grounds and the civilian populations of the city had already been ordered to evacuate days earlier so there was no hope for a safe haven. If there were her country's soldiers around then their existence would be as prisoners of war. And there was always the danger that one them could point out who she really was and then the whole game would be over.

Decision made the princess decided for once that complying with the Lord would be a good idea. She went back to the bathing area to change. Clean and slightly refreshed Jza walked back to the sleeping chambers hoping the man would not be back but unfortunately he was waiting for her. He was out of his soldier's outfit and instead wore a more formal blue suit with a gold sash on one shoulder.

A neat circular gold band was placed on his head. There were no jewels inlayed in the crown but only an inscription in a language she did not understand.

"That's more like it," The man nodded at her appreciatively but Jza crossed her arms and looked away. Her hair was drier now and plainly combed down. It was not fashionable to have a lady let her hair down but Jza had more pressing concerns to think of.

"Your eyes," His spoke softly, "I have seen them before. I never forget a face."

"My eyes are my own and since I have never seen you before, you have never seen my eyes," Jza hissed moodily.

"Maybe. Now tell me your name?" The Lord asked brusquely.

"I shall never let my name cross your lips."

Tarquin smiled irreverently. He crossed the room and placed his hand against her neck even as she stumbled away from him. The girl twitched under his touch but she knew the touch was nothing more than a warning. His thumb slowly pressed against her throat. Jza started to feel breathless.

"Your name," He asked again patiently not a even a hint of threat in his voice so pleasant was his mien.

"Never," Jza hissed, her hair swung wildly. She knew she was going to have more bruises on her neck.

He pushed her away in disgust.

"I wonder if the name you hide has something to do with who you are. Is your name easily recognizable?"

"My name is none of your concern," Jza coughed weakly. She pushed herself away from the wall.

"A man leading a Lady to dinner should at least know her name," Tarquin smiled widely looking disarming, a heavy shift from his usual broodiness. He sat on the edge of the bed nonchalantly as if he hadn't been just strangling the girl in front of him.

"You can call me Miss Ashbrook," Jza replied softly and looked away. It was not a lie. It was the name she went by before her true parentage was revealed to her when she was thirteen. Her uncle had given her his name to deflect any criticisms or questions. She never had the status her cousins had at the farm but she was still treated better than some of the other farm hands.

"Miss Ashbrook, I expected more of a fight or is it not your true name?" Tarquin peered into her eyes trying to search for some fallacy.

Jza coughed again, her hand tenderly gripped her sore throat. "Some things are not worth a battle."

"Good girl, you are learning fast. Now, be a dear and reveal your first name as well," Tarquin raised his eyebrows.

"I have heard it is custom that no man in your Kingdom takes the name of women they do not call family," Jza mentioned haltingly hoping she could make him quit his incessant questioning.

"I hail from a small country with little contact with the outside world. It is interesting you know of such customs," Tarquin's gaze became more calculating as he stood up.

"Books are worth more than aimless talk," Jza replied curtly.

"I agree," Tarquin turned around, "My soldiers' are waiting for their first meal in this castle and our aimless talk is making them hungrier. Come on."

The man held his arm out as if he expected to take it.

"Take it or you shall have to get by without any more food for today," He spoke without turning around.

"Why can't you just leave me be. Why must you parade me in front of your minions," Jza spoke harshly scrunching her nose in disgust.

"What would be the fun in that?" Tarquin arched an eyebrow as he turned around.

The Lord walked towards her and firmly placed her arm around his. Jza pulled away slightly but she already knew in her mind that without food for a few more hours she would lose any energy she had.

Tarquin did not give her any time to make any more choices and led her out forcefully. He walked with much longer strides making it harder for the Princess to keep up and struggled along with him. He finally led her to a door she knew to be one of the banquet halls. It made sense a large dinner was to be served there.

The doors were closed and yet she could hear every sound being made inside. It sounded like the men were roaring at each other like animals. It was quite unlike the polite dinner parties that occurred when she had attended them in the room.

"Open the doors," Tarquin demanded of the two men guarding them. Jza instinctively latched onto her captor's arm, worried about having to face the same leering men again. Tarquin gave her an amused look which she did not appreciate at all.

As soon as they entered a chicken leg piece hit the doorman, on Jza's side, squarely on the face. The stunned man gripped his nose immediately with a low groan.

There was silence as soon as the rowdy men noticed the new entrants.

"I understand so many days camping and crawling though forests has left your manners a little lacking but is this how the cream of the crop of my army behaves," Tarquin's voice was soft and steady but the expressions of fear on the men's faces seemed as if he were shouting at them.

"We have a lady present and I would suggest you behave accord-ingly," Tarquin finally announced carelessly. Jza felt a pang as she realized the man would be taking her father's empty seat.

"I see my own seat but where shall the lady sit," Tarquin sounded like he thinking out aloud but his men knew that it was an indirect order. One of the men swiftly left the seat next to the King's and rushed off to find a seat elsewhere.

Lord Tarquin helped Jza into her seat and finally sat down on the King's rightful place.

"Need I say anything?" Tarquin eyed the occupants of the room and the men started wolfing down the food.

The Princess was shocked at the ill breeding of the man next to her. She could feel the flecks of gravy from his mouth reach her. Even she hadn't been so uncouth when she had first been brought to the castle. She had been a willful, uncultured farm girl with very little training on actual cutlery but she had never thrown her food around quite like that. Jza imagined her old governesses face looking at the carnage before her.

"Animals, all of them," Tarquin eyed the men with disdain, "No wonder my nation never prospered before I was crowned."

"I have never met a man who talked poorly about his people," Jza asked curiously.

"I only speak the truth," Her captor steadily sipped on his soup in a complete contrast from his men. His table manners were as refined and as any of the former Royal family.

Jza delicately brought the spoon to her lips and was surprised at the taste. It was sour and salty with an underlying taste of cucumber.

"Rassolnik soup only tastes good when it is made at home. The veal added to it is of such poor quality," Tarquin criticized but Jza found she was uninterested in defending the veal. Far more important things needed defending and veal of her country did not make it to that list.

Jza was hit in the shoulder by her other neighbour, who so busy with a portion of the main course that he didn't even notice what he had accidentally done. Jza took another sip but it was interrupted by the slam of the doors opening. Every head whipped towards with equal amount of shock on their faces.

An extremely beautiful woman was posing at the doorway with a very dazed footman holding the train of her dress.

"Have we missed the party?" A woman grinned broadly at the room. The crowd inside went wild. Jza winced when her other dining neighbour wolf whistled spitting everywhere.

"What is she doing here?" Tarquin hissed to himself.

"Who is she?" Jza asked urgently.

"She is the leader of my Harem," Tarquin informed her as if were talking about something as normal as the weather.

Chapter 5

"Sofiya," Lord Tarquin stood up and addressed the woman closest to the table. Jza noted the interaction between the two of them still trying to grasp the concept of a harem. It was unheard of in her country but she knew customs in countries around them varied wildly. In Lord Tarquin's country uttering a woman's first name was considered sinful and yet keeping a harem was not. It was so baffling it hardly seemed true.

"Do I need to even say anything?" Lord Tarquin announced to the room which had grown silent. Jza looked back to the woman and found herself already being scrutinized. The beautiful woman was utterly expressionless but her eyes radiated an unpleasantness difficult to ignore. It was fortunate that Jza did not have any problem with pointless posturing and gave the foreign woman a challenging look of her own. This was her domain after all and these people were mere interlopers.

"But the dessert-" One soldier protested still holding onto his spoon.

Lord Tarquin sat down on his chair and crossed his arms. Whatever look he passed to his men instantly made them jump up, some even letting their chairs fall backwards. They quickly evacuated the room in a stampede of wildness. The women took up some of the places vacated by the men.

"And ladies, what brings you here?" Tarquin eyed the new arrivals sternly although his tone was much softer.

"Where ever you go we follow. It shouldn't be so difficult to understand, Tar," The woman called Sofia crooned coyly. Jza snorted highly unimpressed especially since she was the sister of the famous beauties and they could teach anyone a thing or two about looking coy.

The man closed his eyes as if summoning patience from a non-existent spiritual place deep within his heart but when he opened them back it was obvious it had eluded him. His eyes narrowed in annoyance observing the five finely dressed women in front of him.

"This is a warzone, Sofiya. It is still too dangerous to be frolicking in such a volatile area," Tarquin uttered, sounding as if he had little interest in their safety.

"And yet you find yourself wining and dining with one of the local beauties at great ease," Sofiya gave a short, condescending laugh before picking at someone's leftovers from the plate in front of her.

"Hardly," Tarquin gave Jza a bored look. He focused his attention back to the women and started asking about the climate back home. The Princess tried to follow the conversation but the two started speaking in an odd mixture of what was her own language and theirs. She caught a few words but not enough to form a coherent story.

The other silent woman continued to eye their King's captive with beady eyes but Jza ignored them for her own meal. She absentmindedly looked around and was startled when a hand fell on her shoulder.

"We are leaving," Tarquin stood up and sharply tugged Jza's arm so she had to stand up in consequence without much free will. The rest of the women remained in their places.

"Boris will have your rooms ready," Tarquin announced curtly and Sofiya gave a subtle nod. Jza didn't have the chance to even look back at the harem members before being dragged back to the room. A few loitering soldiers saluted as he whisked her through the corridors. A guard opened the door for them and she was shoved inside.

"I've ordered some tea. We shall have it before getting ready for bed," Tarquin informed her as he closed the door behind him and Jza wondered where she was to sleep. The man was settling down for the night and there was no talk of letting her stay elsewhere. There was only one King sized bed in the bedroom so she imagined he would make her sleep on the floor and if he wanted her to be anywhere closer then she would have to put up a fight. A gentle knock on the door disrupted her most violent line of thought.

"Anna, what are you doing here at this hour?" Tarquin spoke as he opened the door.

"Sofiya sent me with a message, Miliy moy," A dark haired girl smiled sweetly leaning in close. She had not been there in the room of woman making Jza assume Anna was not of much importance in the harem. The Princess wondered how many women he had in his harem and shuddered imagining millions. What a pitiful life these women had.

"Fine," The Lord shook his head with an amused look and invited her in.

"Tell me when the tea gets here," The man ordered before dragging the woman away to his bedroom. Anna giggled as he shut the door.

Jza sat down with an impatient growl in the living room and waited until the night tea was brought in by a young looking servant. The servant had taken after his master; entering with no expressions or sound. He brought in what she remembered to be expensive china, used only for important events, and left without acknowledging her.

The Princess got up and knocked on the door but there was no response. She tried her luck again and her loud knocks echoed in the room but she only got silence as a reply. Jza huffed and poured herself a cup of tea.

She took one sip and then another before deciding she would not be ignored any longer. She marched up to the entrance of the bedroom and opened the door hoping the pair was done discussing whatever missive Sofiya had sent them. Before she could even get a word out of her mouth the sight before her shocked her enough to step out immediately, slamming the door shut behind her, with the feeling that her eyes would pop out and roll away into a dark corner from embaressment. She had seen sheep give birth; observed maids giggling with the farm hands in quiet, dark corners but this was too much information even for her.

Tarquin's hand had been inside the front of the woman's dress and his mouth latched onto the neck while he had stood bare chested in the middle of the room. Jza gasped, when the door she had closed in panic, opened.

"The Lord is calling you inside," The woman smiled at her slyly correcting the front of her dress with no shame.

"No," Jza protested unthinkingly and back peddled away with her face contorted with disgust.

Anna with her gold painted nails clawed into Jza's bare arm and pulled her forward. Her smile grew even more sinister and she threw her captive in the bedroom. Jza landed on the plush carpet right at his booted feet.

He held his hand out. Jza swallowed audibly but decided to take it seeing as she had little choice; she was surrounded. He helped her up and her eyes trailed over his naked chest up to his face with trepidation. Lord Tarquin's eyes assessed her probingly. The ends of lips were curved only barely but that slight bit of expression spoke volumes to her and she wanted to smash his face in for daring to look so smug.

"You need to get used to this if you must stay near me. I am not going to shy away from my nature just because a Lady is in my presence. Your missish ways a nuisance for me," Tarquin spoke casually with a tilt of the head, "I admit I was thinking the arrival of my harem couldn't have better timed because I intended to send you to them."

"I would never ever-" He put his hand on her mouth and emptied the bottle in his hand in one quick swallow before throwing it backwards.

"Quit whining. You wouldn't be part of the Harem, of course. You are not to my taste," He shrugged, "I just thought it would be convenient to place with you with my women. Much better then my men, no?"

Jza didn't know what to do she stood there stoically with his hand on mouth. She thought about biting him again but this time he knew her tricks and gripped her mouth so tightly that there was no space for her mouth to even open.

"But, my plans have snagged in the middle. My harem has refused to give you shelter for reasons that could only be known to those tiresome women and I think I shall have to keep you at my side till more savory women from my country make their appearance,"

Tarquin snorted at the look in her eyes, "Until then get used to this. This is a half naked man's chest. It shan't hurt you."

The man unabashedly pointed at himself and Jza averted her eyes with loathing. He clutched one of her hands and she tried to pull it away but his larger hand enveloped hers completely in a fraction of a moment. Her eyes widened when he flattened her hand against his bare chest and she tried to struggle more intensely but it did not deter him what he intended to do with her. His hand effectively trapped hers under his and tugging her arm did not do any good. Tarquin held onto her gaze before slowly letting her hand slide down his chest under his own. She could feel the definition of his skin and the strength in the muscle but what disgusted her most was the heat emitting into her hand.

It made her more aware that she was touching a living breathing male. Jza would have rather pretended it was an obnoxious wall of bricks and mortar but the sensation under her hand would not let her believe so. As the hand grew lower her panic grew and she let out a strangled plea and he stopped; right at his naval. He abruptly let go of her mouth and her hand at the same time.

"See touching me did not damage you-" He stated as if were merely presenting some scientific theory but was interrupted in the middle. Jza had slapped him soundly on the cheek. Even half turned he had a smile on his face which infuriated her further.

"How dare you!" She snarled at him clutching her tainted hand with the other protectively.

"I can dare as much as I want because you are under my protection and hence my rules are to be obeyed, understand?" Tarquin spoke lowly as he leaned in close with a smug smile.

"No," Jza spat out knowing how repetitive she was becoming but her mind was not prepared to think of better replies.

"Trust me, you are safe with me no matter what you think of me," Tarquin spoke suddenly and this was not the angry retort she had expected. She was still arching away expecting a slap in return.

"You have a harem! What should I think of a man like that?" Jza asked.

"And your country has customs that allow multiple wives. What should I think of people like that?" Tarquin mimicked her unflatteringly.

"When a man takes a woman as his wife he gives her respect. If he falls for more than one woman then he gives them all honour rather them turn them into common whores," Jza argued as he pulled her outside towards the empty sitting area.

"Surely as a woman you would understand the concept of monogamy. One man, one woman; together forever; I bet that excites your domestic little socks off," Tarquin grinned meanly.

"The king had three wives and he treated them all well. Their domesticity was not interrupted by the other marriages," Jza spoke slowly, resolutely, before getting pushed down on the sofa. The man took a seat on the matching armchair and picked up the untouched tea cup. The girl wondered whether tea and alcohol would be a good mix but dispelled the thought.

"Three? I have only heard of two," He asked with narrowed eyes.

"T... there were rumours that he possessed another wife; a maid or something equally disreputable. His mother banished her without the King's knowledge and forced him to marry again. It sounds like something out of a storybook so I would dismiss such claims," Jza babbled quickly hoping he would not start questioning her on this issue and cursed herself for not keeping her mouth shut.

"Ah, Royal romance," Tarquin muttered, rolling his eyes.

"It would have done you no harm for you to indulge in one yourself. Why didn't you get married to one of the princesses? It seems much more logical," Jza asked suddenly, toying with her half drunken cup of tea. This was a thought that often troubled her. The kingdom did not have a male heir. The strongest husband of one of the Princesses seemed like the likeliest candidate. The war was completely unnecessary.

"What is the bliss in a conquest when it's done by diplomatic endeavors? The win would be far less satisfying," Tarquin answered easily. It was obvious he had thought on this issue as well.

"You cruel beast," Jza's temper flared by the glee in the man's eyes, "Why are you so determined to spill the blood of my countrymen?"

She picked her own cup and downed the hot liquid and settled the cup back ungainly, hand trembling from the force of her temper.

"Because it's fun and only fair. They spilt mine first and I shan't rest until all of Goridon is under my rule," Tarquin chuckled darkly sipping onto his tea.

"But your country was always neutral-" Jza tried to argue. His country had never been in any major wars until now so his comments about blood and fairness were a complete mystery. She tried to remember anything from the old history books but her head began hurting disallowing any further analysis.

"Enough chatter. Finish your tea," Tarquin grumbled, interrupting her tirade.

Jza tried to reach for her cup but she felt the humming in her head increasing manifold. She clutched her forehead and collapsed on the ground with a furious cry. She tried to get up but the pain paralyzed her.

"I," Jza gasped, "Can't breathe."

The man's face filled her vision.

"You lips are turning blue," Tarquin laughed, sounding very amused, "I fell for the oldest trick in the book."

"The what?" Jza groaned feeling nauseous.

"They poisoned you; that's what," Tarquin answered, still chuckling

"I'm dying?" Jza moaned feeling disoriented. Her throat hurt worse than when Tarquin had strangled her and she couldn't stop trembling.

"Not when I'm by your side. Sofiya wanted to send me a message and apparently she succeeded," Tarquin mused to himself before hoisting Jza up. The girl in his arms could barely stand and she bonelessly dangled against him.

"Oh, hush," Tarquin scolded and placed his hands under her knees so he could carry her.

Jza was barely aware of her surroundings. She sensed the door opening and heard chatter but her vision was a blur and her head was bursting with agony so all information was lost to her. She was lulled a little with the rhythmic sway of the man bearing her burden but once she was placed on a soft surface she wanted to start screaming.

A hand grabbed onto her neck and she thought it was choking her before she realized that the locket around her neck was being pulled away. She tried to protest when her locket was snatched from her but she passed out before she could continue her struggle.

Chapter 6

Jza opened her eyes with a bleary moan but squeezed them shut again as a shaft of light pierced through her vision, hurting her eyes. She blinked a few times before adjusting herself to the cheery sunshine.

The weather had taken such a glum turn during the siege that it had felt like the sun hadn't risen in so many months. Dark storm clouds had taken over the horizon like a bleak blanket pouring down upon the battered soldiers mercilessly making their lives a hundred times miserable. How ironic it was that on the day fighting had officially ceased the sun had decided to make its appearance as if waiting for it to be safe to come out. Coward, Jza thought meanly before turning around to look at her unfamiliar surroundings.

The room was sparse and not one she had ever been into so her confusion was justified. Her head buzzed faintly; unpleasantly and the world lurched precariously and it took a few moments for the it to steady itself. And then it hit her; she had been poisoned last night.

Jza was hyperventilating over her brush with death when an elderly man entered the room with a scowl. He did not address her in any fashion and rudely jostled up her, prodded her as checked her temperature.

"Where?" and she stopped realizing the question was stuck in her swollen throat.

"Zis is ze Infirmary," The older man crocked with disdain, his accent making a mash of her language.

"This is not the infirmary. I have been there before."

"Da," The man raised his nose higher with a twitch of the beard, "Goridians have no concept of natural harmony. Zeir previous infirmary possessed such chaotic energy zat itz a wonder anyone got out of zere alive."

"I see," Jza answered skeptically. She knew of her enemy's traditions were seeped in superstition but this was ridiculous. Jza patted her parched throat idly when she noticed the absence of a very precious belonging.

"Where is my locket?" She asked the old man with narrowed eyes.

"I know not what iz it you speak of."

"Where is my locket?" She growled quietly. The slow deliberation of her tone was enough to catch the man's attention. He looked up but before he could even twitch she caught him by his collar and pulled him towards her.

"Do not make me repeat my question," Jza threatened feeling her heart pounding a million times a second. The old man spluttered, horrified to be in his position. He had imagined her to be a meek, ill girl but his current state refuted all his assumptions.

"Tsk, tsk, threatening a defenseless old healer, Miss Ashbrook," Jza looked at the door and Lord Tarquin stood there with an easy grin adorning his face.

"I want my locket back," She urged feeling a tremor run down her body. Half of her wanted to be vicious and violent while the other half wanted to break down and cry. It was not easy maintaining a calm face when all she wanted to do was fall apart. Without the locket everything was lost.

"Don't worry, it's safe. Here," Lord Tarquin patted his front pocket.

"Give it to me!" Jza urged wondering what he was waiting for.

"Why?" The curves of his lips twitched in blatant amusement as he pulled the chain out and tangled the locket around a finger as if studying it.

"Because I will choke this man if you do not do so," Jza threatened not realizing how close she was to tears. Her eyes were filled to the brim and her vision blurred violently.

"Do it. Pavel is getting far too old for active duty anyway," Tarquin shrugged uncaringly, ignoring Pavel's groan of dismay. Jza released the healer roughly now that she knew her threats were futile. She knew the Lord well enough to know he would soon be giving her pointers on how to strangle someone more effectively than actually save a life. A tear slid down her face in despair. It was over.

"I would have given this back to you if you hadn't created such a fuss," Lord Tarquin played with the chain absentmindedly while his eyes were fixed on her face. Her despair was vastly disproportional to what the worldly worth of the locket seemed to be, "I know, it is very pretty, and girls love pretty things, or do you not?"

"It is my father's," Jza explained hoping to reduce his curiosity and explain her reaction as a case of female sentimentalism.

"If it's that meaningful then I shall keep it with me. Your precious object is far safer with me than in your delicate hands," Tarquin smiled cattily.

"You don't understand," She gritted her teeth furiously trying to keep the anger from boiling over.

"Shut up, you're getting on my nerves," Tarquin dismissed her and turned to the healer, "I gather she is well enough to get back on her feet."

Pavel nodded frantically hoping to excuse himself from the room as soon as possible.

"Good, I need her to be ready in the next hour."

"Where am I to be taken?" Jza interrupted.

"You shall find out on your own good time."

"Then at least tell me why," Jza paused to clear her throat and spoke again, "Why was I poisoned?" Her hand inattentively clasped the empty place on her neck.

"Because you were seen as a threat to my little Harem. It was a warning for me to stay in line and not touch girls not part of that revered group," Tarquin rolled his eyes.

"You follow their rules?" Jza asked with surprise.

"The womenfolk have always ruled behind doors. It is no secret," Tarquin smirked, "They know I do not mind their games."

Jza felt her anger rise at the thought that being poisoned was a game to all of them. This just proved that the whole race was irrefutably insane. Before she could speak he interrupted her.

"There is an execution today," Tarquin's face had a barely concealed smile.

____

Jza sat in the podium with an extremely vacant expression. She was wearing a simple pale blue gown and had light, satin ribbons in her hair. It had taken her an hour to loosen the tangles in her hair which had been a mindless task that kept her busy from going into hysterics.

"Thirty brave men from my country are to be executed tonight and I am dressed up as if I'm going to have lunch with one of my sisters," She thought tensely. She had bruises scattered down her arms in a purple array of colours and her face was no vision of beauty. She had never matched her sisters in perfection but in her current state it looked like a war had not been fought in the land of the kingdom but on her face.

Tarquin was conversing easily in his own language with three burly men who were listening to their leader intently though from time to time Jza could feel their gaze upon her. She wondered what they thought of her and imagined all sorts of filthy names attributed to her right now. Tarquin had placed a hand on her knee as soon as his commanders had stepped into the podium. After this day the rumours would not be considered unfounded. This non-verbal mark of territory had obviously not gone unnoticed though thankfully no leers or innuendos had been sent her way.

The three commanders had only vacated their places after the Harem had made their appearance dressed in flowing, gaudy jewel toned robes. The colours floating around her made Jza see red. How could these people treat an execution with such callous disregard?

Tarquin laughed while making small talk with Sofiya who had come bearing servants holding trays full of treats. The younger Harem girls had instantly reached for the sweet treats.

"Will you not partake in the kind offer made by my friends?" Tarquin placed an arm around a stunning brunette looking at ease in the surroundings.

"Would you blame me if I said no? My last experience did lead me to the infirmary."

"You mustn't hold it against us. If we wanted you dead you would have already been cold and grey," Anna giggled as if relayed a funny joke.

"Is that supposed to allay my fears?" Jza snorted in cynical amusement.

The Lord rolled his eyed and picked up a miniature fresh fruit tart. He took a medium sized bite and then offered the piece of food to Jza.

"Here, if you are too craven then we must share food. We are already sharing a bed," His hand hovered near her mouth and before she could protest the sweet fruit was touching her lips. Jza pursed in lips in disapproval. She wanted to rant and release her anger but his hand was steady impediment. She took a minuscule bite and felt her ears going red while the Harem girls tittered around her.

"We are not sharing-" Jza growled but he snapped his fingers at her.

"Silence, they are bringing your disgraced soldiers out. Do you not want to see their faces before they are executed," The man grinned and pushed the girls draping all over him, "Better yet let us go greet them into the arena."

"I doubt I can change your mind," His captive murmured. Jza felt herself shrink under his touch as he pulled her arm around his in a parody of social norms. In her vision she could imagine the fate of her father and the royal courtiers all standing in line waiting to be guillotined.

"You can try," He whispered in her ear too low even for his precious Harem who looked as if they would like to be trailing behind the pair. Tarquin smirked enigmatically and led her down the dark stone stairs into the dirt covered arena.

The soldiers of the beaten army were being dragged in chains wearing their torn and bloodied uniforms. Jza could smell their filth from the distance she was standing but she could not recoil from them; not for the men who had fought in her father's name and led to the slaughter by their own commander.

The small group of men was forced onto their knees by their handlers.

"Ah, the right place for you filthy animals," A very short, bald man walked out from behind them looking as if he owned the world. He had a whip in his hand and he would slash it in the air whenever he sensed weakness.

"Yes, in front of their rightful Lord," One of the other commanders from before grinned nastily.

The young men kneeling in front of them looked defiant, angry and scared in equal parts. Jza worried for anyone of them who dared who stand up against this boastful statement. They did not have the advantage of her gender or a ransom.

The men also stared at her and she wondered if they even knew who she was. Her face was half swollen; distorted beyond recognition. At least they could not have thought of her as the woman of the enemy.

"I have no last words for the scum of Samuel," Lord Tarquin eyed the dusty, bloodied men with disinterest.

"They are the sons of Samuel," Jza spoke softly before Tarquin could lead her away. In the silence her words sounded as if they had been yelled. None of the defeated men spoke for they were too stunned to speak. She had probably looked too conquered, too overpowered to have word of defiance left in her. The shorter man looked as if he wanted to whip her into silence but Tarquin waved him away.

"Let it not be said Samuel bore no sons for he had so many. All his children fought for him. They lived for him and they died for him. Brave soldier remember our motto, the brave never die."

Her words were punctuated with solitary claps from the only person who was insane enough to let this farce continue.

"Beautiful words. Very touching. I was almost moved," Tarquin smirked and held his hand out to her but before he could reach her a soldier broke the line and fell on her feet. His hand met his and she felt something small being placed into her palm.

"Please, please, I beg you, give this to my mother, please," The fair haired man sobbed incoherently as he was led away. The whip hit his back slicing skin with a gruesome slash.

"Beg, I am sure you're itching to plead oh so beautifully for these men. You want to. I can felt it," Tarquin led Jza away to the inner exit. Jza was momentarily relieved she was not being made to witness the execution itself.

"I shan't. They deserve better," Jza spat out.

"What did he give you?" The Lord's hand dug into her arm another set of bruises. It was not even surprising to see his mood shift so decisively. He pushed her against the inner rooms of the arena. There was only a small slit of light coming though the gap between the roof and the walls.

"Because he wanted to give me this," Jza hissed as she held up what turned out to be the broach, "I am supposed to pass this onto his mother. I don't know if she is dead or alive but that poor boy had faith that I was would be able to pass it onto her."

"Boring, I was hoping for something more-"

"How would you feel if your mother was waiting for you to return and you had lost," Jza hissed.

"I don't lose hence I shan't ever be in the position. My mother would be nothing but proud," Tarquin pushed her into the wall aggressively.

"Oh, I bet she's proud, having such cruel beast for a son."

"Stop talking about my mother!" Tarquin roared, amber eyes flashing.

"It hurts doesn't it?" Jza smiled meanly and he let her slide down the wall. His fingers wavered and he released her from his grip.

"You say one word..." Tarquin's face scrunched in anger and Jza felt triumphant watching the finger he pointed at her shake. She had finally found his weak spot.

"You will do what?"

"Oh, I don't know," Tarquin seemed to have regained his calmness and looked at her dispassionately, "Maybe teach you the ways of the world my Harem knows so well."

Before Jza had a chance to react he pulled her close and let his body push her against the rough wall. His hand scrunched the sheer blue material of her left sleeve and yanked out the slight material.

Jza's round eyes watched him decimate the sleeve in shock, "What.."

"Miss Ashbrooke, you see, there is one of you and one of me, in this room, all alone. You can fight me for as long as you want but I shall be the one victorious when it comes to the matter of strength," Tarquin crooned lowly before bowing his head close enough to give her bare neck a soft kiss.

"Stop," Jza struggled to get her hands out from between them but Tarquin was in no mood to comply. He sighed almost contentedly as if he was with a lover on a mutually amorous excursion rather then forcing himself on a lady, "Please stop."

He raised his face sharply and Jza gauged from his flinty eyes that it was all a game to him. He was enjoying tormenting her more then the proximity to her which almost relieved her rather than offend.

"So, we have an agreement. You say nothing about my mother and I don't make use of you on whim, deal," Tarquin cocked his head lazily daring her to disagree.

"Deal."

As soon as the words were out of her mouth he pushed himself off her and wiped his hand on his trousers as if he had touched something particularly grotesque. Jza wondered if he would go gargle afterwards so he could rid himself the taste of her skin.

"A shame I had to rip such a pretty dress."

Jza did not reply when the man pulled off his jacket and placed it onto her shoulders.

"I am rather surprised you have not asked the history of this place. We are hardly a race who has need for blood sports. It was a practice of the Barbarians where slaves were used as participants of these particular sports," Jza spoke suddenly.

"I see. And you think maybe its time to revive this practice," Tarquin's face was half hidden in the shadows. Jza said nothing. Maybe she could prevent the execution after all if the Lord was enticed by the idea of bringing back blood sports. He was certainly blood thirsty enough to enjoy them rather than a boring execution.

"I think it would be best if we went back to our quarters," He spoke after a pregnant pause.

"And I think it would be best if you return my locket?" Jza asked curtly.

"I mean to keep it safe on my person in my pocket because I wonder whether prying hands can keep themselves off it." He trailed off, "It's not safe after all."

Chapter 7

It was quite the odd parody they made. A courteous gentleman leading a genteel lady for a stroll in the garden was a perfectly polite, socially acceptable situation if it weren't for the bruises on the lady's face, the iron strength grip on the lady by her captor and the decaying garden. It had rained often enough to leave behind greenery that identified the garden itself but no flowers grew in the desolateness.

Every so often a solider would stumble around them, gaping at the odd pair but none dared approach them. With a quick bow and a nod they would race off. The silence became overbearing for the princess who soon realised there were no songbirds accompanying them in their garden strolls. Everything was dead.

The jacket around her shoulders was loose and smelt strongly of the man. It should not have bothered her. Each individual had their own peculiarities she had never bothered to notice but it was unbearable now. It felt like he enveloped all of her senses like physical vice around her neck. She shuddered, overwhelmed.

The man abruptly paused in front of a long empty marble fountain and graciously settled her against the seating place. His pleasant mien was just farce which changed according to his mood. She never knew when the winds would change and his hand would reach out to strangle her throat or worse his lips... Jza squeezed her eyes shut at the horrifying possibility.

After a moment of silence when her heart steadied from its rambunctious pace she opened her eyes to find her captor sitting across from her with a bored expression. Jza averted her gaze and mutely noted the peacock bench had lost its head in the battle. The fountain should have been surrounded by roses but there was no life or colour in them any more. All that was left in the beds were rotted roses littered with cobwebs. The man plucked a brown wilted rose and fiddled with it for a moment with a strange smile on his face.

"Battle cries, sword clashing with sword, brutal defeat and the winner is raised high in the sky. What glorious battles must have been fought in that arena."

"Gaping wounds, torn ligaments, broken bones. There is nothing glorious about fighting," Jza grumbled with a grimace. Her whole body ached terribly from her previous days of trauma and all the pain was numbing her mind.

"So you say," The man retorted with his usual quickness.

"It is as I say," The girl met his eyes defiantly.

"You remind me of this flower," Tarquin uttered with a light tone after a pregnant pause, "all brittle and bruised."

"But don't make the mistake of forgetting the thorns."

Instead of retorting the man touched the rose lightly on her cheek. The most vicious bruise adorned her face on that side and even the light touch was irritating. And why he needed to needle her with his provoking behaviour was also a vexing thought. The man ended his dalliance with the rose by tucking a strand of her brown hair behind her ear and placing the rose along with it. The gesture was shockingly intimate but what could a person expect from a man who had no social boundaries.

"I could have salves ready for your face," The man uttered conversationally while Jza scowled back. "But vanity was never your thing, was it?"

The need to reply surged through her but she bit her lip instead. She knew the man would find a way to squeeze out all possible information from her. It was still a mystery how he had found out she wasn't a commoner in the first place. What was it about her that gave her away?

Tarquin's hand picked up one of hers and gently examined her softer hands as if they held a solution to the mystery. Soft they may have been but they were no less abused than the rest of her body. Small cuts littered the surface along with a discoloured bruise or two. Jza tolerated his probing touch as best as she could until she had enough of being treated like a cattle up for sale.

"Would you cease pawing at me. I am not your toy to be fondled as such."

"Never had a toy in my life so I wouldn't know," Tarquin smirked roguishly but it was his words that made her pause and not his handsome countenance. The Prince could be some master reader of other humans but that did not diminish her own skills of observation. His words added more to his mystery rather than resolving any of it. The little clues he left behind did not add up.

"Then you must refrain from treating like an object. I will not be treated thus!"

"You do not have the power to tell me what to do you weak helpless fool. You are mine now. I am your lord and master," The man spat out harshly, his mood changing like tumultuous clouds. He stood up and turned away from her with his strange eyes flashing, "One more word and I shall-"

"You'll what? Force yourself on me?" Jza sneered back. Her insides were feeling just as corroded as the wasted garden around her. Emotionally depleted there was nothing he could do to make her feel anything but annoyance at the moment.

"Yes, why not, I'm often bored," The man shrugged easily and turned around without a frown marring his well formed face.

"We made a bargain," Jza warned hoarsely. If he even took a single misguided step towards she would run. Her body was tense in anticipation. Her hands were as good as tied behind her back but she would not let him gain the satisfaction of abusing her.

"Of course," Tarquin replied pleasantly,"I shall do exactly as the lady bids me to, that is until she entertains me with the barbarian customs she seems to know so much about."

"Is there not a more capable person in your retinue then this bruised, little fool," The princess sneered.

"Yes, but what's the fun in that," The Lord replied, ended the argument decisively and Jza deflated under his pointed stare.

"There- there is much I do not remember but I have the basic ideas," The princess said warily her eyes still darting towards the marble archway that could have been her last hope for freedom. At the gesture the Lord made she haltingly started speaking; about the customs; the rituals; the battles. She continued until her dry lips cracked.

"And that is how Galios conquered the barbarian enemies. As they say the rest is history." Jza ended her tale while the Lord had watched her quietly absorbing her every single word. Jza felt goosebumps rise on her body and the single minded forcefulness of his gaze, "Wouldn't it be best if we leave for your rooms. It will be dark soon."

Instead of replying Tarquin nodded, took her hand and helped her up. They took a very comfortable pace and led her down the marble pathway that entered the large archway of the main entrance. Jza shook her head, "No, that is perhaps the longest way back to the rooms. It would not do."

"Of course, I shall follow your guidance since you know best having lived here all your life," The Lord said amiably.

"How do you know that is a fact. Maybe I am some noble's base-born daughter making her way in the world as a scullery maid. Have you not thought about that? Maybe that's why I was left behind, excess baggage you see. All alone in the world."

"I doubt you would have fought with such devotion for your father's last memory if he had rejected you," The man patted his shirt pocket smugly as Jza watched with his movements with narrowed eyes.

"Maybe, I am the needy, desperate type grappling with my only sense of identity," Jza retorted.

"No, you would have spat in his face. You would never grovel."

With those words he motioned for the guard to open his rooms. Inside Jza was met with a short, petite girl waiting for her with a large hair brush in her hands. The girl bowed sharply at her Lord and circled his captive with narrowed eyes. The two exchanged words in their own language as the maid pulled off the jacket to examine the damaged sleeve. There were already a few dresses laid out for her use.

"She will prepare you for dinner but do not exert yourself trying to talk to her. She knows nothing of your language," Tarquin said and sprawled across the bed facing her. Jza was propped in seat in front of the mirror by the industrious little maid who immediately tackled the problem of her tangled brown hair. The maid did not know of what to do with the dead rose still perched on her charge's ear so she threw it in the vicinity of the bed.

"Do I even need to make an effort? I'm sure your Harem will provide ample femininity to the table. What will they all think if I turned up dressed to the nines?"

"That you're my whore? They already believe so," Tarquin said, flippantly.

"Of course they do," Jza tried to keep her voice even but the mirror blurred in front of her. That little bit of respect she had yearned for all her life as the illegitimate daughter of the farmer's sister was washed down in that moment just like her tears. She blinked hard to get her composure back and her first clear view was of her captor. He was looking at her with such an intensity that she shuddered. She looked away immediately feeling like he was a demon who could steal her soul.

The maid continued to brush her hair languidly unconcerned by the tension simmering in the room. The Lord soon left the room and the women to their own devices.

Dinner was a quiet and sombre affair. The harem members were behaving more soberly for reasons only known to them. Jza had no idea where the rest were residing because only a few of the women were in attendance. They talked among themselves in their own drawling language leaving her with no comprehension of the contents of their conversion. And with her voice hoarse from the hour of talking there was nothing she wanted to say.

The princess was wearing a soft and gauzy evening gown with her hair held up. It was oddly reassuring to feel so well groomed again. The siege had left her with no spare moment for herself and this sort of normalcy when her circumstances had flipped so dramatically was surreal. She knew the ladies in her vicinity had noticed the change when they whispered among themselves, pointing at her rudely. She ignored the curious harpies and kept her gaze firmly fixed on her lap.

When the first course was served Jza remembering the previous attempt on her life found her appetite had left her entirely. Surrounded by the enemy she was never ever going to feel comfortable letting herself trust another innocuous meal again. She tried to lift her spoon up to her mouth but let it drop back into the bowl.

As she stared gormlessly at her soup a hand from her right picked up her spoon. Tarquin casually took a sip of the warm carrot broth and placed it back in the dish with a pointed glance. Jza blinked back until her brain registered that it was the only way she would feel safe enough to eat or drink anything.

She warily picked up her spoon and took her own first sip. The meal continued in the same vein. The Lord would taste each course on her plate with such nonchalance it would have been unnoticeable for those too engrossed in their own meals to care but unfortunately none of the Harem were particularly interested on what was on their plates. Each time the man leaned onto his neighbour's plate the girls' eyes would narrow at his public display.

After the dessert was served the man took a large, slurpy lick of Jza's delicate trifle from her silver spoon.

"A nibble would have sufficed," The Princess rumbled grumpily snatching the spoon back, "I am not used to sharing my cutlery."

"Now what would be the fun in that. A true man always enjoys sharing bodily fluids with lovely young ladies."

"I thought I wasn't your type," Jza's looks were lethal.

"Bruises are not my type," Tarquin replied with a distracted glance. He turned his head away and began a very lengthy and intense discussion with Sofiya. The conversation was once again incomprehensible to her ears and it gave her an opportunity to observe him stealthily. The man had a thin, angular face; slanted almond shaped eyes; a pointed nose. He truly did not look as if he was the part of the nation he ruled. The eyes themselves gave him away instantly but there was something more; a level of aloofness she could feel. It was same sense of outsiderness she exuded in the presence of her captors. She missed most of her dessert while ruminating over this new realisation. It was only when everyone other than herself stood up that she noticed the dinner was over.

"So, you will take the girl with you," Sofiya's sharp nails hit the wooden table periodically.

"I thought you made your position clear about what you felt about her, Sofiya," Tarquin's voice was the chilliest thing in the room even surpassing the cool dessert.

"Yes, I should have thought you would have taken note."

"Do not test me," Tarquin pulled his captive up by her arm dragging her to the door, "You have already disobeyed me once. I will not make light of it again."

With those words he pulled the Princess out of the room.

"I will sleep in your quarters then," Jza motioned around the room as the door was slammed shut. The rooms were devoid of all others as the maid had already vanished. The guard outside their room had not been expecting them and had fumbled while opening the door only causing his master to radiate his ire.

"Argue with me at your own peril. I will send you to the barracks if you desire different company," The man was still quite agitated with his encounter with Sofiya.

"Why don't you? Your life would be much easier." Jza grumbled angrily.

"You are a crafty little katyonak. I have a feeling you shall somehow get away. Best keep an eye on myself" Tarquin entered the bed chambers and pulled his captive alone, "You can sleep on the floor for all I care but I shan't let you go anywhere else. Not near my harem, not my soldiers, nowhere but here."

"You are not worried I will slip away in the dead of the night? I am sure even a blood thirsty man like yourself sleeps."

"Like a complete baby but I know you are going nowhere, and certainly never too far because you will never want to be parted from this little bauble," The man pulled out the shiny locket tantalizingly.

"Give me that," Jza barked, the pain and aches of the day all but forgotten, and sprang towards the man ready to claw his eyes for it if she had to.

"I think not," Her captor grinned and dangled it much higher above her. She jumped on her toes and nearly knocked both of them down.

"You stupid sod, do not play games with me," She pushed him backwards with utter singlemindedness while the man laughed at her daring. He backed away until his rear hit the wallpapered wall.

"You will do anything to get this back," He smirked while keeping his arms raised high enjoying her helplessness.

"It is mine and I demand it back," The girl brushed against him giving him impertinent ideas.

"Come closer and I'll give you what you deserve," His voice was breathy and laced with so much innuendo even she could not ignore and sprang back with an oath.

"I will not be a participant to your vulgarity," Jza hissed with fire flamed eyes cursing the very day he was born.

"You were the one groping me. How could I resist." The man answered innocently and to add fire to the flames wore the locket around his neck. The piece of jewelry taunted as it twinkled in the lamplight.

"I-I- You intend to keep it on, for the night?" Her hands itched but she kept them to herself her face going blotchy and red under her captor's scrutiny. She had behaved like a milkmaid, touching the man with such uncouthness,"I shall sleep on the floor, of course."

"As you wish but I shan't be surprised if you join me in bed soon. You can hardly control yourself, now."

"Keep dreaming, you beast. "

"Indeed, I shall," Tarquin replied mysteriously.

Chapter 8

Jza tried to make herself comfortable on the floor but there was no respite to be had. The stillness of the night was making it difficult for her sleep. As strange as the thought was the castle had always been thrumming with life. That energy, that feeling of life everywhere, was gone. The drunk courtiers, the chattering servants, the youthful bark of laughter from the soldiers had been completely wiped away. She could feel nothing and it was that nothingness that made sleep impossible for her.

Her restlessness got the better of her and she sat up hugging her knees, with her back against the wall. The room was unlit with only moonlight deftly highlighting the corners and plains of the room. Her eyes trailed onto the only other living being in the room, if one did not count the spiders. Her captor was snoring away on the right side of the bed. He was flat on his back with one arm resting on his eyes and the other on the pillow next to him. Her locket was resting right in the centre of the man's bare chest, mocking her.

Jza's jaw clenched as she made up her mind. That locket was hers to protect. Any more time with it and the man might figure out exactly what it was and war would be lost completely. Her father would sacrifice everything except for his daughters. She would not let him suffer the indignity of defeat. She got up slowly, silently, hoping her soft cotton clothes would not make a sound.

Her bare feet sunk into the plush carpet as she quietly walked to the bed. Jza tracked the steady rise and fall of the muscled chest and wondered if her plan would succeed. She leaned down and touched the locket reverently but before she could do more a hand landed on hers.

"Am I dreaming?" The man's soft, sleep laced voice was incredibly amused. He grasped her wrists firmly and pulled her towards him with a jerk. She landed right on top of the man, "I told you, you would join me."

"Let go, you foul beast," Jza pulled her hands away with a tug and glared down at the man.

"Oh, ho, such hypocrisy when it is not I who is straddling anyone."

Her hand covered his mouth to stop his infuriating chatter but she could feel him smiling underneath it which made her pull back immediately.

"Stop being so infuriating. Just give me back what's mine. That's all I want."

"I had no idea I was in such demand. I can claim a hundred women as my property but never could claim they own me in reverse," Tarquin placed his hands behind his head and made himself comfortable. He was a slim man but in the moonlight the corded muscles of his shoulders stood out prominently.

"I don't want you. Just give me back my locket," Jza's attention was once again taken by the locket but that was a mistake and in the blink of an eye she was flipped and became the captive once again. Tarquin had bared his teeth with a dangerous smile as he loomed over her, the locket hung between. The cool metal gently kissed her bare neck in small intervals as they both breathed.

"Don't mistake me for your kind, merciful, ruler Lord Samuel. I am not a weak and vain fool. I will never give this locket back until you tell me who you are."

"I am a nobody," Jza averted her eyes. The strength of his probing eyes made her feel as if she would blurt out all her deepest darkest secrets.

"Are you sure? Are you not a spy sent to keep an eye on me?" The Lord asked forcefully making Jza squirm. His grip on her wrist would leave another bruise.

"If you think me a spy then why have you kept me so close. Have you lost your senses?" She retorted trying to shake free, "And I hardly am some skilled warrior infiltrating the enemy camp."

"Women have their own talents," The man replied simply with his amber eyes lingering all over her. They trailed from her bitten lips to her collarbone all illuminated enticingly under the moonlight.

"Can I even persuade anyone with this face?" She scoffed, unknowingly giving her bosom an attractive heave, "I am not known for my womanly talents, I assure you."

"Maybe I can be persuaded," Tarquin's voice dipped low as he exhaled on her face, blowing the errant baby hairs off her face. Jza felt the man leaning in closer while the locket scraped and finally settled down on her chest. Instinctively she kicked him on the groin and pushed him off.

"I have no interest in leading you anywhere with my charms," Jza braced herself for retaliation as she leapt out of bed. Her open brown hair scattered everywhere in the frenzy.

The man was face down and showed no reaction until he started moving. He rolled over and revealed he was shaking with laughter.

"If this is where the path you leads me to this, I fear I will have nothing left down there," Tarquin snickered looking harmless as if he hadn't just loomed all over her with vile intentions.

"Then stop following me around. I have nothing of value except my father's last memory. I cannot trust you with it if you can not even behave," The girl's face contorted with frustration.

"I am fully chastised, Miss Ashbrook. I have never had a girl dive in my bed without certain expectations," The Lord apologized in a mock polite tone.

"But you will not give me my locket back until I tell you something about myself. Fine. I took care of the library, if that's what you want to know," She mixed the truth in her words. An outright lie would be caught much quicker.

"Is that who you are? A library keeper?"

"No, I am also a farmer's niece, a devoted daughter, a passable archer and a good friend," She may be a Royal Princess but all of these things defined her as well. If this unraveling of her person was required to get the locket back then so be it.

"A good friend to the famous beauties?" Tarquin cocked his head, while still lying prone on his bed with amusement still lingering on his face, "They must be your age."

"Oh, no! They despised me," Jza shook her head with bitter smile. She was always the interloper to them; that half sister who appeared out of nowhere in their lives.

"A resounding recommendation, then."

"No need to flatter me. I shall forever despise you," Jza stated with a raised brow.

"Not exactly the words a man wants to hear when a woman wants something from him." The Lord languidly got up and walked towards still as unclothed as before. The girl wanted to take a step back but stood her ground. She knew exactly where to aim if he tried to intimidate her again.

"Your sense of duty and honour would compel you to ignore any transgressions?" The brunette clasped her hands and blinked faux-innocently.

"Perhaps? But I want something very important from you."

————————————————————————————

Walking into the library was like a surreal dream. It had been Jza's personal haven during times of crisis, and she was back in her worst situation yet. Ironically she was no great reader. It was just that many of her peers, sisters, courtiers shared the same idea about books and rarely visited the place. It was the solitude she had yearned for and the sense of responsibility that helped her keep it under control.

The battle had taken its toll on the entire cavernous hall. It had been cleaned of the former debris although half the windows were missing. Entire shelves had disappeared. Jza had managed to hide some of the more precious volumes in a vault specifically built for the rare book in hopes they would survive a fire. She was optimistic they remain intact. The surprising thing was the paintings of her ancestors were still hanging intact from the walls behind the librarian's desk. Identical brown eyes peered down at her. They reminded her that she was the key to the survival of their family.

"I have a purpose here for you beyond whatever you intend to do. I want you to collect all the Barbarian books in existence. Those that were written by them and those that were written about them," Tarquin ignored the guards stationed at the doors and addressed Jza only, whom he held at his arm. They strolled down the gallery both wearing navy blue outfits. Jza's maid seemed to enjoy making them match.

"I know some of the books but not the entire depth of accumulated knowledge. It will take time. None of the books remain in their original place."

"Of course, but I must know details, dates, everything," He counted off looking distracted. She noticed his eyes kept trailing back to the Royal portraits. Maybe he had ordered them off and some servant had forgotten.

"I am still not a researcher. I am merely the librarian. Surely someone else with a mind made for research would better suited for the job," Jza stilled them in front of the librarian's desk.

"While we may seem fluent in your language not everyone can read it. Those who can I do not want here. You my trapped mouse will perform much better, no? After all there is much to lose," The Lord pointed at the locket still hanging from his clothed torso. The entire morning Jza had spied on him and the man had not taken it off even once.

"Of course," The Princess replied and walked behind the desk. She rummaged through her drawer and found a book that had just been returned. It had been the one she had been lazily reading through when the announcement of war had happened. How could she have known this book about their Barbarian predecessors would be the one life line she could cling to.

Jza glanced up and noticed the Lord was still fixated on the images of her father and their ancestors before looking down at the Barbarian man's etchings on the book's front page.

It was then the realization hit her. Lord Tarquin was part Barbarian. He looked nothing like the folk of his country. His eyes, his face, his hair; it was so obvious she was amazed she had not discerned this earlier. Almost everyone else, from the common servants to his harem women, was pale haired with large, light eyes. He was pale as well but the rest of the colouring was quite the opposite. Now, his comments made sense. If he descended from the Barbarians he would feel it was duty to avenge them.

Blood for blood that was the Barbarian motto.

She sat down on her creaky old chair in shock.

Chapter 9

Tarquin's attention was removed from the paintings as soon as she made too much noise while sitting down.

Their eyes met and Jza 's gaze shied away immediately. She knew her face gave away everything and letting him access her eyes was akin to letting him step into her mind. She hastily started shuffling papers around. For a desk that had been through a war it was remarkable it was still in exactly the same condition she left it. It was obvious the new owners of the castle had not bothered to even try accessing information via the library. The recent clean down was clearly in anticipation of their Lord's visit.

The Lord's gaze was still upon her but she pretended to ignore his attention. While settling her things in the right places she thought about her new discovery. Tarquin's reasons for his brutal takeover were clear to her now. He obviously had a Barbarian ancestor and to avenge him required this kind of destruction.

Barbarians had scattered after the war. Some had adopted Goridian culture far away from the capital but most had left the country completely. Tarquin's country, Somerluian, must have taken in a fair share of Barbarian refugees. But how was it that a Barbarian was able to marry into their Royal family?

The Somerluians were obsessed with purity of blood. They only took a single wife and only her children were considered their father's heirs so their choices of wives was very narrow and particular. The previous Lord of the Somerluians was not of Barbarian blood. Jza may be ignorant to her country's neighbours but it would have at least been common gossip if the man had Barbarian blood running through his veins. So it must have come from Tarquin's mother; that illusive creature who seemed to be the only person that had caused the man to show true emotion.

"Some rise and some fall. Their blood fades away into nothingness," Lord Tarquin mused as he sat himself on top of the desk, opposite from where Jza sat. Clearly seeing her ancestor's portraits had led him into a philosophical mood.

"But blood lives on forever in ones children," She replied curtly.

"Maybe that is why I intend to capture all of King Samuel's progeny," Jza's heartbeat rose at this statement. The man already possessed the key to his goals. Would this be the day he realized what power was in that locket.

"Surely telling the enemy's spy of your plans is not wise," The girl met his gaze briefly before looking down at her papers.

"Why hide my intentions when I have no chance of failing."

"So, you will kill them then?" Jza asked with a sneer.

"Maybe."

"You can still marry one of them. They could be an asset rather than a burden," She asked quietly still trying in her own way to save her sisters, "Who better than a Princess to be your one and only wife."

"What other virtues do these famous beauties posses that might tempt me? I have only heard of their many attributes in song and I never found the taste to follow flowery poetry," Tarquin asked, jovially, leaning closer all over the desk.

Jza cleared her throat as she leaned away, "They possessed great beauty as you know. They will produce the most beautiful children."

"But surely they had other virtues beyond their looks. I am only an ogre on the inside. I don't fear the chance of producing ugly children," The man smirked while his companion gave his audacity an appalled look.

"The eldest loved horse riding and her hunting skills were impeccable. She along with the others could sing, dance, sew, play musical instruments. They were all accomplished young ladies," Jza continued ignoring how much more closer he was leaning in now.

"And what of you?" The man asked abruptly.

"Me? but I am not of the famous twelve beauties. I am nothing in comparison to them. I never was," The brown haired girl shook her head wistfully.

"Surely all young respectable women learn these things. I am sure even you could play a pretty piece."

"I could try if you want to lose your ears. I grew up in a barn you see," Jza accidentally revealed far more than she had intended to. Her heartbeat thrummed in her ears. If the man wanted to hear music all he needed to do was place his ears close to her heart.

"And your father let you grow up in a barn?" Tarquin loomed near to her face. His nearness was an effective scare tactic as anything else.

"M- My mother was dead and they had been estranged prior to it. I was raised by my uncle. He- My father did not know where I was until... until... I have throttled enough chicken with these hands," Jza wriggled her ten fingers with a slight manic edge. The man was asking too many probing questions.

"And now they hold these precious books," The lord murmured slowly, absorbing her stiff posture and forced expression.

Jza got up abruptly and pointed behind her. Her hand shook as she turned towards her destination.

"On that section was where I know books about the Barbarians were left behind. Should I show you in case you want to ever access them yourself?"

"That would be wise," Tarquin did not ask about her obviously strange behaviour. He slid off the desk and took her hand gently and placed it on his arm. Her fingers clenched, trying to find some solid ground, even if it was only her enemy's muscled arm but she stopped herself.

"They were not always called the Barbarians," She volunteered the information with an unsteady voice, "Their original name fell out of use years ago."

"Of course, it was," The man replied with a scoff and followed the girl's lead to the book shelf.

"Oh good, they are still here. Books on Barbarian culture, art, history, oh, and even war. There's a lot more then I thought I would find," Jza was engrossed by her discovery to let her troubles go for now and also the man's arm. She found a book on Barbarian textiles and flipped through it.

"This is beautiful," She whispered as she paused on an intricate pattern. The book writer had used vivid colours to imitate what must have been rich fabrics.

"Yes, it is," The Lord replied, even though she had required no answer.

She raised her eyes up at him and found him looking at her. With a glare she snapped the book shut. The man just smiled back serenely, distracting her completely from her worries.

——

Jza's days as a captive had been quite mundane. Her routine had revolved around her task in the library. It had taken so many days just to make a comprehensive list of the Barbarian related books and now she had taken to noting every of interest down. It was a solitary task because she had no helpers except for her assigned maid who lugged around heavy books from their shelves. Since the maid spoke nothing of her language Jza had become adept at getting things done via sign language.

In spite of his pretense of a relaxed Lord with a bevy of beauties at his beck and call Tarquin was quite an involved ruler. He spent most of the day either attending multiple war meetings or jotting down correspondences and although he never spoke about his progress Jza had sensed he was gaining momentum over her father's army in other provinces. There was a certain solidness of his shoulders that a defeated and frustrated man would never carry.

Their sleeping arrangements had remained the same. Every night the captor and his captive would close doors behind them and fall asleep in their own usual spots. One on the bed and the other on the floor. Jza suspected her maid had a much more comfortable place at night but she wasn't going to complain. The man would offer the space beside him with a roll of his eyes and that was unacceptable.

Once again as always Jza started her day in the library. Her maid was dozing in a corner while she was jotting down notes from a Barbarian book about dances. It was odd but Tarquin had been adamant everything including frivolous behavioural observations needed to be noted down.

"...And then the men would encircle their partner's waist and lead them on the dance floor..." Jza read and wondered what life would have been like under the Barbarian's rule. They seemed more relaxed and had fewer rules of propriety. And her thoughts drifted to the Barbarians who had to move to their neighbouring country which was even more restricted especially regarding women. They could not even marry on their own accord while the men could keep hordes of women for their own pleasure. The Barbarians must have felt so alienated by the oppressive cultures that dominated them.

Jza rubbed her eyes and broke the trance of the image of gaily dancing men and women etched behind her eyes. She needed another book about Barbarian etiquette to add to her notes about their dances. The freedom of gender mingling obviously altered how they danced and how their balls were conducted.

The Princess got up from her squeaky chair and walked to the relevant shelves. A slight shuffling from the room's corner broke her concentration.

"Is anyone there?" Was on the tip of her tongue but a quick look at her sleeping maid made her pause. There was no point in waking her up from her slumber for something so pointless. The brunette stood on her tip toes on the flagstone floor, swaying, stretching her arms to get to the book when a large book on her right fell. She peered down, her nose scrunching in confusion when another fell and then another until it seemed a waterfall of solid, hard covers cascaded down on her. The girl quickly shielded herself but found herself under the entire contents of the shelf.

She heard her maid yowling in alarm and was quickly pulled away before the bookshelf creaked and fell to the floor with a loud thud. Books, papers, and dust flew everywhere. The other girl gestured frantically at the mess and at her.

"I am fine," She whispered softly at the girl forgetting that she could not understand her words. The maid decided to take matters into her own hands and began prodding her charge to check for damage.

"How utterly bizarre. How did they even fall on me?" She exclaimed, observing the damage. The Princes limped a little as her maid supported her away from the chaos. Three guards slammed the door open and ran inside, equally as alarmed by the distur-bance in the room as by the screaming maid. They surveyed the room in alarm as they were told the entire tale by the servant girl.

"You should go back to your rooms immediately," The guard spoke haltingly, his accent slurring the words.

"I should help," Jza said with a grimace painting her face. The guards quickly waved her away.

"We will handle the situation. Lord Tarquin has very strict orders about your safety. You must leave immediately."

Jza was surprised by the urgency in the man's tone,"I would like you to tell her to bring my belongings, my pens and my notebook back with me. I shall complete my assignment back in... my rooms."

The man conveyed her wishes to the other girl while Jza slowly left the hall. The dust was still swirling in the air making it hard for her to breathe. She eased herself through the door and sat down on the bench outside with a weary sigh. The bruises on her face and body were almost healed but apparently an unblemished appearance for her was not meant to be. Thankfully only her arm only ached from the barrage of books.

"Hurry! Tarquin demands the papers immediately. He will be an utter brat about it if we delay any further," A masculine voice hissed from behind a corner near the library.

"Hush! Someone will hear you and your insolence will end in your blood," Another voice replied and Jza strained to see exactly who it was. She could see shadows flickering under a torch's light.

"What does it matter. Half these illiterates do not understand the Goridian language. We can use it with ease," The first voice clarified with a drawl.

"He will find a way and have your head. A man who would can kill his father can do anything."

Chapter 10

The renovation project of the arena was nearly complete. The princess peaked through the curtains as the masons were laying stone on the last few steps. She did not know if it was a bane or a boon to have given Tarquin the idea of performing the age old Barbarian ritual of blood sports.

While her soldiers had not been given their death sentences that maybe prolonging their miserable lives would not make them grateful. But no matter, what was done was done.

Her head throbbed with an intensity she was sure would keep her at night but she had more pressing matters to think about. Her eavesdropping had led her to the incredible discovery that all was not what it seemed in Lord Tarquin's army. He did not have absolute control because he had killed his father. What kind of heartless soul was he who had no respect for family bonds. He could kill for his mother but could not give the same courtesy to his father. Was he so power hungry that he could not wait for the crown to come to him?

The moral dilemma of whether to reveal the conversation was weighing upon her. She wanted to ask him the impertinent questions swirling in her head but shed oubted he would take kindly of her questioning. He would once again threaten to slaughter her head and that would be the end of that.

Jza's headache grew exponentially as Lord Tarquin sauntered into their shared quarters playing with a red apple with his fingers. He was dressed in blackhead to toe but his face was bright like a furnace. It was so typical he was enjoying her pain.

Their eyes met and the crushing secret in her heart made her feel deathly afraid. The library situation was but a faded memory by now and only the new revelations swirled in her head.

"I heard a certain librarian was crushed beneath a pile of books. It would have been the most ironic death this palace has ever seen if those books had succeeded."

"Hardly," Jza shifted her stance, "Just a shelf that came down. Must have been damaged in the attack and gone unnoticed during the renovation."

"And you suffered any injuries?" Tarquin asked.

"Nothing of import. I am as bruised as I was before."

He sat on the bed and took a bite of the apple as he surveyed the damage. It was true, bruises upon bruises were difficult to decipher.

"Are you sure?" His voice was much quieter. His face lost the smarmy expressions. He handed her the apple and she absent-mindedly took a bite. It was turning into a habit to have him feed her his leftovers. The threat of poison was still constant and ever present. The Harem had not warmed up to her at all.

"I see the arena is being set up for the battles," the girl shied away from the conversation about her accident lest she blurted everything out. Also knowing him he would make fun of her weak reflexes for weeks ahead anyway.

"You should be happy you saved your soldiers. They were never meant to live longer than the day of the execution."

"They will be fighting in the true barbarian fashion, I suppose," The girl murmured wistfully.

"It will be an honour for them to indulge in such noble activity," Tarquin mentioned proudly.

If Jza hadn't figured out his heritage she would have been baffled by his insistence to glorify Barbarian traditions. The Somerluins were a proud race and they certainly would never have allowed another culture to prevail over them. The man dominating her thoughts flipped though her notes and materials that were lying allover the bed.

"Are you well versed with the subject of Barbarian Balls?" The man asked sharply.

"Yes, I am quite sure I have the length and breadth of this subject tightly by the neck, why?"

"Because I shall be holding one very very soon."

Jza could not fathom how her captor found time to run a war and then plan a ball on top of that. He apparently even took time to visit the kitchens regularly to dictate his food plans for them and she had seen him wandering through the gardens with the gardener observing the desolate situation. He would have been the perfect housewife if his gender had been altered since his ability to multitask knew no bounds. His future wife would have absolute luxury because he would leave no chores for her to do.

One day a week after her incident in the library he ordered that she accompany him instead of heading towards the library. She barely finished her ablutions and hurriedly followed him out their shared rooms knowing his temper would flare if she wasn't there at the right time. Her maid ran behind with her hair comb but there was no saving the mess on her head anyway. Her hair hung loose behind her.

"Who shall even be attending the ball?" Jza asked curiously as he finally slowed down and offered her his arm. She took it without protest. Her life was much easier if she chose her battles. She could bide her time until she got hold of the key, "Surely you won't be allowing your uncouth soldiers near your Harem."

"The Harem will not be allowed near this event. My people shall by populating the grand hallways soon. The wives and families of the army men will make up the female population of the ball. The Harem never mingles with the rest of the population. Their husbands will not allow their wives to be in such company."

"Interesting. Are they happy to bring their families to an active war zone though?"The Princess could not hide her surprise. Her father would never have allowed any women folk to traipse into a situation so dangerous.

"You may not wish to hear it but your army ceased to be a challenge a long time ago. My army is proud of its accomplishment and they wish to show their wives this fallen city. It is just a temporary outing but a well deserve done. These wives have been separated from their men for a long time"

They crossed the hall of the Royals on their way to the banquet hall Tarquin had deemed suitable for the ball. The Princess was surprised the artwork still remained intact. Not only were the portraits still hanging of their ancestors but also the current family.

Suddenly the hair at the back of her head stood up. Was it possible she had made it into the gallery? Could her father have commissioned a likeness of her without her knowledge? She had regularly refused his attempts at making her immortal in paint but who knew which artist had targeted her from a distance.

The duo passed by many cameos, paintings and etchings of the royal family. The twelve beauties featured prominently in them. The girls were eager to have their accomplishments displayed and remembered.

Jza kept an eye out for her likeness to be staring back at her but mercifully there was nothing that incriminated her. It was just an inundation of the girls either posing gracefully in a scene or being shown accomplishing various tasks.

"They are very common looking," Lord Tarquin wrinkled his nose like a spoilt brat.

"Pardon me, but did the war addle your brain? None in even your Harem could match their beauty," Jza was aghast at his declaration.

She half expected to be hit in the head by the man but he had stopped wishing her bodily harm ever since she started working in the library. Maybe the information she collected was worth far more to him than she had realised.

"Plain, plain,plain," The man ignored her protest and rebuking words.

"Oh, Lord, I imagine you whither at the sight of me. I was notoriously not in their league," The girl laughed self deprecatingly.

"You are correct in your assessment Milayamoya ," The Lord smiled at her indulgently. His eyes travelled over her face and Jza wondered whether she should take up the veil to conceal herself from his criticism. How horrendous he must think she looked like.

"What do you call me? Is it an insult?"She asked. The man did seem in a pleasant mood so he might just answer her.

"Whatever is it you want to believe," He answered instead, mysteriously.

Jza was relieved as they walked out of the hallway realising none of her likeness existed. There was an inkling in the back of her head that deemed it improbable but who was she to question her good luck.

They walked into an empty ballroom that was far smaller than the one she had been captured in. It too was marble clad from top to bottom but had a solitary chandelier hanging in the middle instead of multiples as there had been in the largest hall. While not the largest entertainment area it could easily see to a ball in here. As a matter of fact she had seen quite a few. Her sisters had held many parties here with a ridiculous amount of guests. The room was surprisingly in good shape with no signs of wear and tear. Either the war had left no scars or Tarquin's men had been hard at work far beyond the time frame she had been informed of the ball.

The hall sparkled in the chandelier light and Tarquin's amber eyes gleamed along with it. Today his eyes were speckled with more green than usual.

"Miss Ashbrooke, I am in need of your expertise. What do I need to do to make this ball a success."

Jza rambled in her usual way about the food, decorations, clothing while the man listened intently, "...you also must have the musicians out in the open. No hiding them behind curtains like we do. The Barbarians like to hand them money for any performance they adore. There is of course the matter of the dance. It is different then what we do at least."

Lord Tarquin beckoned her close, "Teach me."

Jza should have fainted at his words because she did not believe he was capable of asking for help but instead began to narrate what she knew.

"Your hands will be on the lady's waist and she will have her hands on your shoulders. Keep your hands fleeting. No one likes a man who uses a beautiful dance for his own pleasure."

"What if I do wish to be suggestive," All his perfect teeth glinted in the face.

"The Lady would have no qualms putting you in your place. Barbarian women were adept at combat. The Lady would already be carrying her own weapon to place at your throat."

"I remember you too had some ideas how to put me in my place," Tarquin smirked.

"Unfortunately hand to hand combat is not my forte. I am only useful with arrows," Jza said ignoring his expressions.

"I should teach you soon," He breathed in her direction. Was he flirting with her or did he seriously mean it? The man was a master of innuendo. He exhaled suggestive thoughts like cascading water out of a fountain. Sometimes it was hard to understand when he was being literal or not.

She placed her hands delicately on his broad shoulders without acknowledging how he was making her uncomfortable. Sometimes she wondered if all his posturing was a test to see how soon she would lose her temper. Did he laugh at her helplessness during his private moments.

"You would have a hard time then. I am not that easily teach able," Jza replied, primly.

Tarquin pulled her closer in response until all she could smell was his scent. Jza kept her eyes on his chest but Tarquin had the gall to pull her face upwards, hooking his finger under her chin. Jza tried to keep her eyes unmoved by his intense stare but she felt the urge to pull them down. Her sudden shyness at their closeness made her feel inadequate.

His fingers on her waist were not subtle at all and that broke the camel's back. They gently dug into her flesh making her squirm. She tried to get away from him but he held on firm. His hands tightened around her. Jza heard an ominous creak but ignored it to glare at the man.

"Ugh, must you be such a beast all the time. You have a harem to take your frustrations out on so stop harassing me. Talk to me like a human being and not some loose piece of muslin," The girl growled.

"Do not test me. I am being very patient. You do not know how many times I have come close to pushing you down the nearest staircase," Tarquin warned, looming all over her his mood incredibly severe. Jza pulled herself away from his grip.

"My patience is the one being tested. Who knows how many times I have thought to fling myself off the roof of this castle. Maybe I should go ahead with my plans."

There was another creak from above and the princess looked up to see the chandelier swaying.In that instant she realised what was about to happen. In a fit of insanity her body accelerated into action and ran towards Tarquin. With a grunt she shoved his firm chest and managed to push him aside using all of her bodily strength. Behind them the chandelier careened down and smashed into the floor in a glitter of glass and light.

Jza landed squarely ontop of Tarquin with her face buried in his chest.

Chapter 11

Jza buried her face in the soft material and exhaled. Behind her the glass was still tinkering as the multiple layers of chandelier dismantled slowly after the explosive beginning and settled into the ground. This was a dramatic turn of events and the Princess willed her heart to slow down. She was content to lay there trying to get her bearings when she heard another dull sort of thudding sound. She raised her head up realising it was Tarquin's heartbeat.

The man stared back at her with a shocking lack of expression. Was that his default expression she wondered before shaking her head. No, she had seen enough of him to know he was a master at hiding what he felt. She pushed herself off him and surveyed the destruction behind her. The chandelier was a beautiful mangled mess. Jza brushed off remnants of the glass on her person.

"You seem to have gotten more accident prone of late," Lord Tarquin was up on his feet in a heartbeat while she still struggled to straightened her skirts. He watched her endeavours to get on her feet blandly. Behind them multiple guards ran into the room with varying expressions of shock.

"Accident prone? That doesn't seem like an accident at all. If I were a betting person I would think someone just tried to kill you," Jza asserted.

"Kill me? It would be best if you keep away from gambling since you would lose quite poorly. It was not I who came under an entire book shelf, recently."

"Surely you don't think-" Jza was cut off with a sneer.

"Take her back to the quarters," The man ordered and like an unruly child she was walked back to their rooms. The last thing she heard was him angrily growling orders in his own language.

Jza woke up gradually. Her head felt heavy but a soothing pressure nearly lulled her back to sleep when her eyes sprang open. Was that a hand on her head? The Princess found herself reclining squarely in the middle of the bed with two pillows propped under her head. She looked around and found Lord Tarquin lounging on an uncomfortable chair a comfortable distance away from her.

"When did you come back? You should have woken me up?" The Princess glanced at the curtains and realised it was night time already. How long had she slept for? She certainly had spent a great while pacing in her rooms before feeling completely drained and deciding to take a nap. She noticed an untouched plate of food on one table.

"That's the least I can do for you after what you did today. What do you want from me?" Prince Tarquin said, curtly.

"Pardon?"

"Your services must have a price. Everyone must have one. Other than freedom what do you want?"

Jza's brown eyes travelled to his throat. The chain around his neck dangled down to his chest hidden from view even in the informal outfit he only wore in their rooms. Both of them knew what she would ask for.

"No, I cannot allow you to have the locket either."

"Why? It has no significance whatsoever," Jza lied, "I do not understand your fascination with a meaningless bit of jewelry."

"You will run the moment you get it. I cannot allow for that to happen."

Jza nodded and conceded defeat. That was exactly what she would do although she wanted to ask why he even needed her presence. To him she was of no value. She did not know any military secrets, nor did he know her true identity. Her presence only caused him difficulty if she was honest. He spent much time making sure she wasn't dead on his watch.

"Then you could do me a favour and be less of a brute. It is not befitting your station in any case," Jza glared at the man. After all it had been his wandering hands that led them to quarrel before the chandelier fell. She had thought him an improved man after his initial introduction but apparently that was not so.

"Oh, ho, you think you know what a man of my stature should behave like," Tarquin laughed.

"Yes, you have a duty to your nation. They will want someone to look up to."

"I do not really care what they think of me," Tarquin's apathy was extensive.

"Handling a noble lady is a skill you should learn for the sake of your future wife. No Lady of quality would be wooed by wandering hands. You would only be left with the ones who's own moral values are very low. Have you not be taught so? Your tutors should have been vigilant," Jza implored.

"How should I know how to treat a noble women? I was raised in the Harem. I have known only but a few noble women," Tarquin's throat worked as he stood abruptly, "Enjoy your meal. I have already tasted it. It's rather good."

The man left the rooms in a flurry without so much as a look.

Jza watched the doors closing shut and placed her head on her knees a few moments later. Somerluians were very strict about their women folk. Like the man had informed her earlier the men kept the true and proper wives and women away from the Harem. It was not possible for a prince to grow up in the Harem unless his father was begetting sons left and right with his playthings. Was he a bastard? Was that why he looked different from his subjects? Was that also why he had to kill his father to get the throne. The proper Somerluians would never let a Bastard much less a half Barbarian bastard lead them so how did all of this come to be.

In all this confusion she forgot to eat once again.

____

The Princess sat primly among the guards awaiting her turn to meet Lord Tarquin in his office. He had called for a meeting with her and she had obliged. She could hardly say no thought the illusion of choice was appealing. He could have asked her to give him the full list of Ball related items in his rooms but he had disappeared since the day of the chandelier accident. He would barely make an appearance once in a while but it seemed he had decided to make the Harem's rooms his permanent abode.Was it because she had scolded him about propriety or because he did not want to face her after his revelations of his upbringing, she did not know.

A guard motioned for her to follow him.

The rooms she entered were neat even though they were full to the brim with parchments, lists and maps. The desk was not the one her father had used but another set up in a grander fashion with carved feet and curved, gilded edged. It contained many locked drawers and she imagined space for hidden compartments. It seemed Lord Tarquin kept his personal belongings close by.

She looked down at her extensive notes, waiting for the man to make an appearance when suddenly her attention was caught by something in the corner of her eye. She looked towards it and was faced with an image she had never seen before. Right in the middle of the panelling sat a portrait of a girl holding an arrow. The sun streaked through the middle where the bow and arrow met.

It was her.

Painted in broadstrokes with fetching greens and browns swirling around her image it could be no one else. The artist must have been inspired when she won the archery competition against the commander. There was no title under it although she wondered maybe it had been removed. Her heart was in her throat and she nearly crashed in the Lord who had finally made his appearance. He smiled at her terror.

"Did you think I would stop trying to find out who you are."

"You still do not know my name," Jza guessed. If he knew he would have wasted no time in addressing her with it.

"True, but for how long? I have my ways."

"Is that why you called me here, to see your triumph," The Lady was incensed at his games. He had hung her portrait where every one of his senior staff could see. She wondered if they could recognise her since her bruises were taking time to fade.

"I never thought you were the vain sort," The man hummed ignoring her fury. He sat down behind his desk languidly.

"I did not know any likeness of me existed."

"These are not the only ones," The Lord stated watching her closely.

"Truly?" Jza was stunned. She had never seen anything of the sort. How stupid had she been to imagine the multitude of artists under King Samuel were not capturing her every move. Had some silly fool placed a false version of her with the Royal family?

"Yes, but first we need to go over the workings of this ball. The dates are getting closer," The man switched the subject with the finesse of a blind cat.

"You are more determined to hold a ball than a mama with a spinster daughter,"Jza allowed him the change in topic.

"I need to show my might to both the Gordians and the Somerluians. I shan't let them doubt me any longer.

Chapter 12

The very next day she paced on the stone library floors wondering how could she get to the bottom of the situation. The tap tap tap of her gait echoed in the cavernous room. She could ask Lord Tarquin bluntly of what he knew of her but the infuriating man was not the most easy person to talk to. He would either throw the information in her face or conceal it enough to make her quiver with wrath.

Jza was certain Lord Tarquin did not know who she was. His temperament had not changed in the slightest or maybe, just maybe, he was playing her for a fool in his wretched game of trying to break her. It haunted her mind the implications of his discovery. Was it possible he had found more paintings of her. Were any of them with the Princesses? She barely spent any time in their company so there was a chance she could have been eliminated from any group portraits.

Even her rooms were far removed from the Princesses because of how severely they ostracised her from the beginning. They would spill their drinks on her new gowns and let everyone believe Jza was so uncivilised she could not keep them clean for an hour. They would hide or break her belongings and call her irresponsible. It was when they started misplacing their own belongings and blaming her that she was taken away from their shared quarters.

Her father had been clear it was not as a punishment but for her own protection. He knew she was truthful.

Her own room was smaller than her former one. It had no separate seating room but one combined with her bedroom so she could only entertain her most closest friends. It also had no balcony and only a small window but it had the peace she yearned for. She was safe in her own little space with her meagre belongings. Her father had asked her to decorate it with her own choices and she had chosen green, silk wallcoverings to adorn her cosy room.

Jza continued her pacing feeling the rope tighten on her neck. The man was just too curious to let her identity be a non-issue. He was hunting her as he had hunted her since the day they had lost this castle to him. She could sense his metaphorical teeth at the nape of her throat just itching to draw blood. His moments of calm were just a facade. He would not rest until her identity lay on his feet for him to stamp on.

Her feet paused as she realised there were no shadow under her door. She looked outside the massive library windows and discerned the guard was switching with another fellow. They tended to do so at this time of day. It was in that moment a thought flitted through her panicked mid which was so stupid, so selfish. If caught she would most certainly lose the tatters of freedom in her grip.

She placed her book on the desk with false calmness. Her head and mind were bursting with the possibility that she could use this moment to escape. She was rarely ever left alone and if there was going to be any chance this was it. Her maid was also absent that day due to one ailment or the other. This was a chance in a million.

But what about the locket she thought. How could she think to leave it behind. Another selfish thought marinated in her head. Surely the man was too dense to figure it out. To him it was just a sentimental bauble of no worth. If his immense curiosity had not led him to the locket's truth now then why would her absence. She could escape, hide, find her father, who would consequently defeat Tarquin and take the locket off his dead body.

Before she knew it her body had crossed the room and near the door. Her hand shook as she touched the intricate door handle and then the world exploded in a bright disarray for colours. It was all in her mind since the room was quiet as it had been. Jza's limbs burned and she fell to rough floor with an ominous thud.

————————————————————————————————————

The world swayed when she opened her eyes. The gold and green blurs danced across her mind as she blinked, trying to clear her vision. Her hand reached her forehead and it was damp to the touch. Her head was resting on a silk pillow.

She knew he was around. He always was around when there was trouble. Her eyes finally began to clear up and the dark blob at the edge of her vision began to solidify.

"Good Afternoon, my Lady Ashbrook?"

"Not quite," She replied primly smoothing her skirts. Her bare feet greeted her from the end of her clothing and she found herself amused imagining the great Lord Tarquin at her feet, prying off her shoes, like a lowly servant. She expected to be in familiar surroundings but the blood drained away from her face as she looked above. The greenness of the room left her nauseous. She leaned heavily against her pillow trying to catch her breath. It was done. He had found her room. She should have escaped as soon as she had the chance and now she was caught.

"H- How d-did?" She could not complete her sentence the knot in her throat blocking her voice.

"I'm getting closer, aren't I?"

She closed her eyes and strengthened her resolve. Maybe all was not lost and she chose her words carefully, "Maybe."

"My industrious little servants were busy examining all the rooms and look what they brought me," Whatever he held in his fingers he brought forward. His feet were soundless on the hard marble.

It was a painting of her during her come out ball. It was a sweet little sketch done by a courtier's young daughter who was only learning how to dabble in the arts. It was hardly accurate since all her features were exaggerated to make her look like a beauty of the highest order. She was not and had never looked so ethereal but the bashful girl had been so pleased with her creation Jza had not uttered a word of criticism. She had kept the painting on her desk under the glass.

The Lord watched her with his amber eyes.

"Are you delighted at your new finds? First my paintings and now my room. You must have searched it thoroughly to seek my identity. Do you not have a war to win?"

"I have my hobbies," The man shrugged casually, "It was not you my men searched for. You are not as important as you think. All the rooms are under scrutiny even the attic space. Information is all the power one needs to win a war and I have vowed for it to be all mine."

"You had Raymond to thank for then, for helping you capture the castle? I know that cur betrayed us."

Tarquin smiled with all his teeth on show as he folded his arms complacently, "If you think he is the only traitor... Not everyone is like you, ready to die for the country and King."

Jza limbs burned at the memory of the moment she had tried to run. How ashamed was she at thought of her traitorous mind to just run into the wild and abandon the Royal Princesses to their fate. Even now the regret of being unable to leave the room at that moment was a disappointment. She nowhere as noble as the man had implied.

"What is the vow that you speak of?" He asked still watching her bruised face.

"Me? I daresay I do not know what you speak of,"The Princess was still puzzled by his question. She tried to sit up but her limbs still felt heavy. The man's hand darted forward to steady her but he stopped himself swiftly.

"I found you unconscious, feverish in the library. You were speaking gibberish as I carried you here. I only understood just one word from your mouth."

Jza was struck by his words. Was that the reason why she could not escape? Was the vow she had bonded herself to making things difficult. Was the bond so sentient it would injure her if she dared to break it. She knew of the ceremony and of how it was performed but she did not know the consequences of not following through with the bond.

"I have vowed many things. How should I know what I remembered in my moment of fraility."

"My Lady, I am sure you do not mistake me for a fool. You were talking about bonding to a vow. It is not child's play you talk off."

Jza noted his change of address as well as the lack of sarcasm to her title. Her rooms were not in the Royal quarters but they were close. He now knew she was not a plain little miss. His speech indicated his new knowledge.

"I know very little about bonding to vows," She replied truthfully.

Tarquin eyes glowed with barely contained fury but he paused. His hands unclenched and his body relaxed like a puppet divorced from his master, "Stop missing your meals. I do not care if you starve yourself but finding you lying prone here and there is not what I wish to do in my free time.

The man instead walked up to her ornate wardrobe and started browsing through her belongings. If he wanted some signs of her identity in her more plain outfits then he was looking in the wrong direction. She did not keep her jewelry in her room nor any important papers. Everything was in her father's multiple safes and she was certain her father had disposed of all the parchments before he left the castle. Tarquin might have been luckier in finding information if his father had been a more lax ruler.

"Have you not made any bonds to your vows as yet? To your country, I mean. King Samuel bonded his vow to the kingdom when he was made king," Jza looked at her captor's sharp profile with curiosity.

"No, Never. That is not meant to be. I just have one vow to make. Why waste it on what is already mine."

"Are you saving it for your future wife?" The girl was incredulous. In her society people only saved vows for two important things. Either their professions or their marriages. It would be amusing if the man was a romantic.

Her words entertained the man greatly. His shoulders shook with mirth, "Finish this Ball and maybe I shall show you."

"No one finds a wife just by attending a Ball. While I'm sure the candidates are there, you must court the fine young Ladies. It will take time," Jza lectured him on propriety. She needed to save whatever poor young girl that caught his fancy.

"I told you I was raised in the Harem. I know nothing of social niceties beyond what was taught to me by the women there. You should tell me all there is to courting. I should add that to your Ball research."

Jza made a sour face. How was she going to turn a brute into a gentleman? That was an impossible task. He should have just asked her to give him the moon.

"How come you do not know polite society? The Somerluins would never allow there crown Prince to be raised with the Harem. I know at least that much," Jza asked before she could stop to consider how inappropriate the conversation was. He would never expose something so personal to her.

"I was not always the crown Prince," He revealed, much to her surprise.

"They say you killed to get the throne," Jza did not have the courage to mention she knew about his father. But it was implied. She knew that he understood her meaning.

He did not look the least bit surprised that even in her confinement she knew more than he had presumed. His eyes caught hers with a gaze that could freeze lakes in the middle of summer.

"I would kill anyone for my mother's honour. My father was no exception."

Chapter 13

"**Y**our mother must be very precious to you. Will she be coming to the ball?"Jza asked after an eternity of silence.

Lord Tarquin gave her a look that was pure stone. He lips did not move and her question was left unanswered as she had expected. He instead continued to rummage through her wardrobe. He pulled a gown out of her meagre collection and placed it on her bed, next to her. It was some sparkly number she had never gotten the opportunity to wear.

"You must wear this to the Ball," He finally spoke, irritating Jza to the core. He was more persistent than her governess at bettering herlooks.

"Will I be attending? The brown haired girl asked pulling her feet towards her in an effort to sit with more dignity. She took great pains to keep her legs covered under her morning frock.

"You believe I would ask you to organise the entire Ball and keep you away from it."

"I am just your lowly acquisition. Why would you keep me at your side at the Ball. Surely the Ball attendees will be mortified to be in my company." Her words caused a frown on his face. His nose wrinkled as if he smelt something unpleasant but he lost the animation in his face as soon as he caught her gaze.

"I do not care what they think."

"But you do. The Ball would not be happening if you did not. Don't deny your very human feelings."

The man pursed his mouth with another frown dancing on his forehead. It was a small victory but Jza basked in the win of rendering him speechless.

She went back to manoeuvring her gown modestly and tried to carefully set her feet on the floor.

"I can walk," Jza uttered stubbornly knowing the man would tell her off but her still weak knees buckled under pressure and his arms were around her before she could blink. He took hold of her limbs and picked her up before she could protest.

"You should look after yourself," The man's pale face loomed near hers, "Is that your intent, to slowly let yourself die?"

"Why should I? I may never see my family ever again. I may just lose my will to live eventually," She spat out more furious at herself than him at how fragile she felt. Lord Tarquin it seemed had decided to take her back. He opened the door with his elbow and cautiously eased her out through the doorway. There was no doorman guarding the door to watch their awkward movements.

"I won't let you die on my watch," He words breathed through her loose locks of brown hair. She continued holding her gaze up ahead trying to ignore his presence. Their current path also seemed empty which she was grateful for.

"But you shan't set me free either. I am merely your captive, your slave,"Jza exhaled.

"Don't sully the protections I offer you in this time of war. Your luck has been most gracious to let you fall in my hands. You would be lost without me. You are nothing in the grand scheme of things,"Tarquin stated blandly.

"You don't believe that. I would not be under your protection if that were the case," Jza argued finally locking her gaze with her captor.Her face tinged pink noticing how closely he was following her words.

"I am not in the habit of capturing young women. I would have kept you even if your were more worthless than a scullery maid," The Lord said in his own defence.

"But the Harem?"

"The Harem is an ugly leftover from my forefather's time. They killed the men and stole their woman even those they should have been honour bound to protect after treaties and so forth," Tarquin looked away for once looking disgusted by his ancestors.

Here he was talking about honour all over again. Jza wondered why where it had suddenly come from. Where was the brute she was so well acquainted with.

"Then why not be rid of it once and for all," She asked catching his eye once again.

"Where will they go? The level of fear they command is only afforded to them because I allow it. The society has no place from them."

Jza accepted his answer. It made sense. They were fallen women. It would be hard for them to find employment in her own kingdom much less her enemy's.

Tarquin stopped at the doorway of their shared quarters. The guard outside their door was startled to see the way they made their appearance. He swiftly opened the door not letting himself linger on the spectacle in front of him.

Jza sighed having gotten used to the humiliation of being considered a fallen woman herself. She wondered if her household would accept her back after sharing a room with her captor. No one would believe her loyalty to her country or her claim to virtue. It abruptly hit her that there may be no place for her back. Things would never go back to normal. Oh, what a mighty price she had paid for being her father's daughter. She felt a kinship with the woman of the Harem she had never felt before, knowing their choices were just as limited as hers.

"If you're truly trying to kill yourself should I stop wasting my time?"The man uttered breaking her reverie.

"You have your own burdens and I have mine. I cannot afford to lose, not even my life," Jza replied as he walked them into their bed chambers. It was dark with only a single burning on the mantle.

"I am already carrying the burden of your weight maybe that is why you strain my limbs," The princess' captor barked a laugh at his own joke, "Maybe you should share since I already support all your burdens."

"You are my foe. You are the last person I shall share it with. I may falter with my own self but I will stay true to my cause until I can since I am only made from human flesh."

"Oh, I know." He gripped her harder. He smiled at her with intentions as plain as day. His clean breath washed over her face.

"Beast," Jza dug her nails in his neck's flesh, letting him know she was onto his games," I promise you the day I break, it will be the hardest day of your life."

They stared at each other as he laid her down on the bed. She was steadying herself and arranging her gown down her bare ankles with his gaze still on her. She faintly wondered if he meant to join her.

His amber eyes glowed in the candle light with intent, lingering on her face as if he could not decide which part of her face he should focus on. His slanted eyes narrowed even further on her lips but he moved away to fiddle with the matches in a stilted fashion unlike his usual self.

He had been tempted, she knew. There was nothing she could have done to stop him, not now when she weaker than a newborn kitten but he did not lunge for her as she had expected. Was he honouring her request to let her be in exchange for saving his life?

"I believe you," Tarquin answered softly.

She barely heard him above the beating of her heart. It raced faster than a war horse. Her captor was maintaining the distance between them as he looked on from the shadows. He lit the match and his face shone brilliantly. Their eyes were still locked. Nothing it seems could break their connection which made Jza more frantic.

The Lord took pity on her and with a sigh looked away. His fingers curled up into fists as he denied himself the temptation to join his captive in bed.

"I was not allowed to talk to anyone when I was young. Only the servants and the Harem girls. It is not easy to be the outsider. It is also why my address is unacceptable to you."

"I know the feeling of being an uncouth outsider," Jza gave a bitter laugh, "I grew up in a farm. Transitioning into the palace was painful."

"Did your father pay his penance for abandoning you too? He after all abandoned you to a barn until he could not longer afford to ignore your existence."

"No, he just did not know I lived. My grandmother made sure of that. My father was my saviour. He came looking for my mother but only found an offspring he never knew existed. He cleaned the muck off my fingers and handed me gold and silver instead."

"I am sorry I undo his good work," Tarquin said abruptly and walked out of the room without ceremony.

Chapter 14

Her captor knew too much. Jza could not deny that extended time in his company was making her foolish. She was saying too much. Maybe that was why he had managed to retain the crown when his blood was not even pure. Instead of forcing her to reveal anything about herself he was clearly using a gentler technique which was obviously working.

But was she not privy to information no one else in her kingdom knew? The exchange of knowledge between them was equal in that sense at least. His questionable family history was almost in her grasp. While the titbits of knowledge he fed her were not enough she knew his biggest weakness. His mother. While he knew not who her father was she knew who his mother was. She vowed to find more books pertaining to his history from his Somerluin side of the family tree.

Jza blew out the candle on her bedside. In the dark her mind wandered to the memory of his eyes on her. Her hands shook as she grabbed her silk sheets closer to her. Her heart beat once again deafened her. It was a wonder it did not echo in the high ceilings of the room.

The look in his eyes had petrified her more than anything she had ever endured in his capture. He had never given her such a transparent look of longing. His eyes were usually veiled as much as his tongue so she never could gauge what he thought of her other than overt displays of disdain. Today had been different. She did not know if she could look him in the eyes again.

———————————————————————————————

The next day started without incident. The weakness in her limbs was minimal enough to be an afterthought. Jza dressed in her most staid, grey outfit and pulled her brown hair up plainly much to her maid's exclamations of nyet nyet. She was sure whatever he saw in her could be hidden behind ugly clothing. The bruises that hid her face were disappearing much to her woe. As much as the pain hurt her they had their use.

In the gigantic library she started her search while her maid stared at her nails. The books about Somerluins were scattered all over the library. There was a reason it had taken her weeks to find information about the Barbarians. Nothing was in any sort of order about this subject. The books had been squashed inside whatever space the soldiers could find on the shelves. She found a number of books she dared not bring to her desk. She placed them together on one shelf and brought the one without a distinct cover out in the open.

She settle herself against a pillar on the cold stone floor with her dress spread around her and started her study with a quick look around. Her maid was still engrossed in her own thoughts and no one else observed her.

The book was unusually dry. There was no mention of any royal murders or any intrigue of any sort. Just a scattering of dates. Jza mentally chided her father's librarian for keeping such bare bones of information on what was now an important state. She was sure there was information in the other books but she needed time to search without making anyone suspicious.

She quickly found the name of Somerluin king before Tarquin. Lord Ivan. She skimmed over his life and paused over Lord Tarquin's birth announcement. His mother's name was Altani. She raced past his life and found the entry she was looking for. The year and month the seventeen year old Tarquin murdered Ivan.

She saw the dates and her puzzlement increased manifold.

Lord Ivan had married the Barbarian Princess Altani the day he had died. That very day Tarquin had been proclaimed the new Lord. The crowning ceremony King Samuel had attended happened months later when the blood on the throne had long been washed away. The implications were all too clear. His mother had been a married woman for only a few hours before her son had killed his father, her husband.

Jza set her book down in confusion on her lap. Why had Lord Ivan, a man of advanced years, married anyone when he had never shown the inclination earlier and much less to a woman from his Harem. The Somerluins did not believe the woman of the Harem deserved the respect of marriage. Did he want to finally legitimise his heir so he could pass the kingdom onto him? If Tarquin would have gotten the throne as it is why did he need to resort to patricide?

She turned to the book and flipped back the pages to see why a Barbarian Princess was in the Harem in the first place. Jza's own ancestors had displaced the Barbarians from the land so they must have tried to settle in the neighbouring countries. She found the dates to a Barbarian treaty and months later to a public execution. She suddenly understood why Tarquin had mentioned broken treaties and stolen women when explaining the existence of the Harem. His mother was one of the captives of King Ivan.

Melancholy overtook her. It was not difficult to see the parallels of her situation but that was not what disturbed her. Her situation was not even close to being as traumatising as this Barbarian Princess' looking for a fresh start in a new country.

The brown haired girl broke her gaze from her book feeling like she was being watched. Her captor was standing in the middle of the room. How he had managed to walk on the cobbled floor without making a sound was beyond her.

His amber eyes this time around were more focused on her outfit. He rolled his eyes and gave her a hand. She took it without pause since it had been infinitely unwise to sit on the floor when her limbs were still sore. She felt the scar she had left on him. The sign she had injured him and left a mark gave her a strange sort of thrill. Was this the feeling successful warriors felt slaying their prey.

"We have work to do," Lord Tarquin informed her and walked briskly out of the room, letting her follow him. His clean shaven face held no signs of last night. He had barely looked at her while her eyes were fixed on his profile. For a moment she wondered if she had dreamed it all but no she knew something had happened.

She followed him silently and soon realised they were heading towards the ballroom. She was relieved he had meant what he said. They were only meeting to discuss work.

Jza entered the room and her heart escalated beyond her expectations. Scattered along the room was members of the Harem like colourful, murderous peacocks. If there was anyone she wished to never share the room with it was them.

"What is she doing here?" Sofiya snarled in her direction. The Harem would rarely speak her language. They would revert back just to offend her sensibilities just as they did now. Jza felt lucky her sisters were equally as venomous and their words could not hurt her. Their poisons were another matter...

"Wrong. This is a question I should ask you. I don't remember inviting you here."

Jza kept her mouth wisely shut. This time around the tension in the rooms had nothing to do with her. There was already dispute brewing before her arrival. The women had been standing with clenched fists and frowns maring their pretty faces.

"We are your women, Tarquin. We have supported you since you were born. How dare you give this interloper the place we rightfully deserve," A harem girl Jza could not place spat at them.

Tarquin switched to his own language. He clearly had no intention of including Jza in the conversation.

"Is this the payment to all our loyalty. She is as much of a whore as we were. Why are we not included in the ball preparations?"

The Lord's eyes narrowed at her daring but he continued in the language of his father without hesitation. He called Sofiya towards him who obeyed very reluctantly. Her hand movements told Jza she was not about to be pacified anytime soon.

"You cannot have him," Anna hissed near her face before Tarquin could notice her movements. The mint in her breath wafted over Jza's face.

"You can keep him." Jza wrinkled her nose with disgust. Where he spent his nights was none of her concern. The jealousy Anna was showcasing was unnecessary and unwanted.

"You are just like those Goridion Princesses, writing to him, begging him. A traitors to their own country is traitor to us. You will stab him in the back, I just know it," Anna's eyes glistened, anticipating a rebuttal, but Jza was too shocked to respond.

Chapter 15

Jza stared at Anna's fetching face unable to form any words out of her mouth. The Harem member was pulled away by her companion presumably to bear witness to Sofiya's altercation with Tarquin. Jza stood numbly in her spot barely registering the words echoing in cavernous banquet hall. Harsh words were being exchanged but it was mere noise to her.

As the daughters of exceedingly wealthy Noble women the Princesses were of selfish stock. They lacked for nothing and yet never seemed happy with what they had. They wanted more clothes, more jewels, more pets and baubles. They always wanted more. Jza had never thought their greed would have led them to this path. Jza wondered what could have been said and what had been revealed. Were her sisters even aware of their surroundings to know any state secrets? There was a chance it was all lie Anna concocted but why would she?

There was no male heir and succession was tricky. Jza was not privy to how it would be done once her father passed. She was sure the council and her deceased grandmother had thought of some way to ease succession without leaving a power vacuum on the throne. For a nation that had male preferred primogeniture it was ironic her grandmother had been the true power behind her father's reign. It was only after her death had he been able to come into his own and found out about the existence of another daughter living at her uncle's farm.

"I am disappointed, so very disappointed that this young Shlyukha is the cause of our dispute. Think with the head on your shoulders not..." Sofiya trailed off with innuendo.

Any other time her words would have struck profusely but the Princess was too numb to register them. Jza watched Tarquin's amber eyes narrow with stone like hatred and for a moment it seemed he would strike Sofiya. His hands shook but he composed himself in a blink of an eye and gave all the girls a very pointed look.

"Leave, now," Tarquin's voice was so soft it seemed almost jovial, "I will not responsible for the consequences if you do not obey me immediately..."

Sofiya huffed but conceded. She backed away with a false sense of importance and walked out in the swirl of her emerald green gown. The rest of her girls followed behind looking far less composed. The varying looks of anger and torment were all focused on the captive as they stamped their feet in defiance.

"You may go back to your rooms if you please," Tarquins's words were still low and pleasant sounding. His back was towards her leaving her with a view of his pale brown hair.

"N-no, I can continue. The ball is in a week. The kitchen has already begun the preparations. We cannot pause for even a moment."

Jza babbled further informing the back of Tarquin's head of the ongoings of the preparation she was incharge of. In her thoughts she wondered if that was why he searched for the Princesses when his army had stormed the city. Had he vowed to make one of them the queen or was their fate to be like Raymond's. She suddenly cruelly wished they had been caught so they could have been meted out the punished they deserved. How could they be so selfish to destroy their own country? She vowed she would expose her traitor sister.

Jza's legs buckled beneath her as she completely lost feeling in her limbs. Her knees hit the marble floor barely giving her a chance to brace herself. Her amber eyed captor was by her side in a heartbeat. She looked at him through the wisps of the hair coming undone around her face.

"I - I do not understand," She stammered bowing her head in disbelief. Her thin hands splayed on the white marble trembled as she tried to move.

"You are still unwell," The man uttered kneeling next to her.

"I am not- not at all," She whispered and closed her eyes. She felt hands around her waist trying to help her which she struggled against.

"Leave me. I can - can do this," She felt oddly out of breath. He ignored her protestations. He pulled her up along with him. It was an ode to his strength he did not look the least bit strained. She was smoothly propped up again him.

"Leave me, you beast," She hissed,once realizing he had her in his embrace. His breath mingled with hers as he peered into her face with a slight slant of his mouth. He was enjoying her anger.

"Krasavitsa," He murmured with a small smile.

"This had better not mean what I think it does," She growled trying to make her limbs cooperate. Her feet had no strength even now.

"What do you think it means," He asked curiously.

"I am not your.. plaything or whatever they call me, you know, your Harem. I believe I've had quite a few slurs thrown at my face in your language. I do not need you to add to it."

"Believe me I know. I know how I spend my nights."

His expression was an incentive to push him away roughly and she fell to the ground in a heap with a staid grown looking even more crumpled.The pain of the fall was worth it. Tarquin gave her his hand which she looked away from. She did not need his help is he was only going to manhandle her.

"Now, now, no need to be fussy. I will only touch you if you deign me worthy of the honour." Her captor continued sarcastically. He watched her look away from his still outreaching hand.

"I cannot feel my legs," She finally uttered, explaining her predicament, "Have they poisoned me once again?"

Lord Taqruin frowned at the mention of her Harem. He hunched down next to her and examined her feet. Jza tried to scoot away but honestly she had no strength.

"Can you feel my hands?" He delicately pulled one foot out of the slippers and prodded it carefully.

"I can feel a pressure but- OW did you just pinch me, you pisspot!!" Jza's voice echoed in the hall. The man did not look even remotely remorseful.

"You will recover soon," He nodded and unceremoniously picked her up, "It shall be for the best if you rest for now."

Slowly and steadily she was starting to feel the warms of his limbs around her.

"I have a duty to perform. I cannot rest when there's work to be done. I have written everything down in a journal. You should find it in my- our room if I do not regain the strength in my limbs on time."

"You should have said so. You are unwell. You can barely stand.. Maybe it's' time to let go of your duties. There will be no shame in giving up. I will continue without your physical presence though it will make the job far more charmless."

Jza shut her mouth in vexation as he carried her across the threshold into the hallway.

"What do we have here? The false king with his whore."

Jza felt Tarquin's muscles tense as he laid eyes on a man standing against the stone wall further down the hallway. His face was hidden in shadows but he soon leaned forward and his pale face flickered with torchlight.

"Anatoly," The Lord murmured while his captive strained her neck to see who had dared to talk to her captor in such a manner.

"I have much to say to you, Tarquin."

Lord Tarquin replied in his own language but as usual his subjects were keen to exhibit his foibles to her and the fair haired man replied in their common language.

"Busy then, busy now. I will not be silenced. I will not let you usurp the throne with your polluted blood."

The blond man aggressively marched forward with absolute fury raging in his eyes. Jza instinctively hid her face in Tarquin's shoulder but before she could scream Tarquin had pulled out a dagger from his sleeve and punctured the attacker in his heart. Anatoly swayed in shock and pain. The Lord kicked the injured man and his prone body slammed against the ground while his blood spilled at his murderers feet.

Chapter 16

J za breathed in Tarquin's scent as she found herself at loss for words. She pulled herself away and saw the opponent was listless, quite utterly dead. She had to force herself to look away.

Tarquin did not even pause to examine his prey's dead body. He swiftly moved on leaving the gruesome scene behind. He said not a word while he walked towards their common resting chambers while his companion could not formulate any words. There was an uneasy silence cast around them. Jza belatedly noticed the splatter of blood resting on her captor's face.

"The weather is forecasted to be clear for the ball in a week's time," Tarquin said, as he placed on his bed.

"The weather?" Jza found her voice, "Are we not going to discuss what just happened?"

"That was politics," The brown haired man replied nonchalantly. He examined his appearance in a mirror and pulled out a handkerchief to clean up stray specks of blood.

"I have seen a fair bit of politics in my life and this is not how I have ever seen it being done," Jza continued incredulously.

"Not when you have to snatch a throne," Tarquin displayed his pristine teeth mirthlessly, "There were quite a few bastards left behind."

"What an odious man. How could a king make no effort to plan what happens after his demise. He should have known his heir the day they were born."

"And you think King Samuel knows what to do with his dozen daughters?" Tarquin argued.

"He has a plan, I'm sure of it!" Jza said decisively although remembering her father reminded of her sisters' folly. It seems her father would have to revise his will considering he had a traitor in his bloodline. She just had to find out who.

Tarquin continued his ablutions, clearing up his handsome face from the unsightly red covering it up. He started untangling the shirt's knots at his throat in preparation to change his outfit and Jza broke her gaze away from his form. She reached out for her notebook from her side table to distract herself.

The man whose presence she was ignoring entered her vision from her left and made himself comfortable on his side of the bed. Jza clenched her teeth in frustration but continued to pretend she was reading her notes as the feather mattress moved under his weight.

She made an effort to at least try and read her own dates for the Ball's deadlines when she felt herself being watched. Completely forgetting she was deliberately ignoring the man she looked to her left and instantly regretted it.

Tarquin was lying on his side with a hand under his head just staring at her. She could have noted his newly laundered clothes still untied or his wet hair but none of the changes could compete with the sheer power of his gaze.

Jza felt her cheeks and ears heat up as her hands fumbled with the pages. She looked away, blinking furiously. His face contained no particular emotion, just a narrowed eyed focus on her.

A hundred things scrambled through her brain; words, emotions, insults but none reached her tongue and before she could gather her thoughts the brown haired man furiously sat up from his reclining position and got to his feet. He gave her one last consuming look as if he intended to devour her with his eyes and walked out of the room with fists at his sides.

Jza clenched her knees through her dress and wondered how without saying a word he managed to leave her so flustered and distraught.

————————————

The day of the ball was upon them and Jza could see the tension in the air. The staff looked as grim as if they were to be massacred by the end of the day. The food was already prepared beyond expectations and halls swept every hour or so to keep the dust at bay. She knew nothing of how the guests were being hosted since her only responsibly was to organise a Barbarian Ball of incredible standards.

The entire week of preparations had been entirely devoid of Tarquin. It was not entirely strange for her to lose track of his whereabouts but she knew he was keeping his distance. He had sent his bilingual men to help her order about the staff which she gladly accepted.

Jza found something nondescript from her wardrobe. She looked more a servant than a guest which was her quest. Her maid was troubled by her refusal to dress in what was sent to her rooms by her Lord but she had not been able to persuade her charge.

In the ballroom the captive girl stood near the servant's hidden pathway as the Somerlian guests started arriving. They were welcomed with Barbarian music and garlands.

The host had wandered in wearing his military outfit after the curious guests had settled in. The Somerlians greeted him with bows and reverence but Jza could sense their disdain for the strangeness of the ball.

If the soldiers and harem girls hadn't created a visual palette of their county then the folks at the ball certainly did. They were all pale with light hair and eyes. There were a scant few variations in the midst but Tarquin was the most visibly different. It was clear he was mixed. His narrow, almond shaped eyes, the high cheekbones and his hair gave away the open secret.

The Somerlians were a sour looking bunch. They were gaudily dressed with heaps upon heaps of fabric and jewels. It was not just the men but the women who were covered in layers of powder and perfumes.Jza had assumed her sisters were masters of indulgence but she was wrong. Their sense of fashion was frugal and sensible compared to these tarts.

Jza wondered if the families were pleased their daughters were being introduced to a man with impure blood. The Somerlians would never mix their blood with any other race but it seemed power was everything because she saw eager mothers push their daughters to the forefront.

Tarquin turned and twirled with the young girls who looked at him with wide eyed curiousity as they stumbled in the foreign dance. Some looked eager to be in his presence while some looked bashful.

The meal after the dances was plentiful and the Somerlians consumed in a fast pace with little pause. They were not in anyway slowed down by the strange Barbarian spices and recipes.

Wine was pouring when Tarquin's roving eye caught hers. She knashed her teeth in frustration.

She chose the coward's path and entered the servant's corridor on her right. She hoped he would not be foolish enough to follow her but she was wrong.

"You look like my matron. Did you forget the outfit I chose for you?" Tarquin's words slurred. Jza was instantly on edge because no matter how much spirits he consumed he never lost his composure. She turned around to face him.

"I have to make sure this ball moves smoothly. I have no time to play dress up," She answered with fraying impatience.

"You would have looked charming with your hair running down your back. It was a pretty dress," He noted, trying to look bored but failed.

"Now, you sound like my governess," She answered.

Tarquin laughed leaving her completely astonished. It seemed her assumptions were correct. He had indeed consumed far too many spirits because his inhibitions were running far too low.

"How much liquor have you consumed? You should have left some for your guests." Her voice echoed in the narrow passageway. She could barely make out his face in the dim light.

"Enough to tell you that even in that outfit you tempt me more than you'd like," Tarquin's voice was almost too low and gravelly to be heard.

"Have you gone mad? This is hardly the time and place to make such a ... declaration," The girl hissed, taking one step back while the man took one step forward. She looked away with a grimace.

"Am I that terrible you won't even deign to look at me?" Tarquin continued with the strange tone of voice.

"You destroyed my land, my home, everything! You underestimate my sense of honour to throw everything away for a handsome face," she replied venomously.

"Oh, believe me, I know of it. It is my only impediment. If you would only let me-"

Jza slapped him with all the pain and fury that consumed her being and marched away furiously, leaving him standing against the wall. He did nothing to stop her.

Her assumptions had been correct. His intentions towards her were as clear as the sun in the morning sky. He was the beast she had always knew he was. What did he think of her to acquiesce to his demands just because he was not unpleasant to look at.

She was so furious if she had the strength she would rip down a tapestry on the way out of the hidden corridor.

What was to be done she wondered in despair. She needed to plan her escape. She needed that key that nestled near his heart. The importance of which eluded him so complely.

But first she needed to find those letters her sisters had written to him. She needed to relay to her father what was being done behind his back.

Chapter 17

J za was dying.

It was slow but the pain radiating within her bones was spreading.

She broke her vow to protect her sisters and now she was facing the consequences. But if the kingdom needed to be saved then the vow had to be broken. She had no choice.

She pressed herself against the stone balcony and looked down from the highest point in the castle. She wondered if throwing herself off the balcony would make the end easier and the girl nearly roared in pain as her body betrayed her just for her vow breaking thoughts.

Every other time she had fainted her vow had been punishing her but unlike the other times she was awake and aware to suffer the consequences. Perhaps this time it was because she knew the pain was coming.

She had known it the moment she had decided to break into the study. The pain in the body had grown and grown as her actions led to exposing her sister. The vow did not like that Jza was going to reveal her sister's treachery.

A stray pigeon flew around her scattering the pages in the wind. She had read them as fast as she could and dispatched the ones most important ones on the various pigeons that sat in their little perches on the roof. Tarquin may have unravelled so much of the castle's working but he had failed to realise the importance of the pigeons. They did not just take mail from one place to the other. They could also reach King Samuel where ever he was. Some peddler had given her father command over his livestock once upon a time.

The princess had dispatched all the important strategic enemy documents along with her own note briefing her father of current events and her own observations. If the pigeons found her father he would know the locket was around her captor's throat. That was probably why her death at betraying her sisters was not instant. The powers that be were deciding what consequences her actions were going to have keeping her in a strange sort of limbo.

She looked down at the rustle at her feet and sat down to examine another one of her sister's love letters to Lord Tarquin. It seemed ridiculous calling the traitorous notes anything else but the Princesses were wooing the man. They were flattering and evocative, begging him to conquer the land and make them his queen.

Not all of the girls were involved. At least she hoped not. But the five of them who embarked on the ridiculous journey to compete for the throne had jeopardised all of them. They were a miserable reminder what her sisters had done to annihilate her kingdom for their own selfish gain. The Princess had with a heavy heart sent her father samples of those letters. He needed to know the truth no matter how harsh.

"...My Beloved.... We must snatch... Father is a fool.... the only worthy heir.... Come after winter when the reserves of food are low...." Jza's eyes teared up once again seeing how poorly her eldest sister had behaved. She noticed a pair of feet in the periphery. For someone caught in the act of treason she felt quite calm.

Tarquin watched her lean against the wall in pure silence. He was still in his military uniform but everything was subtly out of place. It looked he had run himself ragged searching for her. After finding his upturned study be must have grown even more frantic.

"You have been busy," His eyes wandered over the remnants of the parchments she had stolen from his study.

"Your guards were imbeciles. They left their posts or showed up utterly intoxicated," Jza tried to hide the pain in her voice. It had been ridiculously easy to smash the lock outside the study with the potted plant next to it. That was when the steady hum of pain had heightened, leaving her on her knees. she had known for sure she was choosing death by giving up her own safety.

Tarquin picked another errant letter touching his shiny shoe and examined it carelessly. There was no mistaking the disdain on his face.

"So, you found out the truth about King Samuel's ridiculous daughters."

"Those stupid girls. Proclaiming love for a man they had never met. It seems they led you here. Is that not the truth?" Jza growled.

"The Princesses were hardly an enticement. I have no interest in associating with foolish girls with no pride or honour. I only seek vengeance because of my heritage. You know who I am; a half breed. It's a shame I do not know who you are.." He trailed off without the anger she had expected from him. He was far too calm.

"You will never know my name. Not until I am your captive.." She trailed off blinking back tears.

"You have his eyes. King Samuel's. You have noble blood in you. Of course the discovery of your room confirmed my hypothesis. I am sure I was will discern everything in no time."

"Are you trying to convince yourself that killing me would be mistake? That I am important enough to keep even after what I did," She breathed heavily.

"I like your resolve. I admire it. You are a puzzle I need to solve but perhaps I should have heeded the advice. Perhaps you are too dangerous to keep alive."

"No, I have no resolve; none. I am failing tonight. I have broken the vow I made," She inhaled noisily and collapsed very suddenly on the floor. She idly noticed the blue in the sky was losing the fight against the reds and the purples.

"What is it? What ails you?" He was at her side before she could exhale. The man lost all composure as he watched her take shallow breaths. She was impressed her slow death filled his eyes with genuine fear. She had hoped revealing her truth about the vow would hasten her demise but it seemed she was stuck dragging out this painful moment for as long as possible.

He cradled her head in his hands and lay it in his lap. His face looked over hers as he searched it to understand the situation.

"The moment I decided to break into your desk in the study I knew I was making a choice. I knew I would be caught, and I would be hanged. And the promise I made my father, the vow I made for him I could not fulfil when I chose death." She rambled incoherently. The tips of her nerves were losing feeling. She did not know it but her lips were turning blue.

She closed her eyes and faintly heard the last words she would thought to hear again.

"I promise thee, as I have promised heaven above that I shall fulfill my duty...." Tarquin's voice followed her to the darkness.

Chapter 18

The icy cold breeze roused her from her slumber. She tried to hide her face in the warmth beneath her but froze as she inhaled the smell surrounding her. Death smelt like him.

Jza lifted herself upwards and found herself face to face with her captor whose pale face shone under the moonlight. His hair was in mild disarray, his clothes crumpled and his eyes shut. Jza closed her own as she marvelled at her mortality.

She was not dead but why? She had broken the vow to protect her sisters twofold. By putting herself in danger with her obvious treachery was the first way she broke her vow. She was the only one who knew where her sisters were. Putting her own life in peril meant her sisters would have been lost forever. If this had not broken the vow for her then revealing her sister's treachery most certainly did. Treason was death in their kingdom and so was the consequence of breaking a vow you were bonded to it. She had not known the consequence back then but she did now.

Jza heard the steady heart beat under her ear increase pace and for a second wished the moment would not end. She wanted to lie there in peace and forget her woes. She was just so tired.

"When am I to be executed?" Jza murmured with her eyes still closed. To her surprise her captor's chest rumbled with mirth.

"Why would I go through the motions of saving your life if I was only going to hang you," Tarquin answered with an amused snort.

Jza lifted herself up again and stared at his face. Was he the reason she was still alive? Her wet eyes widened as she remembered the words he had uttered right before she had lost consciousness.

"What have you done?" She hissed, furiously as she unconsciously held onto the man.

"Why do you presume I had anything to do with.. this," Tarquin casually remarked, his voice low from their shared slumber.

"I was dying! I do not need to read from a book to know this. The metallic taste has not left my mouth," The Princess' voice shook with emotion.

"Once the vow is broken the justice is swift and instantaneous. It is a sure death. I have seen the end of many a coward. It is true you were losing the battle but far more slowly than usual. Your vow must have been a unique one to have such an effect."

"I heard your words.. the ones they make the vow with... Why did you need to say them?" Jza asked after a moment's pause as she pondered over his words.

"A bond for a bond. That was the only way to save your life. You chose a very dangerous path bonding yourself to an unpredictable vow you could not keep. You would have died had I not reached you when I did," Tarquin explained with a strange look in his eyes..

Jza pushed herself away with confusion bleeding thorough her anxiety, "I do not understand. How is that even possible? How could another bond save me?"

"Let me tell you a story about a Princess trapped by an ogre," Tarquin sighed wistfully as he looked at the stone floor, "He made her bear him a son for his own ego. Over the years her son watched him destroy her. He brutalised her until he chipped away her sanity and she was just a fragment of her former self.

"Her son knew he had to slay the ogre and capture the throne for himself before he robbed her life like he had done with her mind. The boy accumulated friends fast but his foes were equal in number. They found out his plans and took his mother away.

"That night there was more bloodshed in the palace then there had been in a century. The boy ran and ran all the way to the temple. His spies had informed him the ogre had married his mothet but he was not done yet. The ogre was to bind himself to the Princess. If the son killed the ogre his mother would die too. The boy's swift feet won that night. He reached there mid vow and slaughtered his father in front of the high priest."

Tarquin had a faint smile on his face as if reliving the bloodshed. Jza exhaled the breath she had trapped through the story. The realisation of what he had done was numbly starting to come to her.

"Is that what you did? You bound yourself to me like that ogre."

"No! Not like that ogre, never like that ogre!" Tarquin's voice echoed around the stone walls. The fury in his amber eyes was evident even in the dim light. He took a shaken breath in before he continued, "It was the only thing I could think of. People bind their vows to their marriages, careers, ambitions. My father taught me that day that people can bind themselves to people. That's the only way I could remember to steal you back from death."

"Why? Why would you... even attempt ... to save me..." Jza trailed off in whisper. His motives were a mystery. Was could he possibly gain from keeping her alive?

"I- I do not know why," Her captive's words was equally quiet.

"There has to be a reason," Jza leaned in, her loose hair swaying along with her. Tarquin stared at her as if hypnotised.

"It's only fair that I save your life after you saved mine," He said as his eyes were still fixed on her.

"No, no, no. I do not believe you in the slightest. Why would you bind your entire existence to a girl whose name you do not even know," Jza was relentless.

"I am not an ambitious man but I never lose and I don't intent to start with losing you," He bit out with a mirthlessly smile. There was no humour in his eyes. He was deathly serious about his proclamations

"That's insane. You have been so meticulous and ruthless in the capture of this country. Why would you throw it all away for.. for... Me..." Jza was hesitant to put out such presumptuous words out of her mouth.

"I have done what I aimed to do. I have soothed the vengeance of my barbarian blood. I have shown my father's people I am more than worthy of this throne. Why should I not choose to follow my own desires," Tarquin finally looked away. His jaw was clenched as if it pained him to speak.

"I am already your captive. You already have... whatever your heart desired."

He did not answer. It was clear he disagreed with her.

"I thought you meant to use your vow on a girl, any girl from the ball. Is it not true there is only one vow to be had. I may not know much about bonding to vows but I do know this much," Jza asked, trying to make heads or tails of this conundrum. Tarquin had once again caught her eyes and heat of his gaze burnt her. Her face flushed from his attention but she could not look away.

"Yes, one vow for eternity," He paused, "They had no use for me and I had no use for them. They would sell their daughters to anyone but I know what they think of half breeds."

"That's a disgusting word."

"I have heard it all my life. It still follows me when they think I am not listening. They have no loyalty in their bones to a harem girl's bastard," Tarquin snorted.

"And you think bonding us together would be any different. If I am not a traitor than who is?"

"You never vowed for me or my kingdom. You were never mine. I always knew where your loyalty lay and even with your head on the line you would never chose to betray them."

Jza was suddenly embarrassed by his words. She had broken her vow to protect her sisters. If that wasn't a betrayal than what was. Even while living with the man she had failed to take the key back. She continued to fail to do her duty every day she tolerated his existence.

"You won't ask me what vow I broke. It is after all the reason we are.. in this position," She asked, unsure what demands he would make off her now. He had revealed so much of his life to her. Did he expect an exchange of information.

"No. No point in risking you all over again."

"Of course, after all your life is now intertwined with mine. You need me to survive," Jza was deliberate in keeping her voice light.

"Yes," Tarquin said quietly his voice barely audible in the night breeze.

Chapter 19

They sat in silence as the clouds rumbled in a distance. It seemed rain was expected in the next few days.

Jza bit her lip and wondered what her future would look like. She had nowhere to go. If her sisters were traitors then what was she? Her easy acceptance of her living conditions had sullied her reputation beyond repair. On top of that the new complication forced upon her had added to her confusion. Would she drop dead the moment her father executed Tarquin? Would he even care his traitorous daughter was bound to his enemy? What a muddle her life was. Fate was a cruel mistress indeed.

"What should we do next?" Jza asked, trying to banish the image of her father looking at her with uncontrolled wrath. She needed something to distract herself with.

"Enjoy the peaceful weather?" Tarquin exhaled nonchalantly with his amber eyes still closed. He was still reclining with his back to the stone wall while Jza was now sitting cross legged leaning against the same wall. Her view was of the clouds swirling a long distance away.

"An upcoming thunderstorm is peaceful?" Jza scrunched her nose as she spoke.

"Yes," Tarquin paused contemplatively, "It cleanses everything."

"Not the blood off ones hands," The Princess replied sharply. Tarquin's mouth curved into a smile as he looked at her.

"I am only living upto the name you have given me. I am afterall the beast."

"At least you understand what I call you. I never know what to make of the names you refer to me as," Jza complained. The use of the other language grated on her sometimes. He did not leave many clues about what he thought of her. She often assumed he found her helplessness amusing but then why would he care if she lived or died. Was there a human heart beating under the lethal beast?

"A tit for tat then since you are determined to keep your real name from me," The man answered with a shrug before lowering his voice so much so that she had to lean in to hear him, "But I can tell you, my solnyshko, if you so desire."

"No. That is quite unnecessary," The girl said as she straightened her back, suddenly aware of how his voice changed mid sentence. The intimacy in his voice and tone unsettled her more than her near death experience did. Death was always looming on the hori- zon circling viciously in her mind but his altered behaviour always caught her off guard.

"The sun shall be rising soon," The man observed, ignoring her discomfort.

"This may be your castle now but I am sure you do not want to be caught by your guests on a stroll especially with me before daybreak," Jza hinted very strongly they should be returning soon. The sky was indeed brightening and she had no wish to be seen in her disheveled state. She gathered her skirts and rose slowly, resembling an unsteady child.

"Why do you always assume I care about their opinions," The Lord exclaimed looking less pensive and more diverted while he followed her example. He brushed off errant patches of dust on his uniform and offered his arm to the Princess who took it immediately. The weakness in her bones lingered too much for even her pride to burden her.

"It is not wise to completely disregard the worth of their opinions. You could still make many alliances-" Jza lectured as they started taking steps down into the castle.

"I have no inclination to associate with this depraved lot. I have made up my mind tonight about the future," Tarquin gave her a searching sort of look as they turned to the coridor towards the main staircase, "This vow changed nothing."

"Yes, of couse, it changed nothing. It is not as if we-" Her chatter was abruptly cut off as he pulled her into a shadowy nook. One finger was gently placed on her lips.

Jza paused mid sentence mouth still half open. She blinked at him while the man arched his neck to check the corridors.

A drunk guard's footsteps walked passed them as they held their breath. The guard was humming loud enough to conceal any sounds they might have been making.

Tarquin's eyes followed the drunkards movements before letting them rest on his captive. Jza inhaled abruptly with a wheezing sort of noise and he pulled his finger away from her. His touch had lit ablaze her lips and she struggled to control her reaction.

The man obliviously ushered her out of their hiding place and unhooked a burning oil lamp from the wall for their journey since it was still dark in the deeper parts of the castle.

The Lord held an arm around Jza's shoulders and began to lead her down the main staircase. His grip was so gentle as if she would break and crumble into a thousand pieces confusing the girl even further. She remembered the bruises he had contributed on her body and wondered when that had changed.

They reached the room without further incident. Like Jza had encountered earlier most of the guards and soldiers seemed to be enjoying the ball and the revelry it offered them. Even the man usually positioned outside their doors was absent.

Tarquin placed the oil lamp on the dresser and watched Jza's delicate face go through a multitude of emotions.

"Take the bed," He gestured magnanimously.

"I'm fine. I am always comfortable on the floor," The Princess lied without looking up.

"I have work to do, the new day is upon us. I will not inconvenience you," The man whispered at her. She blinked feverishly back at him while she took a seat on their bed.

"Wait," She called out as he turned to leave, "At least tell me what are the implications of... What you did. I only heard a few of your words. I did not comprehend much. I live while you do. Is that correct?

"Yes, always," He answered as if out of breath.

"And vice versa?" Jza steeled herself as she comtemplated the possibilities. Could she end the war by simply ending her own life.

"I haven't a clue so if you're planning to take me down you might be sorely disappointed to reach the afterlife all alone," Tarquin seemed to relish her predictability.

Jza laughed at his words,"How did you guess my train of thought?"

"Oh, I know you, Lady Ashbrook. I know you very well indeed," Tarquin tilted his head with half a smile.

"Not that well. You still have not figured out my name," She countered. The Lord just rolled his eyes and left the room leaving Jza to her ablutions and rest. She changed in her night dress and laid her head down on the comfortable pillows.

The entire night was uncharacteristic of anything Tarquin had ever done. Her comprehension skills had never been as limited as they were now and the entire business gave her pause.

What did he want from her? She had nothing to offer him. Nothing about her appearance or personality warranted a second look much less a first one. If he wanted a warm, willing body he had an entire harem at his disposal so why did he have eyes on her?

She was not dim. It could be an act but those eyes...

Goosebumps ran up her arm as she remembered the way she had caught him looking at her. His earlier advances and roving fingers had never been so intrusive as his eyes. She had no words to describe the intensity and focus, none. It was as if he wanted to consume her whole.

She had never had anyone show a sliver of interest in her and it was strange. She was still scared of him and his intentions, of course, but he had saved her life. It shamed her that this gave her an odd sort of thrill. So, this was why women wanted to be saved by a handsome prince. Maybe, in some other time, some other life... She dared not finish her trail of thought. She forced her eyes shut but could not dispel the image of him gazing at her face.

Chapter 20

Jza woke up far too late in the morning. In fact quick surveillance from behind the curtains showed daylight had almost faded into nothingness. It was not morning at all, as she had mistakenly assumed at first, but evening. Her maid had obviously been warned not to interrupt her sleep which she was grateful for since she had never felt so well rested in her life.

The Princess forlornly noticed the flags raised high above the arena. It seemed like the ball guests would be entertained by blood sports this night. Tarquin would be foolish if he forced her to attend. As singular as it was she felt free even when trapped like a song bird. After facing death everything that could come her way in the future felt trivial. That fear of telling her captive no was lost forever.

Jza quickly lit the lantern left behind from their sojourn to the rooftop. She wrinkled her nose as the smell of oil filled the room.

The girl restlessly waited for the rest of the evening for Tarquin to come back. She had no yearning for his company but it seemed she still had so many questions swirling in her head. Her future actions depended on what bonding her to him implied.

Jza mindlessly flipped her notebook over and over until she found a dried up rose resting gently in the bound pages. She closely inspected it trying to recall when she had left it there. She vaguely remembered some foolishness associated with Tarquin but she was quite sure she had never saved the rose.

Her thoughts were marred by the outer door being slammed open. Startled by the interruption Jza stood and gripped her light source close to her.

To her alarm her maid ran in, red in the face, breathing in large gulps of air, shutting the bedroom door behind her. The woman shrieked in her own language, frantically gesturing with both hands. Even without the word comprehension it was obvious something was very wrong.

The maid kept looking behind her as if expecting something horrific to pounce upon her. Jza inferred somone was coming but before she could make out more there were more sounds outside.

"Sssh," Jza hissed and pulled her maid into the closet, "Hide in there!"

She slammed the closet door shut leaving her weeping maid in the dark. At least her loyal servant could have some protection. Behind her the doors opened and guards stormed in as if ready to battle a rabid beast.

"You need to come with us," One guard had his dagger pointed at her.

"I shall comply peacefully. You needn't fret," Jza took great pains to look unaffected by the intrusion. She gathered her skirts and bearing only the oil lamp she followed the soldier who had addressed her. The other men joined the procession behind her.

Once outside her room her confusion quadrupled as her slippers were drenched in blood. Two guards were slain outside her room. They were one of the few regular guards who could speak in her tongue. Her concern grew stronger but there was nothing to be done but march forward.

The brown haired girl was led to the derelict study which she had breeched what seemed like a lifetime ago. She had certainly not left it in the state it was now. While she had broken into some locks using brute force she had not completely butchered Tarquin's desk. It was now barely standing on two feet. A cursory glance informed her the rest of the room was also in disarray.

"Ah, here she is," A familar round faced commander bared his teeth at her, "The enticement."

There was not an inch of warmth in his icy blue eyes. Lantern still in hand Jza walked in soundlessly trying to see who he was addressing. The light in the room was almost negligible leaving her blinking. The guards around her were dismissed.

"We have been looking for your mother? Where have you managed to hide her? This girl will have to do in the meantime."

Jza reached the centre of the room and her body stilled mid motion. Her nails burned crescents into her skin as she realised it was Tarquin who sat on a chair with his hands bound behind him. His head was bent foward in a slump. His uniform was drenched in dark congealed blood. She would have presumed he was dead if not for her own health which belied the vision set before her.

The Princess saw his chest move as he exhaled his words, "Kill her. I care not."

"Liar till the very end. You have guarded this girl with every means possible. She is not so insignificant as you pretend," The commander meandered around them lazily. Jza placed her free hand on Tarquin's chair.

The girl hadn't realised she was holding her breath until her lungs struggled to work. Her eyes narrowed on her new captive. The man's feet was bringing him closer and closer.

"Where are the papers? I do not know how you discovered our plans but for this war to continue without your presence we will need everything," The burly commander asked. Tarquin only scoffed without even raising his face.

Jza closed her eyes trying to drown the urge to laugh hysterically. The very papers he was demanding she had already dispatched to King Samuel. He was asking the wrong person.

"What are you smiling about," The commander abruptly barked at her.

"Me? I am just an innocent bystander." Jza opened her eyes as her mouth twitched. This was by far the most ridiculous situation she was forced to be in.

"Not so innocent. I know you hold some knowledge. He followed you like a pup everywhere."

"If you want to hold a Barbarian ball I can tell you a tale or two. I am only well versed in Barbarian lore," Jza answered in a sedate tone. She had noticed the fire raging within the commander's eyes as the answers he searched for eluded him. The more serenity she exuded the more composure he was losing.

"Yes, Barbarian balls, Barbarian blood sports... How much degradation must our Somerlians tolerate. It cannot be borne any longer. As the new ruler I shall order all remnants of Barbarian culture to be annihilated, starting with you," The fair haired man jabbed his finger in the air towards Tarquin.

"I am curious. Is this how the Somerlians do it; Dispose off their rulers one after the other," Jza asked uncaringly. Her eyes were still searching for a way out.

"Lord Ivan murdered his uncle. Tarquin murdered lord Ivan. I can certainly kill the half breeds with no repercussions. No one will shed a tear," The commander answered, meanly.

"Interesting. I wonder who will be the one to dispose off your body," The Princess asked with a hint of amusement on her face. Self-preservation was irrelevant when the person who's life yours depended on was bleeding profusely. Tarquins face was chalk white. It would not be long before the blood loss would be irreversible. It may already be too late.

The commander gave a startled look at the bizarre upstart. She was meant to look alarmed, frightened, giving Tarquin pause at his defiance, not adding fuel to the blaze.

"Who are you?" The man asked a very popular question.

"Is this wise? Taking down the one man actually doing his job. Goridian castle is still holding on firm. Without the traitor you are left with no one on the inside to help. King Samuel will use the power vaccum to regain his power," Jza wondered out aloud as she took a step closer.

"We have Goridian castle under control. We will starve them out. We managed this castle, we can manage another," The commander looked flustered by her probing.

"Are you sure? I've read about Ivan. Worthless just like all the other Somelians," Jza sneered. She gazed sideways at Tarquin. The man's lips were curved in amusement. Even caught in a trap like a wounded animal he was still his old self. Some things never changed.

Jza swiftly raced forward with a small war cry and bashed her lantern in the commander's face. Before the man could regain his footing she emptied the oil on his clothes and threw the burning wick on the screaming man. For good measure she picked up an errant desk limb and started slamming it on the rolling man.

"J-Jaza?" Tarquin's breath rattled painfully as he completely butchered her name. It was only then that she paused her beating of her victim.

Chapter 21

"If you do not want to be responsible for dropping him off the mortal plane leave him be," Tarquin's voice sharply cut through the trance as the Princess gaped at the bound man.

Jza dropped her weapon abruptly, startled by her own viciousness. She gave a brief look at the broken man lying on the floor but her attention was immediately diverted by her enemy whose amber eyes were still hidden behind his hair.

Tarquin had his hands in front of him before she could speak. He flexed his bloody fingers trying to warm them after their period of unuse.

"How did you..." She whispered, searching his counatanance for a sign; anything to assuage her he did not know the truth.

"Does it truly matter?" The man took a long rattling breath that seemed ominous. His eyes finally caught hers and they revealed nothing of import.

"Of course it does. And if you've known for so long then why conceal it. You are not one to hide your victories, are you?"

"What an apt description of my beastly self," Tarquin gave her a lazy smile as fresh blood slid down the side of his pale face. He quickly undid the ties around his feet but remained seated, unperturbed by the other man moaning on the ground. Jza glanced down at her murderous hands and took her own shuddering breath.

"Finding errant parchments with your name in your room is hardly a victory," His face was hiden behind the shadows made by the harsh light cast upon them by the torches, "It's a jumble of letters, Miss Ashbrook. How am I supposed to pronounce it. It would not do to say it out wrong."

"And yet here you are mispronouncing it completely," Jza sneered at him but knew time was not on their side. She glanced at the door with frayed impatience, "There will be guards outside."

"I will take care of them," Tarquin's voice was far too confident for a man sodden in his own blood.

"Dont be aggravating," Jza clenched her fists in a frustrated motion, "You are in no position to be battling anyone much less your own turncoats."

"Do you still find by my prowess in battle lacking?" Tarquin asked with a hint of amusement as she bent down in front of him to inspect the damage her loose hair dangling around her face.

"Not really. What I'm surprised by is how they managed to capture you?" Jza's focus was on his injured torso.

"For the first time in my life I had thoughts on my mind that had nothing to do with this forsaken nation," The injured man answered. The Princess could feel his eyes following her hands as they grazed over the multiple holes in his uniform.

"You were stabbed with much enthusiasm. Your wounds will fester if you do not attend to them," She glanced up to find his eyes closed as her fingers brushed over a gaping hole on his collarbone.

"There's a servant tunnel on your left," She informed him while leaning closer. Her hair brushed his face as she examined the wound on his shoulder. This one seemed less shallow and was deliberately done to ensure maximum damage to his movements.

"And there's another one under the desk," He answered back without pause. Jza's lips curved at the man's predictability. It was impossible for him to keep his nose out of anything. She never detected her hair strands transfering tiny, slivers of his blood on her profile.

"Someone's at the door," The Princess hissed, her fingers inadvertently curling around Tarquin's injured shoulders. The sounds from outside were muffled leaving her unable to discern what was going on. He placed his right hand over hers and she scarcely noticed for the sound of her thrumming heart over took all her senses. Her eyes were fixed on the door opposite her instead.

"You needn't worry. The faces beyond that door are friends not foe," Tarquin finally eased himself up with his hand still encircling hers firmly.

"How can I? Not when your friends are my foe," Jza stood upright along with him facing the door.

A heartbeat later Sofiya sauntered in casually as if on her morning walk. The only difference to her usual self was the blood splatter lightly staining her pretty blue dress. Behind her a few unnamed girls loitered outside in the hallway.

"Too late, Sofiya. I have already been rescued..." Tarquin grinned at her loss of composure seeing Jza.

"What in the world..." The new arrival scrutinized the bloody man on the floor who smelt of burnt leather with a wrinkled nose. The prone man was still breathing but it would be a long while till he was back on his feet. Perhaps never.

"That's not fair, Tar, you never let us have fun," She whined and even her petulance was alluring Jza had to concede. The other woman had obviously perfected the art of looking attractive.

"Not my doing," The man easily rolled his injured shoulders and only that movement allowed Jza to notice where her hand was. She tugged lightly but the fingers capturing hers only squeezed tighter. That was the only indication the Lord remembered her presence since his eyes did not turn to her even for a moment.

"I am not having fun in this," Jza announced but her words were like a breeze in a thunderstorm; unnoticed and insignificant.

"You were stabbed obviously. Did he dip the blades in anything in particular? I have all the antidotes with me," Sofiya came in closer and pawed at her master's injured form.

"No, he wanted to stretch my life enough to gain all my knowledge. What a fool he was. Am I related to him? I hope not," Tarquin sneered at his former captive while his Harem leader started tearing apart his shirt. Pins and buttons fell to the floor without protest.

"Gently!" Jza hissed in annoyance having seen the severity of his injuries but she was ignored once again as the man's upper half was swiftly disrobed.

"I thought you would be worse for wear. He never touched your heart. What an amateur. I cannot believe you promoted him over Leonid. This man was so lacking," The fair haired woman tsked with mild annoyance as if the traitor was a knat floating in her drink.

"He did aim for my heart but..." The Lord paused as he inspected his bare and bloody chest. Right in the middle of his torso was Jza's pendant. His eyes locked with his captive's and they needed no words to comprehend the magnitude of what had occurred. That pendant had protected his heart.

Jza wrenched her hand away and fumbled with the chain and managed to free it from around his neck. The man was surprisingly compliant, bending his head to give her access.

"What a thief!" Sofiya's disdain was dripping from her words.

"This is mine! He stole from me," Jza snarled at the wretched woman. Her hands trembled in relief. She had never thought this day would come when her sisters would be back in her grasp.

"Its not theft if you are just stolen goods yourself," She was told with an arched brow but Jza barely heard the words.

The Princess deigned to give her no reply and instead regarded the floor her attention unseeingly, unable to digest the information. Was this truly how fate worked? What did her future hold that she must be saved at all costs by lady luck? First her enemy lost his mind and saved her from death and now this.

"How is she?" Tarquin took no heed of the animosity dangling between the women as he turned to Sofiya.

"You needn't worry. I told you I would find a way. I told you I found an old man; that strange peddler. He had this key..." The fair headed woman explained, hands on his bare chest imploringly.

"I told you I do not trust those peddlers," The amber eyed man showed the first sign of true emotions the entire time they were in this room. His speech was harsh and barely controlled.

"Trust me as I have trusted you. She is safe," The blonde switched to their language of her own violation. After a few clipped replies they stated into each others eyes as if daring the other to protest. Tarquin's shoulders drooped before he nodded, signalling that his companion had won their argument.

"What do we do next?" Jza asked, feeling impatient. She arched her neck in hopes of finding another weapon. Unlike Tarquin she did not trust the harem girls at all.

"We? You are not part of this matter, interloper. We shall go our own way and you go your own," Sofiya rudely cut any expectations she might have had down, "You have been a burden for far too long."

"Alright, then we must part," The Princess replied, calmly. Freedom was just around the corner but she was too cautious to celebrate just yet.

"Alone? I refuse to let you go!" Tarquin's hand found hers with the swiftness of a snake bite.

"Am I still your prisioner? Even now?" Jza asked with a measured tone. She looked down at their joined hands with growing dread.

"No, dusha moya, you're my savior," Her captor replied indulgently with a brief smile on his face and gently let her hand go.

"Please, you would have taken down the man even if I had not been brought in." Jza continued obliviously while she was gaped at by the other women.

"Come now, Tarquin, we await your orders. That tunnel leads you to the heart of the castle. We mapped it out per your command. These stupid men have made it very easy," Sofiya pulled him back into their conversation. She trailed a finger down his face, coquettishly.

"I do not wish to retake the castle," He answered decisively. The slant his mouth took was a bitter twist.

"Have you lost your senses? Is this a call for retreat? I will not be part of the losing party," His beautiful companion was incensed and disgusted by his words.

"No, it is an order for a slaughter. Not one of the traitors should get out alive. I wash my hands of the Somerlians. I no longer want to sit on my throne," The brown haired man replied with a grimace.

"All these years and all that suffering. Was it all for naught?"

"I have vowed for a long time to vanquish the Goridons but what of the Somerlians? They produce tryrant after tyrant and after all this they benefit from my blood and sweat. Nay! Have you not see the gold they adorned on their bodies last night? I felt such fury at their excesses at the ball. These worthless scum will not profit from my success any longer. Let the dark era of Somerlians begin. This is my vengeance," Tarquin's face was thunderous and even

Sofiya took a step back, overpowered by the fury radiating on his face.

The silence in the room was broken by the war lord, "You are free, my ladies. As my last duty to the throne I free you. No longer will you be a slave to me or anyone."

With a sob the former harem girl's trembling form was at his feet. Her cries echoed in the vast room. A few women standing guard outside peered in with alarm.

"And what do you propose to do with yourself?" Tarquin asked after a moment's silence turning his head towards Jza.

"I do not know. The servant's tunnels go to the garden. Perhaps I'll find my own people. I am unsure," The girl replied with her eyes fixed on the weeping woman. It was uncertain whether the tears were of joy or sorrow.

"Your people? The ones that I ruthlessly anhilated? Pray tell where will you find that particular breed."

"Yes, my people," Jza's thought process solidified and she instantly knew where she was going, "My men are locked up in our vicinity that await freedom as much I do. I am glad you decided to keep them alive for blood sports."

Chapter 22

"**Y**ou are being impossible. Why would they help you and even if they do you cannot be certain they shall protect you with success," Tarquin's eyes flashed with simmering annoyance but Jza noticed his stance was faltering.

"You must have fattened them up for the fight. It would not have been entertaining to have them die with the first blow. Am I not right?" The Princess' voice was barely a hushed whisper but it felt like her voice reverberated in the study. She still held so much fury at his deplorable behaviour. Using her men for sport was a sin she could not forgive.

Tarquin looked away with a faintly unimpressed expression. His hand was back at the chair and Jza was now certain he was in more pain than he wanted to show. The injuries on his body were stark against his pale skin. While she was no expert she had noticed most of his injuries were shallow enough but the blood loss could not be discounted. She could not fathom how he even stood on his own two feet with the amount of blood adorning his bare torso.

"Tend to him carefully. He is still losing blood," Jza nodded towards Sofiya and turned her back to the tableau. The girls who had brought clean water and sheets of bandages were now bickering over who would have the chance to caress his chest. She instead faced the wall meant to open up the servant tunnels. There were a series of stones that needed to be pressed she could recall. She taped her fingers lightly trying to get it right.

"He is no concern of yours," Sofiya replied, tartly.

"Neither is he yours from what I've heard just now. He's set you free. Why bother him with your attentions now," The brown haired girl replied with her eyes firmly on her goal. With another light press on the stone the tunnel appeared gradually.

"He was never a tormenter to us but instead a brother. We will always be loyal to him."

"Brother?" Jza blurted with a incredulous smile. "I may not have any brothers but I should hope ones conduct is different from what you've-"

Tarquin abruptly slammed down on his knees making his audience cry out. He blinked multiple times as if losing his vision. The vacant expression on his face was one Jza had never seen on him making her reach his side before anyone else.

"There, I warned you. Do not waste his time soothing your ego. It will not do to be so preoccupied with yourself once you're free. The world ourside your harem requires hard work," The Princess scolded the girls scattered around her.

"What do you suggest we do then? You pretty, pampered, princess are hardly one to talk. After this war ends you will be back to reclining on cushions," The blonde was unhappy with the way Jza held the man from behind; allowing him to rest his uninjured back on her.

Jza eyes widened imperceptibly but the mocking tone was just bitter enough to assure it was just a jest with no real meaning. The word Princess was used as an insult.

"I'll go back to my uncle's farm. I shall milk the cows and wring chicken necks. That shall suit me very well," The girl kept her tone light and unconcerned.

"Charming," Tarquin drawled and Jza felt every tremble running through his body. Her hands slipped over the fresher blood covering him as she readjusted his position. He suddenly rested his head on her shoulder and his brown hair tickled her cheek.

"And what will you do next? You don't fool me with this talk of abandoning the castle. You just want to hide your true plans," She asked, ignoring how close he was that she could sense the freezing clamminess of his body through her clothes.

"Never doubt the firmness of my intentions. I never make such statements lightly," The injured man exclaimed with an odd sort of gravity to his voice, "And I assumed you would be half way out of the tunnels by now. Why do you delay your flight? I will live I promise. I shan't let you die."

His words jolted Jza for she had momentarily forgotten her life was bound by his. Her reason for aiding had truly been an instinct she had not thought twice about.

"Unlike you I am not a beast. Humanity matters more then even my life."

"Beast? He calls you such pretty names and you malign his generosity. He should have kicked you out to the wilderness when he realised you were worthless to his cause," Sofiya was quick to temper at the insult.

"Pretty names?" Jza asked pointedly. She sensed his throat working itself. She shook her head to keep the distracting thoughts out of her head. "His wounds need to be closed. Exsanguination is a major danger here. Does anyone here know how to sew?"

One girl pulled out a medical pouch from the bandages clearly pilfered from the infirmary but none volunteered.

"I am in acceptable condition. I just need time to recuperate. It has been a long day," The injured man rumbled. He let his body rest heavily against his former captive's.

"Hide him!" Sofiya abruply stood from her crouched position. Her eyes were darting to all the exits of the room, "He needs to be taken out of harm's way."

"Do not be preposterous," Tarquin snarled. His eyes too were firmly stuck on the door. Jza clearly was the only one possessing substandard hearing.

"Leave! When you rid yourself the responsibility of this castle you rid yourself of the consequences. We will take care of the traitors. None shall leave this castle alive. I vow it, I swear, I vow it I will complete our vengeance. We need to work under the cover of darkness which is not your style. Leave before the men arrive. We shall take the other tunnel," she hissed and nodded towards the desk.

"Is this goodbye?" The Lord asked, stonily. Jza helped ease him upwards, using a considerable amount of her strength until he stood. Two girls grasped his elbows for support. "For now. Until we meet again," Sofiya's lower lip wobbled dangerously. She pulled out a delicate, gold, chain from underneath her fine clothing and placed it on his neck swiftly,"There, she is with you at last."

Jza's heart suffered interesting acrobatics just looking at the familar chain. It was not identical to the chain that contained her sisters but it was close. Tarquin seemed to have reached the same conclusion because his gaze lost all signs of weakness and hunted down her own. He now knew she hid a secret far bigger than he had imagined. "Hide!" Sofiya whispered urgently as she frantically watched her own small army of girls dive behind the broken desk and into the secret tunnel. Jza and the other two girls brought Tarquin into the other tunnel and swiftly closed it behind them.

"Bring me the honey and then the thread," The Princess said once the Lord was settled on clean sheets. Her lips were a grim line as she observed the wounds now cleaned of the blood. She took one of the lantern from her helpers.

"What are you doing? Why aren't you leaving?" Tarquin asked. He had refused to lie down and instead chose to sit straight.

"What I am doing is losing my godforsaken mind. Damn it all to hell," Jza cursed the situation, alarming her companions as she sat down in a huff. She could not walk away, "The blood has stopped in all the shallow wounds except the one on the shoulder. They still need to be tended to if you are to live."

"Burn it. Use a dagger. I will tolerate the pain," His face twisted in a grimace as the brown haired girl dabbed his wounds in honey. She now sat cross legged in front of him on the floor. She had wrestled with the idea of leaving without a trace but her feet would not cooperate. Behind them the girls gasped in fear. Solid constitutions they did not possess.

"You are not an animal," Jza said, "Cauterisation is not for every wound. The flow has ebbed successfully for most wounds so it's quite unnecessary. Sewing it up shall help you better."

"Am I to presume you have sewn up many wounds back in your day?" The injured man taunted.

"Once upon a time I was a talented seamstress. The only clothes I wore on my body were made by my own hands," Jza replied, patiently although her body shivered at the prospect of such delicate needle work. She undid the ineffective leather band from her hair since most of her hair was really dangling loose. She also pulled out a large needle from the infirmary pouch. The girl behind them wailed hysterically at the sight of it. The other one had already taken to wimpering. It would have been funny if the situation wasn't so dire. Tarquin too shared her thoughts from the look of the smile of his face.

"Hush! Go help your mistress. This tunnel leads to all over the castle and I'm sure you know where to go. We will manage on our own," Jza asked them kindly. Their fear of needles was so palpable Jza could not help but be swayed by their terrified sounds. She needed her hands steady for this task.

"Bite into this," The girl offered the injured man the leather binding.

"I promise I won't scream. You can do whatever you want with me," His voice slurred slightly although his eyes were alert as he watched her every move.

She hastily looked away trying to focus on her task. He was teasing her even faced with the prospect of a painful end. Did nothing scare him?

"Do you have any spirits on your person? If there was ever a time to ingest them it is now," Jza announced hoping he had something to dull the pain but he gave her pointed look as if asking where on his half clothed body could he hide it.

Jza suddenly tasted blood and her tongue darted out to inspect her observation. Tarquin's hand reached out and his fingers slowly mapped her face, following his blood, that had transferred onto her face, until he reached her lip. He languidly thumbed the traces of blood on her lips with slow, searing movements. The look in his eyes burnt her more than his touch did."No intoxication could be as potent as your presence," His voice was gravelly and low.

"Stop distracting me," The girl's hand trembled in what she hoped was fear as she pushed his hand away.

"Am I a distraction? At least I can claim you don't think I'm a beast. You called me a human today," Tarquin smiled indulgenly. He placed the leather in his mouth and Jza pricked him with the needle in response.

Chapter 23

J za fingers were stiff as she slid another stitch into soft flesh and pulled it out carefully. She tried to keep her actions tiny and precise hoping the pain was as minimal as possible but she could not assume anything. Tarquin had his eyes closed and she could almost pretend he was sleeping but his hand would clench and unclench occasionally leaving her sick to her core. It was one thing to nearly beat an aggressor to death in a fit of passion but another to painstakingly inflict such torment on another. The Princess was on her knees now, looming over her patient. She had hung the lantern on the torch holder helpfully built into the wall. The shoulder wound was the last of injuries she needed to contain but it was higher up then the others. She was glad she left it last because her hands were less clumsy now. There was a sudden grumbling sound from deep within the castle which shook the tunnel walls. Jza took a deep breath to keep her hand steady. "It's the harem isn't it," Jza broke the silence, "They're certainly busy. They seem to have survived. I hope." "You're concerned for them?" Tarquin spat out the leather band, voice hoarse from disuse. How many hours had it been since they had conversed. Jza's back twinged from stiffness every time she moved indicating the passage of time. "Of course I am. It is a dangerous task they have undertaken. I doubt I could ever perform with such ferocity. I commend them for taking the initiative to fight for what they believe is right," Jza said truthfully. They may may not be on the same side but she would give credit where credit was due. "Why? You survived on your own under enemy lines. How different is it from what you've done?" Tarquin asked curiously. His eyes wandered over her handiwork before resting on her wane face. He briefly tensed up with another needle stroke. "I had no choice while they chose their path to glory. I was just mistakenly left behind. There will be no valor awards for me for sharing your bed," The Princess' lips were a grim line as she spoke almost to herself. Her hair now truly hung loose and she never did realise how they gently caressed Tarquin's face every now and then. "I'm certain Vladimir has something to say for your valour," The injured man chuckled making Jza glare at him for moving her hand with his careless movement. "They go for the attack without any hesitation. I am surprised, for they seemed like women of leisure," Jza ignored his comment about her time in his captivity. She did not feel proud to have been so compliant and harmless. "They were bored and had the free time to learn something new. I gave them a few lessons but they eventually rid of me to pursue their specialities. My harem was never as active as it was in Ivan's time. They had to submit to no one but me and that too at their own leisure unlike earlier times." Jza suddenly felt embarrassed by the frankness of his words. Their transactions were not something she wished to hear about but she was still curious about his allusion to the past. "Back then anyone could just walk in and..." Jza made a pained face. She did not have the stomach to complete her sentence. "Choose a harem member for their pleasure? Yes. Anyone important at least. If a bargain was worthy Ivan would offer the harem to them like cattle. Nobody was safe from his eyes," The man spoke with bitterness tinging his speech. There was a certain rigidness in his shoulders that appeared that even a needle could not provoke and Jza was now even more horrified by her next line of thought. "You were in the harem too. Surely he would have kept his son as an exception..." "There were unpleasant incidents throughout my life but they only forced me to show a prowess for warfare earlier than most. Ivan began to encourage his political rivals' attentions to my strange and exotic face just to see them be disembowled. I killed my first man when I was ten," Tarquin's voice was stony as he touched upon his childhood. His life history explained many things about his blood thirsty personality. She had also wondered why he had never touched her beyond his manner of teasing. He had no reason to show restraint. She had seen the parallels with his mother's story but it seemed his own experiences sealed the deal to how he treated her. In his own brusque way he had protected her not just from his army but from himself. Her eyes drifted to the chain dangling on his bandaged chest momentarily. His gaze was steadfast when she met his. There was no doubt in her mind they both knew what her chain was. It was odd she clould read him so well with one shared look.

"You know the purpose of this chain. Yes?" He asked. She unraveled the bandage and applied it to his shoulder as best as she could.

"Of course," Jza gave a measured reply, "I shan't ask about it if you give me the same courtesy although I have a fair chance at guessing who you are hiding in your chain. I hope she's doing well."

"I hope so too. If you think to weaponise the situation then remember she is a broken women who barely recognises her own son. My mother is nor aware of anything useful," His words were very precise and biting. After a very long time the Princess could feel a true threat emanating from him.

"Of course not," She replied cooly, "I will keep your secret safe. The war is not meant to attack the innocents."

"I seem to remember King Galios had a different ethos."

"King Samuel is not like his ancestors. He is the guardian of the weak and indigent. His army is routinely reminded to have mercy on the unarmed. He would be disappointed to see me use your mother for his political gains," Jza continued encircling his shoulder with the protective cover until she was certain the wound was safe.

"That's why he lost," Tarquin scoffed.

"No," Jza's voice was forecful, "It was because we had traitors in the midst. Not one but many. You are not having much luck in Goridion castle are you?"

"It is tougher terrain," The patient looked away with a brief frown.

"Don't insult my intelligence. I went through your correspondence. I can read military jargon well enough to understand your continued defeat," Jza finished the procedure and adjusted the bandage around his forhead.

"You're certainly knowledgeable about healing methods and warfare terms," The injured man asked. It was clear the instinct to uncover all her secrets never dissolved like he had his throne.

"We were under seige. I could not sit behind and wait for the menfolk to fight our battles. I was in the infirmary as much as I could," The Princess settled down on the sheets with a thud. She cracked her knuckles with a grimace and only stopped when she found her companion grinning at her. Why did all her actions amuse him so. She was distracted by another explosion that rattled the tunnel.

"Do you truly mean to never go back?" Jza asked with cough. This explosion had been closer and the dust long settled in the tunnel bore down them.

"Of course not. The Somerlians disgust me. I thought after all these years I would learn to tolerate them but the night of the ball made it very clear I did not care whether they lived or died. It's a waste of time to pretend I care," Tarquin sneered. He took the opportunity to lean against Jza who wanted to push him off but did not want to jostle his wounds.

"I did not think you were the person to give up so soon," She asked with a wry smile.

"Oh, I'm not giving up anything. My end goals have changed. I will get what I want even if it takes me an eternity," He said gregariously and Jza found that a very curious comment. What could more important than a crown.

The sat in a comfortable silence for while hearing the consistent booms echoing in tunnel walls. It was a surpise the tunnel hadn't collapsed on them.

"I need to leave before dawn breaks. I should not have let the girls go. You need more care," Jza wet her lips and gave his shoulder a nudge indicating he needed move. The man instead let her bear more of his weight.

"You should take me with you. I am aimless for now," The girl gave him a horrifed look causing her patient more amusement. She felt his shoulders shaking with mirth.

"What about your new goal. How will you achieve it clinging to my side?" The Princess finally shoved him aside and forced him to face her, " I mean it when I say I am farm bound."

"I'll be here all alone. What if Sofiya doesn't find me? What if I bleed to my death. How would you feel but, oh no, you would not feel since you too would be dead," Talk of their mutual deaths positively delighted the Lord.

"You don't fool me," Jza wanted to be unconcerned since the manipulation was obvious as the sun that would rise soon. "But there's a chance isn't there. To leave a wounded man all alone... What would king Samuel say. Tsk tsk," Tarquin mock pouted giving her a very sultry look. The Princess could instantly see some of the learnt behaviour from the harem. His face instantly lost all gaiety as he spoke further, "What better way to regain King Samuel's favour than to offer me as your prisoner?" Jza froze at his proposition. The temptation was so great she feared she would burst. She would regain her honour, her home, her father back all in one go. Could she dare to hope for all she had thought she had long lost.

"You are going to be the death of me," She uttered, giving him a disdainful look. Jza had made her decision.

"You know as well as I do that it's the complete opposite," He replied with an unconcerned shrug.

Chapter 24

They lost their way before they even began. Jza was con-
founded by the similar looking twists and turns while Tarquin
seemed to be in an unhelpful, contemplative mood. He neither
added to her monologue cursing the confusing paths nor gave any
indication he was aware of their surroundings. He slowly strolled
behind her letting her be the judge of the terrain.

"We are still following the wrong direction! This is too close to
the explosions. If we were under the gardens the sound would
have decreased by now," The Princess grumbled, swaying the infirmary bag whose straps were rounded around her. She turned
around with a dramatic flare of her skirts and found her captive
leaning heavily against the wall, breath shallow and sweat dotting
his blood smeared face. With a pitying look she offered her shoulder for support which he took without hesitation.

There was another defeaning boom and the girl could have
sworn she heard a scream. The thought of the human destruction
happening above ground gave her stomach an unpleasant lurch. It
reminded her of the time the castle had been under attack.

"You would slaughter all their children too? They're innocent in
their parents' schemes," The brown haired girl asked her silent
conpanion who was steadily breathing in her ear. The weight
around her neck was heavy but not unbearably so. The thought
of letting the man drape himself over her half naked should

have bothered her but he was injured and compassion overrode her sense of modesty. Besides, the amount of bandages she had wrapped around him meant she could barely feel the heat of his muscled flesh. Barely.

"You're predictable," Tarquin sneered, almost inaudibly. The exhale of breath lightly glided against her pink cheeks.

"If I was, you would have known I would break into your study," She breathed through her nose while she spoke.

"Hardly a surprise. I knew you would do something drastic when I accosted you at the ball-"

"I'd rather not discuss your drunken foibles," Jza remarked stiffly, "Now listen to me. This is my domain, my people. Let me judge the situation. Do not start running your mouth and jeopardise our escape."

"Why do you think your level of generosity would be exhibited by your people? Not everyone would heal their captor's ailments with a steady hand," Tarquin's bitter tones were oddly complimentary. Jza felt the tips of her ears heat up but dismissed the feeling of elation and squashed it beneath her metaphorical feet.

"Do not attribute virtues onto me I do not desire onr deserve. If you die than so do I. Maybe I am more self absorbed than you think."

He scoffed in disagreement, his movement jostling both of them.

In their inattention they never realised they were right at the end of the tunnel. It seemed like there was no exit but a dusty stone wall blocking them but the Princess knew a deft hand was that was required to open the tunnel exit.

"Remember my instructions and keep a low profile. I will handle the situation. I hope the bandage on your face hides your identity well," Jza gingerly unloaded her burden, who took the manhandling meekly, and began to work her magic on the stones.

"Why, yes, my lady. I am your prisoner after all. I follow your every command," The man replied, sotto voce.

The tunnel opened into a low ceiling, dimly lit room. There were full sized, caged prisons lining the room. Inside the cages were multiple men gathered at the ends talking to one another. Jza was grateful they were awake although it would have been shocking if they could sleep through the explosions. She could hear another one reverberating from behind them although it was fainter now.

"Who are you?" A man uttered with an astonshed whisper. Jza gave her silent companion one last look and began the search of the room. She could hear scuffling over stone as the men scrambled to get a better view of the new arrivals.

The princess found a circular key chain hanging on a rusty hook on the wall closest to her making her job much easier. She fiddled with the keys and began unlocking the barred doors one by one.

"There is a mutiny among the Somerlians. Take advantage of the infighting and leave the castle immediately. To repay my debt help me and my companion flee from the castle grounds. That is all we want. We shall be most grateful," Jza replied after the pregnant pause. The too quiet room suddenly errupted with noise. There were many questions and comments thrown her way but one in particular caught her attention.

"He's one of them. He wears the enemy colours." A man with a messy black beard and overgrown hair pointed at the injured man's trousers as he got a closer look.

Tarquin now rested against the wall furthest away from the crowd with hooded eyes. His face was covered in both blood and bandages hiding his most prominent features. There was a tenseness in the man's posture that indicated he was ready to take the crowd down if they so much as looked at them the wrong way.

"We can help you find a way out but why should we save this cur's life? He's part of the army that destroyed our homes, our families, our lives," Another older man recently released from his prison looked cross at the mere presence of the enemy.

Jza closed her eyes trying to summon the words that could convince them. She imagined begging for their lives but failed to imagine a world where she could see herself doing that. She opened her brown eyes and knew it was time. She needed to reclaim her identity back. Her shoulders unconsciously squared making her seem taller than she was. The look on her face made the crowd of men take pause and their chatter died down in anticipation.

"Because my name is Princess Jza, the thirteenth Princess, and all of you have sworn your lives to my father's throne. He gave me charge of this castle and it is your duty to obey my command," Jza voice was made of iron. She cast a look over the audience of sallow faces. The whites of their eyes were stark against the ill pallor of her complexions.

"It is her. It is, dear saints, I would vow it on my life. I was there when she beat the commander at the arrow competition. I thought I was mistaken but it's truly her," The oldest man with a bushy white beard confirmed with a decisive shout. There were other voices agreeing with him.

"Your Highness," The younger boy, who had approached her the only other time they met, exhaled. He fell to his knees in supplication while the others bowed. Jza blinked for longer than a heart beat in sheer relief.

"This soldier is my captive. He is under my protection and I will not leave my prisoner behind. I have vowed it." Jza took a few steps backwards reaching Tarquin's side though she did not have the fortitude to examine his reaction.

"What is it that you propose we do? We are always so heavily guarded. Escape has been futile," The man closest who bore marks of a whip on his forearms asked her urgently.

"The guards should have abandoned their posts by now to combat the castle's destruction. The others have been eliminated for having too much loyalty to the throne. They will be short on men but we must still maintain as much stealth as possible.

"Our first task should be to find resources for our escape. Find all the weapons in the stores. I am certain they have a stock for the blood sports within these walls. The grainery is also at the end of the gardens so we must take our fill and lay waste to it. We shall need food for our respective journeys. Bring everything that can survive a journey.

"Raid the stables before dawn shines upon us. All of you must take the horses back to Gordian castle. Do not take the main roads. The traitor must have pulled his men for the treachery but it would not do to get into battle right now," Jza wet her lips after her long list of instructions. Unbeknownst to her anyone who had doubted her identity was now convinced of her authenticity.

"Reaching Goridian castle is no stroll in the park. The forest, the mountains are treacherous felling even the greatest of navigators. The roads are the only demarcation that lead the rider safely," A bald man hesitantly revealed his fears.

"The horses will find father without instruction. It is not common knowledge but all the animals in this castle will go to the King if ordered so. There is no chance of losing your way. Be loyal to him and the animals will obey you. And that reminds me, find the pigeons! They gather near the fountain. It's best we send him a missive about your arrival," The Princess explained with a decisive nod. The plan was finally forming shape in her head to her satisfaction.

Three of the the men who were not shackled additional to the imprisonment took the initiative to follow her immediate instructions.

"When you get there inform the king and him alone that you are following Princess Jza orders. I do not know if he still has anyone in his midst who will betray his confidence. We lost this castle because of that traitor who played a most evil farce," The only girl in the room explained. She wriggled her finger behind her back trying to regain some feeling. This particular sewing project had not left the after affects even now.

"Why don't you join us, Your Highness. It is only natural you wish to reunite with your father as soon as possible," Another former prisoner asked her kindly while his hands were freed from his shackles.

"I-I cannot," Jza faltered. She unconsciously took a step back with a troubled expression and her back hit the stone wall. Her throat felt so parched after her long monologue. She could feel Tarquin's gaze bearing down upon her.

"What if he asks about your whereabouts?"

"Tell him I went back to where I came from. He will know," She was mindful of not disclosing too much in case they were captured by the enemy once again.

"You are not going alone, your Highness. The man with you is injured enough. He will not be able to protect you if indeed he does not stab you in the back," The oldest man who spoke did not doubt the certainty of his statement. His beady eyes looked over her shoulder letting his loathing reach the so called prisoner.

She could feel Tarquin's muscles tense in affront. She placed a hand on his uninjured shoulder as a warning and felt the tension leech from his body under her firm grip.

"Yes, we will need help for a safe passage out of the city bound-aries but beyond that you are free. You have suffered enough turmoil. Then we shall part," The Princess countered.

"My Lady, you do us grave injustice. How could we face our master with the news that we left you alone to fend yourself with a strange enemy soldier. Let the strongest of us protect you. We have already sullied ourselves for not being able to save you when we knew you were trapped in the castle by that Vile creature, Tarquin. Let us atone for our sins," The younger fair haired boy pleaded.

"I will take your recommendations under consideration," Jza pondered for a moment, "Five, it is. Just five of you will be needed for our journey. We are not a day from my intended destination. It is too rural and nearly barren to be of much interest for the enemy. I do not foresee any trouble."

The leftover men proceeded to argue among themselves who would have the honour to guard the Princess. It seemed like it would take a while.

"I am not so predictable after all." Jza whispered as she gazed at the group. Tarquin remained silent.

Chapter 25

❚❚ .bonnie and blythe their angelic smiles.." Tarquin hummed
• softly under his breath but Jza heard him all the same which
she was certain was his intention. His accent stood out more
prominently now. Hearing Goridans after so long made her realise
how different he sounded from them. The Somerlian language was
a harsh one with gutteral and sharp sounds but ironically when
Tarquin spoke Goridian his accent was very melodious. It was a
wonder she hadn't noticed earlier although being in captivity did
allow her the leeway not to be enamoured by her enemy's voice.

Jza placed her parchment on the desk with fraying patience at
the infernal noise he was making. She belatedly noted the room
had emptied while she had been engrossed in her fervent letter
writing. The rundown desk in the corner of the prison room
proved a good place as any to keep her father abreast of the new
developments. In the middle of the room were weapons the men
had collected for the journey. The mission was for every man to
have at least one weapon on their person.

"Are you truly singing that abomination at a time like this?" The
Princess asked incredulously, unable to contain herself. Tarquin
sat on a tatty chair in his corner looking particularly smug. "It's
not the only song I know about the twelve famous beauties. The
bards were rather popular in my court. I wonder why they never
mentioned the thirteenth princess?"

"When I say I look nothing like them I truly mean it. They are ethereal and deserve many songs written about them while I do not," Jza informed him plainly and tried to divert her attention away from him but failed miserably.

"Liar!" Tarquin said with a callous grin although she could not understand what prompted his exclaimation. He continued, with his gaze fixed on her face, "You have your father's eyes. I knew I could see him in you but I did not know the relationship was that close. My mistake. He cannot have hid you just because of your looks since you favour him tremendously. Was it because of your mother?" "No, he never differentiated between his children and was quite surprised by my decision to keep away from court affairs. He married my mother after all even if it was in secret leaving no taint on my existence. It was my grandmother that hid every trace of my mother and her repeated attempts at communication after my father returned to the castle. Perhaps there would have been more kindness shown if I were a son or had noble blood..." Jza trailed off speculatively. She was glad her old bat of a grandmother was dead and buried long ago. What she had done to her parents was unforgivable. "Would not having a secret third wife and an unexpected child make a scandal?" The injured man asked curiously. "No, not in our country especially with his marital history. His first two weddings were arranged at a very young age. He had his first child at fifteen. No one would begrudge him happiness except his own mother," Jza paused and gave him wry smile, "That is why Cassandra at thirty two is still unwed which is almost unheard of in both your kingdom and in mine. He would not force his daughters into marriages they did not want and certainly not at the age he was." "It was good of him to give you the respectability of his name. I had to bloody my hands to attain mine." Tarquin gazed at the floor, pensively, "Maybe you are correct that King Samuel is the worthier king. His actions certainly show why his people are devoted to his cause."

"It took him a while to uphold the true virtues of the king he was vowed to be. Maybe if you could hone your social skills you could regain your position..." Jza wondered almost to herself. It was turning into a habit to solve other people's problems even if that person was her enemy.

"Are you trying to coax me back to my throne? Surely you do not consider me such a burden you would want a tyrant back in power," Tarquin laughed, harshly at her naive nature. She has cursed his very existence since the day they had met and now when he had rid himself of the troubled weight upon his head she was trying to fix his fallen fate.

"You are not a burden," Jza said defensively with a flush on her face. She looked down at her tidy lettering, informing the king of the situation. "Why not? I know I am the reason why you cannot meet your father. You would have been on your way to him this very second if not for my presence," The brown haired man gave his companion a pointed look.

"Not quite," The girl mumbled, despondently, "How can I meet my father's eyes? What he must think of me I wonder? I am a tarnish on his good name."

"Cease your foolishness! I will ensure your father sees reason. He will know nothing untoward happened in our time together. You showed no sign of weakness and neither did you lose your loyalty despite my best efforts," Tarquin's hissed words did not assuage her. Her dark thoughts flitted across her face.

"My stepmothers will not care. My name and reputation will be dragged through the muck for their pleasure," Jza lips twisted bitterly.

"Those women bore traitors. They will not wish for you to retaliate by sullying their daughters' names. Your stepmothers will be too craven to spread rumours once you threaten them with the right choice words."

"I couldn't ruin their reputation like that," Jza was adamant. She rolled up her parchments and placed a seal on the ends. Finding no other means but the enemies mark she had decided to press her pendant on the wax. It was the symbol of her resistance although she was still not unloading her burden on the survivors. She trusted no one to hand over her sisters to her father but herself.

"Ah, being good and boring is such a tedious chore," Tarquin sneered as he adjusted the bandage across his brows, "If you wish to the survive the royal court you need to flourish the ruthless aspects of your nature. They will chew you up and spit you out with nary a thought if you insist on staying on the straight and narrow. I suggest an alliance with the morally ambiguous if you do not wish to dirty your own hands."

"Why would I even need any help of such sort? I am now firm in my decision to retire from public life. This life is not meant for me and I have no wish to return to it," Jza told him bleakly, not realising how much her decision mirrored his," They all despise my existence anway. You think it is only the harem that has tampered with my food. Fear not because my own sisters were enjoying their torment of me. It is only an actual war that curbed their increasing vendetta against me." "Maybe the older you got the more you were diverting attention from them," The injured man suggested.

"Perhaps. I did gain attention from the archery competition. The painting you had of me, remember? I won against the commander that day. My father was so proud he celebrated it in full form. I will miss the sheer joy on his face most out of all that I will lose."

"You would let them win? Let those foul traitors take free reign of the castle? You belong there much more than those green eyed monsters," Tarquin pressed his lips in displeasure. The injustice of it all seemed to offend him greatly.

"Meet them first then declare them as such. You are just a man and I will not tease you much if you cannot over look their external appearance," Jza's laugh contained no pleasure. She had had the unpleasant experience of having the crimes against her ignored by the court persons at large because their imaginations could not concieve such otherworldly beauties could act with feral intent.

"I have spent my entire life surrounded by beautiful women. A pretty face creates negligible impact on my heart or body. I have seen their images. They have very few charms to divert me," The man rolled his eyes but Jza non-verbally dismissed his claims. She could not fathom a man who did not fall for her sisters. They were sitting in tense silence when the room was quickly filled with the hard working Goridoners.

"We have found many loaves of bread and alongside them were jars of preserves and dry meat to our luck," A very bulky, sandy haired man sat a sack next to the weapons after they all bowed in the Princess' direction who remained seated.

"If there is an excess then it would best if you could regain your strength and partake an early morning supper now. Your imprisonment was a long one," Jza's words sounded too kind to be the order they were.

"We were well fed and well rested, your highness. Out of all our complaints against our enemy food was not one of them," The giant like man answered with a brief smile. His companions started sorting the meals with rations for all the men. It seemed like there was enough to last them for days.

"Good. And the horses?"

"We had a skirmish in the stables but we managed to free thirteen horses. We have sent more resources to free those out on active duty but we might need to ride in tandem. There simply would not be enough for all of us," A red headed man with a newly acquired bruise informed her.

"Take care not to tire out the horses. It's perfectly possible to ride to Goridian castle in two days through the forest but my estimate for five was to give the horses rest. There will no chance to refresh your rides. Do you know how to take care of a horse?" Jza asked. "Not all of us are soldiers. We have three stable boys and four footmen among us," The man with gigantic proportions nodded with a pleased look. "And other survivors?" The Princess asked with an optimism she knew was useless. Tarquin had been too thorough in his search of the castle grounds to leave a trace of the enemy not in his grasp.

"We were the unlucky few who survived. I know my fellow gardeners were able to escape into the tunnel. I believe we are only ones left behind," The larger man informed her surpising by his admission of occupation. As the largest it was expected he would have a different talent but appearances were deceiving as always.

"We have found many abandoned carriages. Apparently the Somerlians were having a gathering," The redhead told her as he packed the last sack of food and weapons.

"Carriage? What would I do with one. It will only slow us down," Jza dismissed his suggestion with a graceful wave of her hand.

"Your Highness, it will be a harsh journey. The sun will be unpleasant along with the dust. You might find greater comfort being transported in such a fashion."

"Absolutely not. I might as well paint a target on my forehead," The Princesss shook her head with a frown, "I know my way around horses. I can even ride one without a saddle if need be. Do not concern yourself by my nonexistent needs."

"I will need a sword," Tarquin intruded on the pointless argument before it could go any further. His voice sounded so foreign once again.

"Not on this earth, I vow it! Your Highness, I cannot in good conscience allow him means to hurt you!" The large man's face turned red with evident fury. Jza sent a pleading look at her prisoner's way but he ignored her wishes.

"I shall be riding with her and surely you would not want your Princess without an armed guard."

Chapter 26

"**A**bsolutely not! The snake will betray us all," The sandy haired man answered. His face was even more redder than before which nobody had thought was possible.

"Now, now, no need to be hasty in judgements," The Princess positioned herself between her prisoner and the Gordioners unconsciously.

"Of course, your highness, anything you want but this turncoat should not be allowed near weapons much less you," Their redhead companion's jaw was clenched at the thought of the enemy protecting their Princess.

"Obviously leaving her at the mercy of a bunch incompetents is the perfect solution," Tarquin couldn't help but needle the easily provoked group. Jza's hand landed squarely on the injured man's newly clothed chest asking him to stand down but his body remained tense. The prisoner now wore truly prisoner garb since staying unclothed would only expose him further to the elements. They had raided the prison closet to find him appropriate garb.

"If there's anyone who needs a weapon right now, it's me. I would like to take that quiver if you please," Jza interrupted any further bickering with a firm glare at the participants. She was handed her weapon of choice immediately which she hung on her left while the infirmary bag hung on her right.

"Have I seen you somewhere before?" A dark bushy, bearded man asked abruptly and for a tense moment the Princess felt herself lose the calmness she had been radiating. She could explain the presence of an unnamed Somerlian in many ways. Her mind had already found a few explainations if she was pressed for more details but expecting them to accept the company of Lord Tarquin was just too much. She would not blame the crowd for beating their enemy to a pulp. He was the cause of all their woes after all.

"Perhaps he has cleaned your stalls now and then," Jza answered carelessly. She picked up a pair of discarded daggers and handed them to Tarquin. He wordlessly hid them in his newly acquired ensemble. "There is no time to be lost. Dawn is upon us. We will lose the advantage if we stand here squabbling. Bring me my ride."

"Am I to go with you?" Tarquin asked and was met with silence and a sea of stubborn faces who were assembling together one by one. They could hear the horses outside being herded.

"I will not share my horse with you," The large gardener answered without any show of mercy. He would have spit on the Somelian if he could although the Lord shared the same setiments. Obviously he had never considered sharing a horse with anyone else but her.

"He rides with me. He is my responsibility and I will take care of him," Jza answered with a sigh. Of course she would be left minding Tarquin since everyone else were loathe to tolerate his presence.

"Your highness!"

"I will not argue any longer," She pulled her damp hair back in a knot as she spoke. They had all taken turns refreshing themselves in the prison outhouse when the men had been out completing their errands. She had hoped she would feel more alive but alas fresh water was no solution for the lack of sleep.

The Princess walked out of the prison rooms with the crowd parting for both her and her Somerlian companion. She found the sky lightening and gave them orders to hasten their flight. She was given a black horse which she mounted easily. Her loose and flowy skirts had enough give to allow her a comfortable seat on the pillion saddle.

"What are you waiting for? Behind me," Jza ordered as she found Tarquin's pale face eyeing their ride stonily. Sensing his hesitation she leaned in and chastised, "Do not argue for your words fall on deaf ears. Please, there is no time!"

Tarquin gave his companion another freezing look before jumping up on their ride barely jostling the horse. Jza felt him settle behind and tensed up as he put a hand on her waist, "Hanging on for dear life since I have no wish to be thrown off."

"You are in safe hands. I am a much better rider than you assume," Jza pulled the large hand off her with a pinching grip.

The Goridians handed out the resources for the stragglers while they waited for the scouts to return. The Princess kept her back straight as she tried to ignore her prisoner's presence. The man hardly fidgeted but she could feel every inch of movement he was so close. Even his shallow breathing caught her attention hypnotically.

"The cowards have abandoned their posts!" One of the stable boys rode back looking elated to have returned alive, "We should have no trouble passing the gates."

"They may have chosen to lay a trap," Jza asked pensively but she had no choice. They must move forward. This was the best time. With a troubled sigh she ordered them forward. The sprightly, more experienced horsemen were asked to take up the rear and front. Weapons out they marched forward. Even though Jza had tried she had firmly been relegated to the middle.

The castle's exit was hidden behind a curve in the path lined with large oak trees and the group was taken aback to find that there was no ambush waiting for them. The archway was truly abandoned. Tarquin hissed what seemed to be Somerlian profanities in Jza's ear. The incompetence of his soldiers was rankling him.

As they continued through the forest Jza kept an eye open for movement but there was nothing beyond the rustling of the leaves in the cool morning breeze. Her heart sank as the view of the village nearest to the castle loomed in a distance. They had no intention of entering it but it seemed to be abandoned and torn apart.

From the corner of her eye Jza spied a shadow moving out from the undergrowth. Her hands went straight for her bow and arrow.

A sun burnt man walked out with his hands raised. He had an oddly cheerful smile as he faced the large procession as if they were a balm for his weary eyes. With his hands now clasped he approached them cautiously.

"What is it do you want?" The Princess asked as her horse came to a halt right in front of the man.

"Some food my lady. We have been displaced by the war," The stranger's accent was mixed. He could be of any nation and they would not be any wiser to his origins.

Jza loathed to go ahead without helping all those in trouble but there was something about the situation that unsettled her. The expressions on the man's face, where his eyes lingered, how he spoke and especially how well fed he looked did not add to the story.

The bow and arrow in her hand were not aiming for the man but they were still tense with anticipation. She was waiting for a sign to prove her instincts right.

The man's hand inched backwards towards something lodged in the waistband of his trousers. Jza's narrowed eyes thought it could be a weapon but when he muttered something in somerlian she knew their lives were in grave danger. In lesser than a second her arrow had disembarked onto the mission and stabbed the man on his shoulder. She was alarmed to see a dagger already embedded in the man's neck.

She was further surprised as her already bloody skirtd were splashed with more blood that came from another source. Another man gurgled foward from thick growth of the trees with a matching dagger protuding out of his neck. Both strangers fell to the ground leaving behind rising dust in their wake.

"Your highness?" The gardener who had taken up the mantle as the voice of the group gasped and for a heartbeat she worried they had ended an innocent man's life.

Tarquin dismoutned and watched the bodies on the floor dispassionately. He pulled out his daggers from their blood sodden bodies in one calculated move. He has acted at the same time as she had so perhaps her actions were not unfounded. It was an odd situation to be in but she trusted the man's killer instincts at least.

The other men also dismounted and turned the bodies around looking for further clues. They found weapons concelaed in their trousers. The strange men were obviously not as helpless as they had implied.

"I knew he meant to attack us. The way he moved his hand towards his back. And obviously the use of Somerlian indicated he was hiding something from us," Jza explained to the gaping crowd.

"My, my, you're learning fast," Tarquin gave her an approving grin as his eyes lingered over her solemn face.

"Perhps being near a blood thirsty killer might be the cause," Jza muttered back.

"You went two steps ahead of me so I could not have been influcing you at all," Tarquin voice increased in volume as he explained, "I merely understood what he said to his companion. And he had no friendly feelings for us at all. It was a call for a surprise attack. There were other men hiding behind us."

Some of their audience started in alarm. They took stances preparing for another attack while two swordsmen bravely inched near the forest edge in search for the accomplices.

"They've run off already. No point wasting our time on cowardly ruffians," Tarquin said loudly although his eyes were fixed on the Princess. She understood his meaning and called everyone back. They were wasting precious time.

Jza made the mistake of glancing down at the blank expression on the robber's face before mounting her horse. Her hands shook on the reins and for a second she wanted to be sick. What had she done? She may not have been the one to kill him but she had played her part. It was her arrow stuck in bloody flesh. To her dismay Tarquin pulled the wooden arrow covered in sticky blood effortlessly. After examining it he deemed it worth being used again and handed it back to her. She placed it in her quiver in a hurry.

"We could pause our journey for now. There would be no harm done if you want to rest," His voice whispered from behind her as Tarquin joined her on the horse. Jza closed her eyes trying to dispell the image of blank eyes. She had harmed enough people in her time in captivity to know she would have gladly completed the act of murder to protect herself and her sisters. It was just the starkness of the end result that disturbed her.

"No, we will take a break around noon as planned. Rest the horses, replenish our sleep we lost and begin our journey right before the sun starts falling," The Princess repeated what she had told her audience before they began the journey. She had wished someone with a wiser head on their shoulders could guide her but even Tarquin had accepted her plan silently. Perhaps he approved which she could only hope. He had the experience leading an army not her.

"I had nightmares for weeks after I helped a friend kill my first man," Tarquin voice contained an edge of sympathy she did not need.

"You were a child," Jza bit out remembering the account of his first kill, "I am a grown woman leading a group of men towards freedom. I cannot afford to be weak."

"No one will view you differently."

"But I would," The Princess whispered almost to herself and began the journey once again

Chapter 27

Jza woke up with a start, clutching her locket painfully. Her dream was lost to her now but the feeling it invoked lingered. The panic and absolute terror left her trembling. She let her eyes remain closed as she composed herself. Her heartbeat soon reached a languid pace and she opened her brown eyes.

The first thing she noticed was her skirts had moved upwards leaving a patch of her calf bare. Cursing herself for deeming it too hot for stockings many hours ago she swiftly sat up and arranged her clothes back to where they belonged. She darted furtive glances around her to make sure no one was watching.

The position she had chosen was as further away from the camp as possible without it being dangerous. The men had not resisted the distance for they knew a lady of her breeding required privacy. She had snorted at the thought that they would be surprised to know where she had slept during her time in captivity.

Taqruin was the closest man to her, sitting only a feet or two away. He sat facing away from with his bandaged face resting on his knees. Jza suddenly realised the strategic way he sat hid her from view especially her lower half. She was mortified to imagine he had taken it upon himself to guard her modesty. The Princess wondered if during the times they had slept in the same room had he ever woken up to her in such a disheveled form.

"You are not alseep?" The brown haired girl asked her guard. His amber eyes were closed but his breathing was not as even and deep as she had grown used to listening in their shared room when he slept.

"I have better things to do than leave this camp under the care of these fools," Tarquin replied, gruffly. He gazed at the encampment with hooded eyes.

"They are not so helpless as you imagine them," Jza answered tartly as she rose from her bed roll.

"What can a gang of stable boys and gardeners do against an army?" The sharp amber eyes glanced at her briefly.

"And what can an injured man stabbed in multiple places do," Jza raised her eyebrow, "Allow me a look so I can replace your bandages."

"Not in front of them," Was the curt reply from the injured man.

"They already know you're injured," Jza rolled up her bed knowing she had no further use for it. The nightmare had dropped her desire for further sleep.

"They do not know the severity or where they lie. I do not wish to expose my weaknesses to my foe," Tarquin informed her leaving Jza surprised. Not by his hesitation to expose himself to his enemy but the willingness to share the reason with her. Was she no longer his foe?

"They are under my command. They will not harm you. I will not allow it, I vow it," The Princess unconsciously allowed the steel back in her voice. She was an indulgent and kind royal but she possessed an inate sense of command even she did not know she possessed. It was also what had convinced Tarquin that she was no scullery maid when they had met. Her stance, her voice, her words had all oozed a sweet sort of power entralling all those that came her way into doing her bidding.

"Forgive me for not misplacing my trust," Tarquin answered, looking up at his captor.

"You will let your wounds fester for pride?"

"No, I will let you look at them, privately. You can do with me whatever you please at your leisure," He gave her a quick grin which she ignored. She smoothed the wrinkles on her outfit instead and walked up to the bruised redhead who was sat at the edge clearly guarding both of them.

"I need fresh water to clean the prisoner's injuries. Is there any available?" Jza asked as the man stumbled to his feet. He clumsily bowed while she watched him impatiently.

"Your Highness, we have the skins available although it would be best if you follow the stream we camp next to. It's mountain water so cleaner than what we have," The man advised pointing in the direction of the water source.

Jza was about to walk away when the man spoke with more confidence then he had shown before.

"I kept a close eye in him while you slept and he never wavered his attention. He is covered head to toe in bandages but he would not rest until you woke. I am beginning to think his loyalty is not in question. He seems devoted," The redhead said in a low and measured voice.

"I would not know. He has never offered me a word of loyalty," Jza replied breezily. She knew what came next and mentally prepared herself for the questions all the men must be thinking off.

"Then how come he is in your company? How come you nurse him to good health?" The words were incredibly predictable.

"He saved my life and now I am saving his," Jza explained. It was the truth after all as it rolled off her tongue, "He was my guardian when I was captured. He ensured no harm came to me."

"Ah, in these situations one does develop a bond," The man replied, understandingly.

"It's not as serious as you think," Jza calm mein faltered, thinking of how close the man's words were to the reality. She steadied herself and tried to keep herself centered, "Once we are safe I intend to let him go. Our debts will be payed."

"Is that wise, setting a Somerlian with dubious loyalty free? Besides in a span of a few hours he has shown more skill with daggers than we all possess combined. He could be useful."

"Unlike Lord Tarquin I have no intention of keeping prisoners for sport," She remarked. She intended to walk away but the young fair headed boy scampered their way holding something in a makeshift sack.

"Your Highness, we found a bunch of strawberries. Please do us the honour of taking all of them," Young Thomas offered the fruit to her like a young puppy greets their master.

"I thank you for the kindness bur I cannot be the only recipient. All of us must have our fill," She answered picking a few in her hands.

"Your Highness," The redhead tried to argue but even he knew it was a useless battle. Once she had declared something she meant it.

"I am of the gentler sex and we do not consume as much as strong young men such as yourself," Jza flattered her company and took her leave. She offered Tarquin the cargo in her hands who quickly took two. Jza then took him behind the bushes where the small stream lay.

...

"I knew one day you would become used to watching the delights of the male flesh," Tarquin's words broke the long silence of unraveling of his bandages.

She rolled her eyes at his unusual innuendo filled speech. She remembered when he had pressed her hand to his athletic chest and felt her ears redden. No, she had most certainly not gotten used to watching the delights of the male flesh. For a second she wondered if he would heal back to his previous fine form.

"Yes, your body has weakened my spitit," Jza answered deadpan without giving him the pleasure of her eyes meeting his.

"Bah, I could never weaken you. Just now you displayed such a saintly sight forgoing your own pleasures for your people. I am sickened by your nauseating sense of honour," Tarquin shuddered for effect.

"Don't be unkind. Perhaps I am watching my figure," Jza replied with a grin. She smoothed her hand down the bumps of the stiches making the man shiver.

"Please, I have seen you dig into clotted cream during breakfast. Gentler sex indeed!"

"I may have to find a husband one day. I need to take care of what I eat," The Princess replied remembering how her governess was consumed with making her marriageable.

"You're going nowhere when you're bound to me," Tarquin replied, darkly. His eyes lost all their earlier vibrancy.

"Indeed, you're right," She gave him baleful look as her touch gave him another shudder.

"Don't tell me you would forgo your men their pleasures," The Princess asked curiously. She was interested in understanding how he ruled his subjects.

"Well, I did keep them away from my harem..." Tarquin trailed off with a shurg.

"Not those kind of pleasures! Its the simpler kinds like.. strawberries. You would not share the loot or would you?" Jza was mortally offeneded by his subject choice.

"I would share if their performance was worthy. A reward is worthwhile to ensure optimal performance," The former Lord replied, wrinkling his nose at the idea of giving away even something small as strawberries.

"Then you cannot accuse me of being too nice. I am just following your conventions of ruling."

"How you rule and how I rule is not comparable. Your forces are loyal, your people content. I had to root out traitors at every turn. Ivan left behind too many loose ends that needed to be dealt with," The injured man replied as he raised his arms allowing her access.

"Eh, my mode of operation is irrelevant anyway It is only under the duration of our march till I need to order these men about. Afterwards I am free from this responsibility my father laid on my head," Jza replied gazing at her handiwork.

"You believe king Samuel will make his return soon," The amber eyed man asked although it seemed like he wanted to say something else.

"He would move heaven and earth to find his daughters. Do not underestimate that," The Princess replied with a snort.

Chapter 28

J za jumped down to the dry ground with a mighty heave, surveying her new abode with quiet resignation. She resisted the urge to stretch out her stiff arms after the grueling ride as her men followed her example. The dust floating around her settled around her skirts as she walked along the barn into the main courtyard. She had spent more than half her life here and yet she felt it was all a dream.

The farm was obviously abandoned. Usually there would be farm hards running to and fro, wheeling in fodder and dumping out the manure but as expected no sign of humans lingering amongst the wood structures was to be seen.

"Something isn't right," Taqruin suggested as he followed her steps. He narrowed his amber eyes, disliking what his observations revealed.

Jza nodded even though she saw nothing out of the ordinary. She trusted the man's intuition and her eyes raced over the abandoned buildings trying to find the source of his displeasure.

"We need to search the area. Make sure there's no enemy lying in wait," The brown haired girl ordered and the men scattered although they did not have to go far since the farm was not generous in proportions. Tarquin stayed by her side keeping a wary eye on their surroundings.

"I must ask you, your highness, why here?" Oliver asked after completing his circuit of the courtyard. She had finally memorised the names of her companions who had fought to be by her side when the small troop had split at the cross roads. The larger group had aimed for Goridian castle while Jza had led her smaller one to this farm. She had been tempted to throw all caution to the wind and reunite with her father but bringing Lord Tarquin with her would have caused the kind of chaos she could not even imagine.

"This is my uncle's farm. Besides the palace this is the only place I have called home," She replied emotionlessly as she lied. This place was never her home.

"Is there anyone here?" Dermort one of the stable boys called out loudly making Tarquin wince at the absurd amound of noise he was making.

To her surprise there was sound of an animal that replied back. Now she could see what had caught Tarquin's attention.

"This is a cattle farm and while usually it would be full of animals but right now, how? Who has been tending to the animals in an abandoned farm?" Jza marched to the barn, following the rattling of bells and stomping of cattle feet.

"The place looks like nobody has inhabited it for months," Oliver rubbed his hands over his beard as he spoke.

"I wouldn't believe so. The cows are alive and well and most importantly bound in place." Jza glanced back at Tarquin as she entered the stall which was a mistake. She lost her balance as soon as she entered but her prisoner was swift on his feet and pushed her to the side. A rusty piece of metal fell down from above without ceremony missing her by inches. Her skirt wasn't quite as lucky and she lost an inch to the sharp machine part.

"You just tripped over a trap wire. We are not alone," The man hissed and pulled her up urgently his fingers digging into her waist.

His dagger was out and the rest of the men raced in behind them, itching for a fight.

"Who is there?" Tarquin spoke, taking the lead. His voice was low but it echoed in the nearly empty barn. Even the meagre amount cattle was silent as they watched the scene from their perches.

From behind the dark corner a familiar elderly woman with two children approached the party slowly. The children, a boy and girl, had their arms tangled around the elderly woman. The old woman's eyes were fixed on Jza. Perhaps the sight of a woman among a group of unknown assailants gave them hope it was not a gang of robbers.

"Get lost!" The boy screamed at them while his sister, identified by how similar they looked, blinked with unshed tears tangled in her long eyelashes. The older woman showed no sign of emotion beyond a bitter twist of her mouth.

"You had better mind your manners, you brats. This is the royal princess," Dermot reprimanded the threesome.

"And yet she consorts with Somerlians," The old woman sneered giving Tarquin a baleful look.

"Greeting, Hyacinth, I would have vowed it we were never to meet again but I was wrong," The Princess spoke with pursed lips. She nodded stiffly as she watched Hyacinth's eyes fill with recognition. She was after all not the short, little girl anymore although her clothes were in as much disrepair as they used to be.

"Where is uncle? Is he safe?" Jza asked taking advantage of the shocked silence.

"They escaped before the armies raided," The old woman replied after clearing her throat.

"I presume they got my letter in time then," The girl asked.

She placed a steady hand on Tarquin's shoulder and gestered for him to sit down. She had been mindful of his injuries the entire journey and it would not do now to tire him out even further. It would be such a waste if he got trapped by the fevers after all she had done to save his life. The man must have been tired to take seat without protest.

"Yes, yes," Hyacinth paused thoughtfully before she replied, "He got your letter."

"Why didn't he take you with him? An old women and children are not ones to leave in a war. Most of the cattle are gone as well," The girl asked as she took her seat beside Tarquin. Her back sorely needed the rest.

"He wouldn't take Bertram's bastards with him. Told me I needed to choose so I stayed. I am old anyway. I couldn't do the distance in the mountains. I couldn't breath very well anyway," Hyacinth's face grew even more bitter as she spoke.

"What filth. I'm glad you've had a change of heart about bastards," Jza replied, vainly trying to keep her anger in check. Bertram was her aunt's wayward brother whom she had never met and now she was glad of it.

"I would've stayed if it was you," Hyacinth replied and watched Jza stand and walk towards them. There was a fear in her eyes as if she worried the former orphan girl was there to take her vengeance. Hyacinth had not been kind to her in the past.

"No more surprises?" Jza bent down as she asked the children. Her knees cracked at the sudden movement. Both children had moon faces that were half covered with light brown hair.

"None, my lady," The girl whispered shyly. She seemed to be in awe of meeting a princess.

Jza turned to the five men who had volunteered most desperately to have the honour of protecting their saviour. Perhaps it was regret for not helping her sooner or the honour that would be bestowed on them later she did not know.

"You can go back to Goridian castle when you have rested and fed yourself. I have reached my destination and no longer require an armed guard," She held Tarquin's unwavering gaze as she spoke," and I do mean all of you."

They all protested and argued that an old woman and two children were not adequate company in such difficult times. They continued the discussion amongst themselves outside. Hyacinth led Philips, the cook, to the kitchen which she had kept running with the limited resources left behind during the evacuation before war started. The small patch of farmland and the small fruit orchard kept the small appetites of the young and the elderly at peace.

Jza left the loud group behind as she toured the other empty barns for materials that maybe of use to her. It was futile trying to discuss her future plans with such a heated bunch. She knew Tarquin, her shadow, was not far behind.

"You need me," The Somerlian uttered as he followed her in and slammed the wooden door of the barn shut. The boarded up windows only let slivers of light inside that illuminated his amber eyes intensely.

"For what. To talk to my father? He will trust my word more than he does yours," The Princess spoke resolutely after a pregnant pause, "If the tale must be told then it shall be my words."

"Would he not need be eased by my corroboration... Would he not celebrate your capture of me?" Tarquin implored. If she was not well aquainted with the man she would have thought he was begging but his shoulders were stiff and his posture arrogant.

"Capture? I have hardly bound you at my feet. You are not defeated in the slightest. You came to me as independent as wily cat. My father is not a fool. He will sense you have ulterior motives. Have you not?" Jza asked taking a step towards him not realising how the man's eyes followed the beam of light tracking her face and neck.

"I refuse to go anywhere," Tarquin ignored her question completely and crossed his arms defiantly.

"You cannot be serious. Just because you're bored and irritated by your people thar does not mean you latch onto me," Jza took another step forward with clenched fists.

"If you do not know why I stay then you are more oblivious than I ever thought possible."

"What is it I do not see?" It was now Jza's turn to beseechingly look into the man's eyes.

"Everything," Tarquin took three steps forward and loomed all over. Jza suddenly remembered their first meeting where she had only seen the colours swirling in his eyes.

His hands as if controlled by an external force came up to her face. Before Jza could take a startled step back his fingers reached her and cradled her face delicately as if he were handling fine china. His sword calloused fingers skimmed over her jawline with a barely there touch that made her heartbeat faster.

Jza held her breath. She did not know what she waited for but she anticipated something. There was too much weight in the moment for it to be all for naught.

His amber eyes gazed at her if memorizing her features making her feel conscious of her looks. She was dirt smeared and dishevelled from their long ride and she wished she wasn't so. With just as much suddenness as before he unhanded her with a jolt and walked away without gazing back. The door opened and closed with a slam and she did not know why her heart felt like it would jump out of her chest.

Chapter 29

T he Princess had flown pigeons to her father as soon as they had settled down from the journey and waited for his reply pensively. Unfortunately the sky showed no sign of the bird's return. Jza's attention was towards the clear skies every morning without fail but she turned back disappointed. She had no way of the knowing whether the troop of escapees had reached King Samuel's terrain. She also longed to know which way the tides of the battle had turned. There was no sign that King Samuel had even received her correspondence to her dismay. The waiting was more grueling than the farm tasks she assigned herself which enabled her to watch Tarquin covertly.

There was an aggitated silence between the royal pair that weighed upon the atmosphere heavily. The other men noticed the frosty air and avoided conversing when both of them were in the vicinity. Tarquin who had not left the Princess' side for most of the journey now found work to be dealt with as far as he could away from her in their modest surroundings.

Jza watched him learn a new task with hooded eyes from her hiding place. He was a fast learner but clearly unused to the drudgery of farm life. She had warned her men the prisoner was not to indulge in any manual labour due to his injuries and they warded off his efforts to help them clean up the farm. Hyacinth had managed to wrangle the Lord into milking the cows. He followed her instructions with a very grim expression on his face but kept what he thought of the process behind sealed lips.

Jza wanted to take him by the arms and shake him into spilling the secrets he hid behind those very lips. She could feel his voice echoing in her head taunting her for her ignorance. She felt the tips of her fingers just right there at the feet of the truth that kept fleeing away from her leaving her chest hollow.

As she sat in the dark cleaning farm machinery the wooden barn door slammed open leading in very red faced men. "Is it the Somerlians?" She asked, throwing iron wool at her feet.

"No, no, it's our banner. They must have come for us." "It's father," Jza pushed the doors open and ran into the dusty courtyard. The dust swirled around the incoming horses leaving her coughing but she did not care. Even many years after that fated day she did not know how she had guessed it was her father leading the troop. Perhaps she knew the King well enough to be certain that seeing to his daughters' safety was paramount. "Jza, my daughter. Is this but a dream? I thought I was parted from you forever," The King cried out as he jumped to the ground unsteadily.

Jza's father looked like he had aged many years in a span of a few months. His hair was overgrown and he had hollows under his eyes his vanity would never have allowed before the war. Her eyes raced over his body and found no injuries worth worrying about although the slight limp was unpleasant to see. Jza flung herself into her father's arms.

"I missed you dearly," Her voice muffled into his shoulders, her eyes dampening his navy shirt.

"I am unsure what this new update is all about?" King's Samuel's voice was made of iron as he watched Tarquin trail out behind the rest of the group. The royal sword was out of its sheath as soon as the Somerlian reached them while he kept Jza tucked firmly under his chin. The Princess placed a firm hand on her father's sword and lowered it. Her father complied her request as he watched her wan face. The girl gestured towards one of the empty barns and both men followed her lead quietly. They entered the room which she closed on the puzzled faces of their subjects who attempted to follow.

Jza was suddenly stricken by how much taller Tarquin was than her father. It was odd how her impression of both men caused the disparity in truth. Her father's strength of character had made him loom all over his subjects while Tarquin's false claim to the throne had made her size him up unfavourably. It did not help the Somerlians were on average a tall race and upon their first meeting she had seen Tarquin alongside with Vladimir who simply dwarfed most men including his Lord.

"He is my prisoner, father," Jza uttered with a shake of her head. She thought it was best to get to the point.

"Prisoner?" King Samuel exhaled, his confusion mounting further. In her letters she had mentioned the presence of Lord Tarquin and even his injuries but never quite indicated how they ended up in their current predicament.

"Lord Tarquin has rescinded the claim to the Somerlian throne. He is no longer a threat to our nation," Jza repeated what she written in her letters but her father yearned for more information. He still could not believe the war had ended with such ease.

"How could that be? They talk of his ambition, the severity of his relentless attack. A man with his fortitude does not leave his rightful place," King Samuel sized up the other Royal with piercing brown eyes. Knowing her father she was certain he was both impressed and disheartened by his enemy's physical attributes. Her father had many virtues to his name but unfortunately suffered from a bout of vanity now and then.

"I have no love for the Somerlians and they have no love for me. I never wanted the throne for beyond avenging Galios' acts," Tarquin uttered although there was a certain deference in his voice Jza had not heard before. Her father did not ask he clarify his statement indicating he knew about his racial background.

"And how come you found yourself possessing such a valuable prisoner?" King Samuel eyes now probed his daughter. "He came willingly. Do not overestimate my skills." Jza sighed and decided she was ready to share the burden of truth, "Father I broke a bond to my vow."

"How is it that you live?" Her father's panicked hands gripped her forearms.

"The day I found myself to be their key keeper I vowed to keep my sisters' safe. I believed at that time it would be best if I strengthed it with a bond. I tried my best, father, believe me! Lord Tarquin had the locket in his possession making escape impossible but he never understood it's function. He never opened it to my knowledge. You must have gotten my letters about my sisters, you know of their misdeeds? Writing those letters broke the bond. I put their life in danger when I revealed their truth to you," Jza could barely exhale her words coherently. King Samuel seemed to be facing the same dilemma as his daughter.

"Ah, the famouse beauties! They were all within a hand's reach and I never even knew it," Tarquin broke the silence making both father and daughter glare at him.

"Of course, not! You were the enemy. I would have died rather than given you the advantage over us," Jza regained mastery over her words and bit out her words with a sour look.

"But how is it that you stand on your two feet? The judgement for breaking a vow is swift and merciless although..." The King trailed off trying to understand how a broken vow could remain unbroken.

"You should ask him. I have little recollection beyond the pain," The Princess pointed at the prisoner.

"I used my vow to bind us," Tarquin said plainly although it was odd how his eyes were fixed to the ground. The itch in Jza's palm urging her to confront him about the contents of his thoughts came back.

"I see," King's Samuel paused far longer than expected, "A touch dramatic for an enemy's daughter."

"I did not know her identity. If I had know I would have never let her too close. If you worry about the appropriateness of her stay you needn't worry. Her behaviour was beyond reproach," Tarquin juvenilely kept a sneer on his face but his eyes would not raise above ground. Jza was certain her father had discerned what she had not.

"And so was yours. He kept me safe and now when I am in the safety of the farm. I am grateful it was you who found me and none of your subordinates," The brown haired girl said softly and the words caught all of Tarquin's attention whose eyes reached hers.

"Your gratefulness is unnecessary. I would never have allowed an innocent woman to suffer the consequences of war. I may not be the best of men but I am not a beast," The Lord hissed out the last words as if he loathed their very existence.

"So, what is the plan for the future? How long do you intend to stay here? If my daughter must stay with you than you know what must be done," King Samuel's words were unusually firm.

"That will be impossible," Tarquin stated though his eyes were on his female companion who had not caught on to what her father was implying.

"Why the protest? You are already married to her, is that not correct, Lord Tarquin?" "Married?" Jza's face lost all colour.

"In front of the barbarian god one does not need witnesses or pomp. Both souls pledge their vows to each other and it is done. It's unlike anything I've seen in our culture where even bonding to marriage vows is not so exteme. This was why Galios succeded in felling the barbarians so easily and then Ivan. If you kill one part of a pair the other dies instantly. He married you the day he saved your life," King Samuel explained and he looked unbearably sadded for that moment that it broke Jza's heart.

"It-it is not complete," Tarquin wet his tongue and continued as if it pained him, "It does not go both ways. I pledged to her my life force, not the other way around. She is free to marry whoever she pleases. It is only I that is bound to her for as long as I live."

"You lied to me when you said he bond doesn't effect you. I could have ended my life to kill you," Jza asked, eyes blazing with emotion. She did not know whether she regretted not knowing.

"Of course, I am not an imbecile to reveal all my weaknesses. It is true one of us dies when the other does just not the way you expected it. If you die then it is I who will lose my life. I stopped my mother from binding herself to Ivan that day. He only married her the Somerlian way. He would have been a fool to tie up his life to hers so completely."

"Why? Why did you save my life. I have yet to comprehend your intentions," Jza asked frantically.

"Comprehend my intentions? I sometimed wonder if you were dropped om the head multiple times as a babe. Perhaps Hyacinth was as ruthless raising you as she looks," Tarquin snorted, deflecting unsuccessfully.

"Why would a man with every advantage pledge his life to a woman whose name he did not know. Logic confounds me!" The Princess exclaimed.

"Delicate feelings are not dictated by logic," The man replied stiffly. His hands clenched and unclenched several times betraying his internal thoughts.

"You have had your eyes on me. I am no naive fool that I do not feel the burn fixed on my form. I assumed it but lust addling you brain," The brown hair girl pointed a finger at her prisoner who was avoiding her gaze.

King Samuel cleared his throat to ensure that conversation remained palatable for his ears but the young pair had forgotten he was even present. He helplessly watched the scene unravel in front of him.

"Do not insult me with your incorrect assumptions. I desire not just your body but your heart and soul. That need to always remain close to you crippled my senses so long ago I do not even know when I drowned in your brown eyes," Tarquin shouted, looking like he was ready for battle not making a declaration of love.

"I really don't think..." King Samuel tried to interject but his pleas were falling on deaf ears.

"You have been the source of my greatest torment..." Jza spoke with immense fragility, remembering the pain and humiliation in his captivity. She closed her eyes in despair not because of his words but because they evoked emotions she wished to suppress completely. She was no better than her sisters.

"And you have been mine but I understand it does not compare, mila moy," The lord's voice had calmed down. It seemed like his hands too itched to bring her close but feared the consequences.

"I hardly think calling a girl affectionate pet names is the thing to do in front of her father," The Goridian King could not stay unheard any longer.

"Affectionate pet names? You truly do not curse me behind my back," The girl asked very quietly. "I would rather plunge my hand in my chest and pluck out my dying heart than give you anything but honour," Tarquin stated so softly Jza could barely hear him over her heartbeat. She looked down at her two feet feeling like she was on the verge of tears. "Your talk of honour increases my wish to see this matter settled," The Goridian King said with a grim expression," I may be going senile at my young age I cannot say but I will not leave my Jza without protection even if it is yours. I will not be able to tolerate if even one word is said against my beautiful and courteous daughter who won the war for us."

"Leave us? I assumed once you understood the truth you would have no qualms about my beheading," The former enemy asked.

The King sighed, "I have formally declared, despite my advisors protests, that beheadings are for all those who did not lay down arms in defeat although the job was nearly done when we arrived. We have already sent the Somerlian womanfolk back although the men have been detained for questioning. The carnage your men left behind nearly rendered the castle unlivable I must say."

"Women. It was women who were responsible for the destruction," Jza added. She could not let the Harem's bravery to their cause be left unnamed.

"Of course. I should have known. The rule of women is upon us," King Samuel gave a brief grin, "You are my daughter's prisoner, not mine. She is to decide your fate. But she is also my daughter and her fate I worry about. I cannot take the Lord Tarquin back for now unless I want a revolution but to leave her alone with you..."

"And why would she stay. I am only her tormenter, a beast. You should have swept her to the castle by now. I should not be into consideration." "My father knows me too well. I am not ready to go back to the castle. I need time. It was my prison even before the war. They will take a look at my war torn face and make the worst possible assumptions. I have no interest to counter the rumours, the innuendos, the politics. Maybe at a later date, one day... But for now my mind needs the rest. I have no energy left. None," The Princess breathed as her father placed a hand over her shoulder understandingly.

"I still worry. Lord Tarquin you must give her the protection of your name," King Samuel sounded as if he were handing over a death sentence. "Father, he never made any attempts at seducing me. Besides, you promised you would never force marriage on anyone," Jza protested.

Tarquin laughed aggressively, "Now you wound me. Half the time in your presence I tried my level best to divert you with my charms but obviously I was off the mark if you do not even count them as seductions."

"Then the harem has taught you very poorly. A missish school-boy would have better sense to attract a lady with such childishness," Jza snorted at his admission.

King Samuel closed his eyes and shook his head as if his brain was well and truly addled.

"I also do not wish to burden her with me. I will not make a single move without her consent. I want her to want me as much as I crave her," Tarquin spoke to the King although his gaze was fixed on the girl.

"Oh dear, I sounded like my mother just then forcing marriage willy nilly. It would be most unfair to force either of you upon one another," The King admitted defeat, "Just remember to not overstep your boundaries. I beg of you."

"Father!" The Princess exclaimed.

"I do not wish to partake in this conversation any longer. I understood as a father of thirteen daughters I must contend with many love stricken beaus fighting for their hands but this talk of passion is giving me gout," King Samuel raised his hand firmly. He turned to give Tarquin a speculative stare, "Your sisters will be jealous. You have taken the handsomest of the lot."

"If I do not give you any favour then what do you propose to do. Will you finally head back to your wayward county?" Jza said as she ignored her father.

"I informed you earlier I had a new goal. I intend to wait for an eternity if I have to," Was the man's reply. Suddenly the girl understood his meaning when he talked of the new goal.

"Even if I chose another man," Jza asked gently.

Tarquin looked away, "So be it."

Chapter 30

"Father, we must discuss my sisters," Jza added after a poignant pause. She was incredibly unready to peruse her thoughts about Lord Tarquin's declaration. She had known in the back of her mind she had his attentions. The threat of committing a fatal misstep that compromised her beliefs had terrorised her so fully it lingered even after her father had given his approval.

"I had my sources there was something wrong with their dealings. Their correspondence was being hidden but I just didn't know the extent of their dissatisfaction or deception. They wrote to you?" King Samuel asked his former enemy.

Tarquin nodded. He looked so uncharacteristically frazzled that he took a seat without being prompted. Did he regret voicing what his heart contained Jza wondered.

"Did you reply back?" The Goridian King asked grimly.

"Yes, although it was my advisors doing the writing. I needed to know what kind of ambush I was walking into," The Somerlian Lord replied with a stony look.

"Ambush?" Jza asked with surprise.

"Why in the name of all things holy would these women start writing to me all of a sudden if it were not a trap," The younger man asked as if it were not the most obvious answer to his predicament.

"Of course," King Samuel sighed with drooping shoulders, "I am aware of the reason. They saw a painting of you. The new painter showed us his older works and one of those portraits was yours. It certainly caused a frenzy in the royal apartments."

"And where was I?" Jza asked with an abrupt laugh. Did all this ridiculousness start because of a mere painting.

"You had barricaded yourself in the library from what I remember."

"Ah, the dead frog incident. Nothing could induce me to stay in the same room as my sisters," Jza answered. It was not as if they would have shared a handsome King's painting with her anyway.

"Nothing could prevail you to stay after that either. I know who owns this farm," King Samuel looked even more defeated. He gazed skywards at the newly patched roof of the barn.

"Yes, I bought this farm from my uncle when I wrote to him about the impending war. I was always meant to move here. I could not abide by the royal behaviour any longer," Jza answered with determination lacing her voice making it clear she could not be persuaded otherwise.

"I did wonder why you were saving your allowance rather than spending it on pretty baubles and clothes but I had my answer when you used it to buy out your uncle. I knew I had failed you that day. It's a pity the war started when it did and I could not devote time to the matter," The girl's father gave her a troubled look.

"It was not your failure," The Princess placed a hand on her father's shoulder hoping to placate him.

"How ones children behave does reflect on the parent. You needn't banish yourself any longer. Your sisters will not be returning to the castle for now. All of them. I have decided the decision to send them to exhile needs to be taken," The King's face reddened with burgeoning fury. It seemed he was resolute like his daughter about his decisions.

"They will be devastated. Even Goridian castle lacked the social life they desired," The Princess answered with a worried expression. Her stepmothers would be furious being separated from their children.

"The time for their whims and games is over. I know what you're thinking," The King addressed Tarquin who was watching them with flinty eyes, "I am soft. Perhaps I am. My daughters betrayed me and I take the easy way out but I find sending them away to be appropriate for now."

"No beheadings across the board. Princess Jza's sacrifices were in vain I suppose," The injured man answered looking petulant. He glared at his nails finding it inappropriate to show his ire to the other occupants of the room even though he dearly wished to.

"Never. Although you should be grateful since my forgiving nature is the reason my daughter survived the vow breaking. I admit my wrath thundered as I read the traitorous letters but I could not in fact kill my daughters even though it is the law passed down from Galios. They were not in true danger even though my vision saw red," The King answered, "Besides, it would be best not to set the precedent of spilling royal blood. Otherwise my succession will be much like Somerlians. All blood and gore."

"Where will you send them?" Jza asked.

"I have twelve holdings all over the land in my provinces. They will be sent away so they can meddle in the courts no longer. Their allowances cut, their activities reduced and they will no longer be allowed to travel as they wish."

"Not all of them wrote those letters," The Princess stated quietly. It seemed unfair to punish those who were not the culprits.

"This is a character building exercise. I have indulged them far too long. They need to know the suffering of their people if they are to serve. Besides, they are the ones that caused you to think about leaving my side. Why should they live any better than the life you want to give yourself in this farm?" The middle aged King replied vehemently. He gave his surroundings a very disdainful glare.

"It will be easier to explain why all the Princesses disappeared at the same time if I stay here. You could tell the court you sent them away for their protection before the war," The girl said knowing she could not give her father what he wanted. He wished for her to return to the castle a victor but she had no such goals. She just wished to remain out of sight and out of mind in her little farm. Her father was silent as he realised he would be losing her as well if he pressed the issue.

"Do you not wish to meet them? They are right here. With me," His daughter pointed at herself. She pulled out her locket from under her overly large clothes borrowed from her aunt's leftovers and revealed it to him.

"I fear facing them," King Samuel replied quietly and Tarquin knew he must vacate the premises. He was no family member allowed to see the Goridian King this vulnerable.

"I hope they haven't killed each other," Jza also ignored her father's statement knowing his vanity would suffer terribly as he remembered his words later on.

"A very real possibility," The King replied, his brown eyes fixed on the gleaming chain, "If the terms of exhile are not acceptable I need to look at a tougher punishment. They can choose the locket or the real world."

Tarquin watched the girl's hair web around her fingers as she pulled the necklace out as if it were deadly. The soft brown hair delicately caressed her pale face as it shifted with her movements. He lost his breath at the vision before him.

"I shall leave," Tarquin stood abruptly and with a ceremonial bow left the room. He could never say whether it was basic manners or Jza who compelled him to take his leave.

....

That night there was a modest feast attended by all the men available. The King and his daughter had emerged from the barn an hour later startling Tarquin. Unlike the other men, who were pretending to do their chores, he had been expecting further company. The Princesses either had declined to step out to the real world or were kept to their confinement. Perhaps it was logistically convenient to pull them out at the castle.

The feast, prepared by the King's personal cook under Hyacinth's watchful eye, was a rambunctious affair. Perhaps knowing the war had truly ended made the men more open in their glee. The sedateness of the dinner had been lost mere moments after it began and people were laughing over tired and abysmal jokes. Jza had a smile on her face that eclipsed the moon shining upon them.

While the farm had managed to adequately provide them with long term resources there were few indulgences to be found in the state it was in. Her father had brought stocks of meat, grain and jams for Jza to fill up her pantry.

Tarquin sat at the edge of the long table, appropriated from the great hall, surrounded by Goridian soldiers. He had never thought it possible and looked uncomfortable as if expecting an attack. The King had made no announcements regarding his identity. He did not reveal his true nature and neither did he shun him. He allowed the Somerlian to sit on the same table as him and that was enough of an endorsement for the Goridians.

The group sang many a song in old Goridian glorifying Galios. Lord Tarquin clenched his fists under the table feeling helpless.

Galios' army had stolen land from his people, killed a vast population, made the survivors homeless. King Samuel's generous nature to his people did not mean the blood on his ancestor's past could be cleaned up at his whim. The atrocities committed in that time still had repercussions to this day. His existence was one of them.

The former Lord stood as soon as it was civilised, unable to keep a straight face any longer. The men had started dancing around a fire and his absence should not be noticed. He walked away into the orchard and wandered until he reached the farm's grain mill. A small stream ran through the room sized mill used for churning out flour although it was currently under dire need of repair. The man heard the soft footsteps before the brown head bent down to get in.

"I need to see your injuries. I hope you have not neglected them while you were avoiding me," Jza asked. She carefully sat on a stone bench beside her prisoner minding her newly altered clothes. She was in the process of repurposing the female clothing left behind and this was her newest piece. He hated the sight of the tatty little thing.

"Not at all, with a mirror I can clean all of them. They're healing nicely. Your needlework is impeccable," Tarquin patted at his shoulder which only twinged mariginally.

"You should thank Hyacinth for inducing such skills in my uncultured hands," Jza said with a nostalgic smile.

Without ceremony the Princess leaned forward and started pulling at the laces of his shirt. The environment was quiet beyond the brook bubbling beneath their feet as she meddled with the finicky threads. Slowly and steadily patches of bandages and bare skin began to reveal themselves.

"I wished I could be the lash that caressed the curve of your cheek," Tarquin proclaimed, speaking without warning.

Jza's hands paused her work but she did not look up. A quiver in her fingers was the only sign she had heard him. She exhaled with a resigned sort of sigh and continued her ministrations

"I wished I could win your favour and you would look at me like I was meant to sit on the throne," The man said. His voice was low and soothing to the ear.

"My good opinion has never been so sought after," Jza said, pleasantly, "Is this conversation appropriate as I undress you?"

"Maybe the sight of you undressing me reduces my mental faculties," Tarquin replied, with faint amusement, "And they were worthless."

"Who?"

"The people who never fought for your opinion."

She gave him a brief glance upwards before lowering her gaze to her task. His throat worked as her fingers ghosted over his bare skin. He barely contained the shivers everytime her fingers grazed over her handiwork. The necklace containing his mother glinted in the moonlight coming in from the bare window.

"They've spent more time with me. Maybe they know my worth better than you," The brown eyed girl said tartly.

"Never. No one could know your worth better than me," Tarquin was adamant. He studied the line her lips made with his words.

"Proximity in tense times creates a bond," Jza uttered, remembering Oliver's words from their first day of escape. She wondered if this was the case and he was mistaking their companionship for something further.

"Then I should have fallen in love with Sofiya," Tarquin snorted derisively, "But there is no one for me besides you."

Her ears heated up to hear the words he was uttering. It was so difficult to pretend she was not affected by his presence, his words.

"I will always be yours," He said, leaning so close his breath fluttered her hair. His hands gripped her forearms in a touch that was barely there.

Jza wondered what would happen if she walked into his embrace and let him glide his hands over her. She knew his touch was not the teasing kind he used when she had danced with him in the ballroom and nor were they hot as the blazing looks he had sent her. It was gentler, more measured. Revealing his secrets had calmed the frenzy that burned within him.

"I did not mean to make things uncomfortable but I could not contain my feelings no longer. You were impervious to all hints I sent your way," Tarquin said, mistaking her silence. He watched as she quietly redid the ties until he was clothed completely.

"I had an inkling. I was unsure of your intentions," she answered, breaking away from his hands.

"You made me feel small. I could have sat atop a mountain and proclaim myself god and I would still feel small in front of you," Their conversation was almost incoherent but she knew the dam had burst and he was revealing all that he could in their silent unchaperoned time away from everyone.

The Princess glanced up and down with a measuring look as if noting how tall he was. He grinned as he observed the faint smile lacing her lips.

"My physical attributes are not in question."

"Of course," She answered, magnanimously, "But I do not believe I have done anything to gain such regard. I have never conquered kingdoms nor fought wars. In the grand scheme of things my mark on this world is limited. After I die who will even remember my name being just another Princess among another dozen. You put too much importance on a nobody."

"You are the reason the war ended, Jza," Tarquin uttered her name tenderly. She could not deny the delicate feelings he spoke of he poured in his speech.

"So, you only stopped the war to win my favour," The Princess asked with an edge to her voice.

"I wished to be worthy. I wished to be your friend rather than foe. Perhaps it only highlights me as a shallow sort of fool but it is my truth," The amber eyes pleaded towards her.

The twosome remained seated on the smooth stone bench in silence.

"Are your sisters not coming out from whereever that is," The man asked with a wave of the hand. He still could not believe a trinket could be so powerful.

"Father has been reticent about what happened in there. I could not go in because I was the key keeper. One person must remain outside the key if they do not wish to lose the ability to come out forever," The Princess explained leaning against the stone wall.

"And you did not ask?"

"I do not wish to see them ever again or hear about their antics although it is not possible in the long run. My feelings mark me as vengeful but I care not," Jza tried to sound uncaring but the hurt bubbled through her speech.

"And yet you stayed outside as the key keeper when we raided the castle even though you should have gone in with them. Now, I understand why your loving father left you the responsibility. He did not know you would sacrifice your well-being for your sisters," The Lord looked grim as the piece of the puzzle righted itself.

"Correct, Raymond was to hold the keys but you can see why I could not allow that," The brown haired girl answered with a dull sigh.

"I have a favour to ask you," Tarquin asked, making Jza sit up straight, "I wish to see my mother."

"Of course. It is an honour," The Princess answered and watched the Lord pull out the glinting chain she had hidden beneath his clothing.

Chapter 31

That night Jza fought her dreams intensely. She woke thrice in her uncle's abandoned bed and found herself surprised to be all alone each time. She refused to entertain the throught that she knew who she was missing.

"I do not know when I drowned in your brown eyes."

Jza closed her eyes to dispell his voice from her head which was a mistake because now snippets of her dreams tormented her instead. Some started with her father overseeing her execution, some with Tarquin dragging her on the floor with chains binding her hands together, some where she being stoned to death by her own people. Her mind was filled to the brim with death and destruction as if peace had not been achieved.

The Princess was relieved to have been woken at dawn to see her father's departure. She dressed herself in a rush and ran out with her brown hair flowing behind her. Her old governess would have been appalled by her recklessness but those days of brutal criticism were over. The underused herald announced her presence but she was in her father's arms before he could complete her designation.

"I shall miss you," Jza said, containing her emotions. There was much left unsaid.

"As will I," King Samuel replied before climbing atop his heavily decked horse. While it seemed imprudent to show off the King, making him an easy target, the man had elected to use the procession as a means of raising the morale of his people. The word had been spread the war was over but to see him with ones eyes would get people out of hiding faster.

The King had many pending errands to run and could not give the farm more time even if he wished most dearly to stay. While his daughter needed him his country could not survive without his presence. Jza's calm gaze as she had bade farewell gave him a sense of peace he had lost before the war had even begun. His daughter had proven she could take care of herself and she would continue to do so. He had nothing to worry about.

For Jza the sight of her father's horsemen exiting the farm's dirt road was agonising but the absence of the gold chain around her neck made her feel like she was floating above air. Her sisters were now her father's responsibility and he could do whatever he wished with them. She was rid of them and their wretchedness with a profound sense of gratitude.

Instead of taking advantage of her elevated position among the new farm hands left behind by her father the Princess chose to forgoe sleep. She knew she could not escape her nightmares even with the sun rising steadily behind the copse of the orchard. She instead chose to inspect how the work continued which had begun even before dawn had broken through the horizon.

As she exited the barn that needed the most repairs she found herself confronted with the vision of Lord Tarquin sat in the middle of the courtyard next to the well. She watched as he brought a red apple, fresh from their orchard, upto his mouth and took a solid bite.

He was accompanied by Bertram's son who was gesturing wildly as he spoke. It never failed to surprise Jza to see the Lord wearing ordinary garb just like all the other workers. His borrowed clothes fit him remarkably well but they were a far cry from the clothing he used to wear in the castle. Over the months it had become obvious he was particularly fond of bold colour and nothing at the farm could provide the richness of the fabrics that he adorned himself with when he was in power.

"You need to take the string firmly else it falls too fast," The twin informed his captive audience as Jza took a detour to the pair. She never even realised her feet had changed paths until she abruptly paused at her destination.

"I haven't a clue how it should stay up in the first place," Tarquin replied, looking engrossed in the conversation.

"They say it's all the wind but I say it's the twist of the hand. You need to keep tugging because if it falls, it goes to the enemy," James, explained while his twin watched from the kitchen door where Hyacinth was making bread. The young girl had not adapted as well to the new comers as her brother but Jza could see how much the little girl wanted to join them.

"Oh, we would not want that," Jza injected herself in the conversation.

"I'll show you how it's done," The boy nodded with enthusiasm at both of them before he ran off to get his toy, "Do not go anywhere!"

Tarquin raised the apple back to his mouth and Jza was compelled to keep staring while his attention was away from her. She could not break her gaze from his profile. It was not the foreigness of his looks. No, inspite of his assertions about the way Goridians had treated the Barbarian people they were still cities full of people mixed with the former ruling race. It was something else. A quality she could not define.

Tarquin handed the Princess his half eaten apple which she promptly took a bite of unthinkingly. She was in the middle of her second bite when she realised what she had done. Tarquin's eyes twinkled at her from where he was seated. She swallowed the remnents of her body's betrayal quickly.

"Old habits are hard to break," Jza replied with a pinched expression. She handed the apple back with an embarassed air. Tarquin did not hesitate to continue his meal with an intent look in her direction.

"Just like your propensity for missing meals," He stated which she ignored. It was none of his concern what she did with her appetite.

"How was it?" Jza cleared her throat as she clarified, "The inside of that door."

She had asked about his mother as soon as he had reappeared but never thought to query what was inside. How could someone spend hours much less months trapped inside a vessel. Could magic be so profound to create an endless landscape capable of keeping a human being content.

"Ethereal," The man answered, "I would not begrudge anyone who refused to leave. My mother thought she was dead. She thought it a blessed plane our people are destined for after death. I did not have the heart to correct her."

"How poorly must she have been treated to find solace away from the real world," The brown haired girl wondered.

"I am occasionally disappointed Ivan is dead. I feel this frenzy of blood lust where I wish to dismember him all over again," The words were spoken idly but there was a fire in his eyes he could not hide from her. The fury did not intimidate or frighten her. She could in fact feel the same sort of flame burning in her heart. She understood what it meant to feel the need to extinguish a life beneath her hands when it threatened the ones you hold most dear.

"If you had laid a hand on my family you would have had the same fate. I would not have forgiven you much less let you live," Jza replied, firmly.

"I know," Tarquin replied as if she had not needed to vocalise this fact.

"You have blood of innocent on your hands," The Princess exclaimed, redundantly.

"I know," The man's gaze was now at his feet.

"Then why do you think I would have you. Do you think me some weak sort of imbecile to fall for a pretty face. I am not like my sisters. Why do you expect me to-to-" The girl lost the words to vocalise the situation between them. No matter how she tried to separate his presence from the expectations in his eyes she could not. It was as if the world was waiting for an answer. The unfortunate truth was even she did not know how the limbo would end.

"Of which I am glad since you were not rendered silly because of a painting," Tarquin replied, "I wish to repent for my sins. I will make myself worthy. Whatever you want I will place at your feet. If you want my severed head then it shall be yours-"

"No, no! Do not let your... Partiality for me do the talking," The girl could feel the tendrils of embarrassment blossom in her chest, "What material items you could win me over with even I do not know."

"Alas, I would have fallen in love with an unconventional woman.".

"I am not so unconventional," Jza replied primly, "I am like all the other women who loves a ball and a pretty dress. I was just raised so frugally that I do not need more than I deserve."

"You deserve everything on this earthly realm and beyond; the sun that is not brighter then the light in your eyes, the softness of the moonlight that is not as gentle as your nature."

Her ears were so red she felt the burn radiating over her face. The girl could not look at him. She felt like she would ignite and burn down to coal if she did. She hid her trembling fists behind herself, her fingers biting into her skin.

James ran upto them bearing the kite and string, releasing Jza from the promise of a reply, with trail of dust flying all around them. The child handed Tarquin his red kite who examined it carefully.

"Are you trying to teach him how to fly a kite? Surely he does not need it. It's a simple task," The Princess said trying to sound indifferent.

"It's simple because you've flown one many times. I have not had the pleasure," Tarquin replied with smug sort of smile.

"You don't know how to fly a kite at all?" James was now wide eyed and mouthed.

"My father didn't believe in toys."

"It's never too late to learn. After all playing with marbles and sticks is the only other thing I'll allow you to do," Jza said, magnanimously.

"Allow me?" Tarquin's eyebrow raised as if hearing foreign words.

"I'm in charge of this farm and what I say goes. Did you miss what my father announced at dinner?"

"Oh I heard everything your father said especially about me," His voice dipped very low before raising itself to an audible pitch, "Ah, the Princess is showing her true colours. She's very bossy, isn't she?"

"Not as much as Hyacinth," The boy replied back.

"I'll get there the older I get," Jza winked and began walking to her destination, "The dry river bed is the place for this sort of an endeavour. I shall be joining you after I finish my chores."

The Princess was accosted by the stable boy who informed her of a pregnant heifer in their stables. The way the cow was finding places to retire to meant the baby was on its way soon. Jza added the new task to her mental list and found Hyacinth in the kitchen sorting herbs for the bread.

"You may have all of them fooled by your youth but you haven't fooled me," Hyacinth's words were as bitter as she remembered them. Jza leaned against the counter trying to see what she could grab for a quick meal.

"If there's anyone fooled it's me. I didn't realise I was trying to fool anyone," Jza laughed before picking up another fresh apple just for herself. She would not be sharing this one.

"I can see you're behaving like a tart with that Somerlian nobody," The girl was reprimanded with a hiss. Young Rose watched their interaction intently as she separated the mint leaves from the stem.

"Well, I'm certainly not hiding anything. The king knows and approves," The Princess answered smugly. This was the one time she would use her father's words to her advantage. There would be no tattling to the King if he had already given his seal of approval.

"Approves? I suppose he can afford to lose one of his daughters to the enemy," The old woman did not want to show her defeat and went back to her herb picking from the pots.

"I suppose," Jza replied barely containing her laugh. The animosity Hyacinth showed her was nothing unusual and she knew not when she had lost the ability for those words to bite her.

From afar they watched Tarquin listening intently to James before the boy led the man away towards the orchard. Beyond the trees there was an incline that led them down to a river that only flowed during rainstorm.

"I was wrong about one thing. He's not a nobody is he?" Hyacinth said, tearing her eyes away from the Somerlian. She pressed her hand to her forehead as if in pain.

"Why do you say so?"

"He's got an uppity air. Perfectly congenial but too high brow. And look at him; can't even play a game of grunt. I saw him looking baffled by the soldiers," Hyacinth informed the Princess.

"Not everyone has perfect childhoods," Jza replied as she finished her apple. She left the core for the compost pile.

"Even you know how to play it," Acknowledging how Jza's childhood was as poor as she remembered it to be. The old woman turned away from Jza as if losing interest in the conversation.

The Princess asked Rose if she wished to accompany her to the dry river which she after some prodding accepted shyly. Under Hyacinth's beady eyes both girls ran from the kitchen to the orchard in an impromptu race. Jza lost by a margin since the young girl was ready to be let lose upon the world. Trampling over fallen branches they slowed down their pace until they reached the incline that led to the dead river. It was a shallow valley carved by a once roaring river. It was now dry to the bone and in the middle stood Lord Tarquin and James at a distance from one another. The boy was holding the kite while his companion the string reel.

Jza watched the man once again feeling her eyes unable to move from her target. Tarquin waited for James to let go of the kite and taking advantage of the slight breeze he pulled the string with a force the girl disapproved off. The kite floundered pitifully and landed in a dusty shallow hole waiting to be resurrected. Hiding her laugh she slid down the dusty slope and landed near the boys. Rose tumbled down behind her catching everyone's attention.

"I am aghast the great Lord Tarquin is abysmal at something," Jza laughed with a sarcastic clap on his shoulder.

"I will master it before the end of the day," Tarquin's face was grim and resolute as he helped Rose up while Jza dusted the girl's clothes. She had noticed the poor child had very few outfits to call her own. She vowed to start sowing for the children as soon as possible.

"I have no doubt you will. Is that how you handle all challenges; With mulish bullheadedness?" The Princess asked with a gregarious grin as she circled around them.

"Of course," The man gave her a brief smirk.

"Is that how you intend to win me?" She asked, watching the children run to retrieve the kite.

Tarquin paused his motions and the faint baring of teeth transformed into a bright, hypnotic smile. He grabbed her hand firmly and brought it to his soft lips.

"I am in the running then," He murmured into her skin. To his surprise she did not pull her hand away.

"Perhaps."

Jza acknowledged both to him and herself that she was sizing him up as a potential mate. The fact that he had bound himself to her without hope of reciprocation just to save her life talked about the depth of his emotion more than anything but it was also the small things. How he interacted with James when even some of the stable boys in their free time had shrugged the boy's attempts at conversation. He could have dismissed the boy away like everyone else but chose not to. Even if he was bored she knew his actions held merit.

"I'll show you how it's done!" Jza took the string reel from Tarquin's hands and motioned for James to hold the kite so she could let it free. With a bit of struggle against the wind she tugged it higher and higher until it floated above them. She motioned for Tarquin to hold the reel from her and felt glee at the delight on his face.

That night there was no sleep for the industrious Princess. She tossed and turned in her ancient bed and wondered whether she would ever find resolution to her current dilemma. After pushing her stone like pillow into position for what it seemed like forever she got up and dressed herself.

Walking out of the doors she saw the night guard sit up straight at her presence but she gestured for him to remain seated. She required no chaperone for her late night walk.

"My Lady, Your Higheness, it is a wonder that you're up at this time. Luck must be on our side. The heifer is settling down to give birth," The stable boy ran towards her out of breath.

"Is it having trouble?" Jza asked. She had watched many births and while most cows did not require any assistance there were some that could get stuck, "Get Hyacinth here now!"

The stable boy ran off to find the elderly woman who had more experience than the Princess and would help guide the way as she had done Jza's uncle. The Princess ran in the newly painted barn containing the cow. The animal lay in the furthest corner isolated from the rest of the cows.To Jza's utmost surprise Tarquin stood over the cow looking as if he just woke.

"What are you doing here?" Jza asked, unprepared to face him so soon after the thoughts of him had lain her asunder.

"Considering I sleep here I could not leave my roommate in distress," He answered, barely glancing at her. His attention was on the suffering heifer.

"She will be fine. She's stout and is doing a good job. If all goes well we will not need to interfere. The cow will do it's work."

The cow moaned pitifully and Jza patted her head with a pained expression, "There, there, my love, you're doing a marvelous job."

"Thank you," Tarquin gave her a cheeky grin. Jza's eyes trailed down his bare torso and baggy sleep trousers and turned away with a huff. How can a person barely out of his bed look more presentable then her?

"I thought there was a bed available where the men sleep. I made sure of that," Jza said, averting her eyes to the animal.

"I do not wish to expose myself to an entire horde of Goridian men. I wonder what they would do to me in my sleep," Tarquin explained and Jza wondered what she had been thinking making such arrangements. She knew the man well enough by now to know he would never let himself be vulnerable in front of the ene-my and yet she expected him to accept the sleeping arrangements.

"They wouldn't dare. I am not like my father when it comes to transgressions. My punishments will not be a slap on the wrist. The price to pay for any harm they try to inflict on you will be brutal," The Princess assured him although she was certain he would never join the common quarters after her assurance.

"Do not let your preference for me do the talking about inflicting pain on your subjects," Tarquin's voice was nearly acidic as he crouched next to the animal mimicking her earlier words. His chain shook with his movements.

"Preference?"

"If you do not have any partiality then do stop staring as if I were a buffet," The man looked at her as if her actions were an affront.

"It's not exactly the first time I'm seeing you undressed. Your accusation is absurd," Jza's indignance was more to do with the fact that he was not oblivious to her actions than his reprimand.

"Exactly! Why you continue to stare is beyond me."

Jza had no answer to his questions. She had not been expecting to be answerable to her actions in the middle of the night when her mind had ceased to work. To her relief the animal suddenly spurt out the water bag with a great gush. The splatter was all over Tarquin, understandably distracting him.

"Where is Hyacinth? What's taking so long? No one will care if she shows up in her knickers," Jza whined as the animal writhed in pain, "It's time!"

The girl positioned herself besides Tarquin who had settled in a heap and watched the cow's hind legs for the calf's arrival.

"We mustn't interfere since it halts the process. If she stalls only then must we forge ahead," Jza explained to the man who was sitting quite still. Perhaps the shock of the birth water running all over him had rendered him speechless.

While the cow moaned and grunted in a prone position Jza could see the feet of the calf appearing. In a timely fashion they began to reveal themselves further slowly and steadily. She gripped Tarquin's bare shoulder in anticipation who barely flinched under her firm touch.

"Shouldn't we do something to help with the pain," The man finally emerged from his stupor.

"This is the reality of childbirth. This is a hurdle women must bear if they wish to have children," The girl answered gravely.

"I have never been more glad to be a man," Tarquin added after a pause. His eyes looked slightly glazed over.

"You let me sew you up without the aid of any pain relief and yet you balk at such a natural process," The girl marveled but the man remained without speech. They were interrupted by a new arrival.

"You've taken your time," The Princess complained as Hyacinth waddled in, looking incredibly put out by the late night meeting.

"I was asleep like a civilised person unlike you lot. Why have you stripped him naked in front of me?" The old woman asked Jza with a rude gesture at the man sitting next to her.

"I-I sleep like this..." Tarquin tried to look small but failed in his quest.

"He does!" The brown haired girl nodded, vigorously.

"Of course, you know the state of his wardrobe during his private time," The old woman sneered.

"His bed roll is right there!" Jza pointed at the mat she had noticed mere moments earlier.

"Humph," Hyacinth was displeased by their existence, "Well, get on it. You, girl, on the front and you, boy, at the back. Not afraid of the blood are we, pretty boy? The stable boy's flat out refused because he faints at the sight of it."

"No, I have no reservations against a spot of blood," Tarquin was stilted in his mannerisms indicating how uncomfortable he was. Jza moved closer to the head of the cow although she kept herself crouched, ready to assist if the man faltered.

"Hmm," Hyacinth made a face at the sight of his bandages, "Bloodletting your thing, eh? Look it's nearly here. Use your muscles, pretty boy and give it a right pull. Ah! There you go."

In a blink of the eye the cow babe sat in Tarquin's arms drenching him completely in the fluids it brought forth with it. Jza quickly helped him bring the calf to the udder to give it the first taste of its mother's milk.

"You can leave now. Not much to be done other than wait for the afterbirth," Hyacinth dismissed them without taking her eyes off the mother and child, "And send the stable boy in if you see him. Time to see how fast he faints now that the crucial bits are done."

"I need to clean up," Tarquin looked like he would lose his lunch soon. He walked into the other half of the barn and closed the large door behind him. There were troughs of water laid out in rows in the feeding area. Jza followed him trying to avoid touching the wet spots on her dress.

The man swiftly poured all the water over his head from the pail in the trough in one go. Water rolled down over his strong shoulder. There was no other way to get rid of the sticky mess accompanying the birth. He fetched more water in a pail and redid the action once again. Jza handed him soap flakes she found in the cupboard. After working the rough soap over his torso not even minding the bandages he once again submerged himself in the pail's contents.

Jza took her time and soaped up to her arms steadily. Her lips quirked at the sight before her. It seemed like he needed another moment to regain his footing before he embraced the water gliding all over again.

"Blegh," Tarquin shivered under the water assault, "I had never thought in my wildest dreams I would help a cow give birth."

"Is it not the best feeling in the world?" Jza asked with a small smile on her face. The exhilarating experience was one that usually stayed with her for many days.

"You and I have a very different definition of best," The amber eyed man shook his head as if embarrassed by her plebeian choices.

"Admit it. Don't you feel the euphoria to bring life to the world? Is it not better than taking it?" Jza asked as she cleaned her hands delicately. She had managed to get away with the minimum amount of blood on her body which was rarely the case in her previous attempts of cow birth watching.

Tarquin squirmed uncomfortably, shifting the weight onto his other foot. It seemed he was sodden down to the core. The man sat on a bench close to the trough but his face did not lose the look of pain.

Jza watched his pensive face looking at the suds floating above water in the trough. The fondness for him burst through her heart. This was a man who had tolerated a cow giving birth on him just for love. The love reserved just for her.

"Yes," he replied gently not meeting her eyes, "It is."

He was hunched over the trough when she placed her damp hand on his shoulders from behind. He dropped the soap flakes on the floor and turned to her.

"I say yes, I will have you," Jza uttered boldly. There was no hesitation in her brown eyes. Her stubborn mind was made up.

Tarquin stood ungracefully and pulled her close, hands still slippery from the soap and planted a lingering kiss on her right cheek mindful that the door behind them could open any time. His eyes blinked as if he was having trouble seeing.

"I am surprised. I did not expect such restraint," Jza said, truthfully.

"Oh, so you know how to truly kiss," Tarquin teased her. His hands quivered with feeling.

"I may have spied on a couple or two. I expected more passion," The Princess said with smirk on her face.

"And what else?"

"More touching and petting," She answered trying to look nonchalant.

"Is this what you want?" Tarquin stalked closer, looming all over her. She took a step back but reminded herself she had no reason to fear him any longer. Her feet dug themselves into the ground.

Tarquin gently pressed his lips against Jza's. His lips were as soft as she had imagined, "Is this better?"

"Yes," She whispered, not realising her brown eyes were revealing the deepest, darkest desires.

"Like this?" He said but her lips met his before he could lean closer. The warmth in her belly was making her act foolish.

"Hmm," She pulled him in again. This time their lips parted slightly. She could taste him. His wet hands held her waist inflaming her further. She could feel the bite of his touch even through many layers of clothing.

"If I continue on this path then I will ruin you," He whispered in her ear before planting tiny kisses down the curve of jaw.

"How so? A kiss cannot possibly do anything serious ruination," Jza tried to breathe like she wasn't out of breath.

"A kiss is only the the beginning and the light petting leads to one thing after another and before you know it I will have you beneath me. Is this your goal?" The man released her from his fingers before she could reply.

Jza shook as the warmth slid up her face. She took a step back finally breaking eye conatct, trying to calm her breathing and her beating heart. What was wrong with her? Was she truly the girl Hyacinth claimed she was.

"That's a dangerous game you're playing Princess," Tarquin said.

"Call me Jza," The girl asked suddenly not caring what anyone thought of her. The reason she had run away from the castle was to avoid all judgement. She had no right to inflict her own when she was doing nothing wrong.

"It's a beautiful name, Jza," The Lord uttered and he was correct. Her name had never sounded so sweet.

"My mother named me after my grandmother," The girl answered. The two stared at each other silently before the man took a step back and began speaking.

"I have pledged myself to you. I have submitted my love, devotion, my entire existence to the worship on your altar. I demand
no less in return. Do you agree?" Tarquin asked with unbridled
emotions swelling to the surface.

"I do."

Chapter 32

They stared at each other as if time had ceased to exist. A water droplet running down the side of Tarquin's pale face was the only indication the sands of time were still cascading down the hourglass. After an obvious intake of breath Jza dropped her gaze to her sodden boots. She could not win against the power of the man's eyes.

There was a sudden tremor of fear that agitated her heart. It was perhaps her own bold behaviour just moments ago but, no, it was another entity completely. She did not regret the decision but instead felt herself lacking the virtues he insisted he could see in her. What if she stumbled over an important matter in the future and the statue of perfection broke to tiny unmendable pieces.

"Am I dreaming? Is it you that stands before me or will you melt into the atmosphere like a figment of my imagination," Tarquin's voice of hushed awe brought her back to the present.

"You just touched me. Is that not proof enough?" Jza asked quietly. She paused the gnawing of her own lip when she found the taste of his mouth still lingered.

"Maybe my mind is addled beyond repair. Maybe I died at the castle and mother is right, that we are on the blessed plane. But I doubt the deity would give me everything I ever wanted in the afterlife."

Jza took his damp hand in hers and brought Tarquin closer with a light tug. He complied without any resistance, letting her lead him towards her.

"Does this feel real?" She asked bringing their joined hands upwards. His fingers skimmed over her hand before delicately touching it to his slightly rough cheek. He then pressed her smaller hand against his lips and gave it a sweet kiss. Jza could feel his smile against the back of her hand. She couldn't help but smile in return.

"You often dreamt about me? Is this the cause for confusion?" The Princess blurted out before she could stop herself.

"Perhaps. Although it was more nightmare than a pleasant dream," The Lord answered with unexpected gravitas. He did not let go of her hand.

"My dream self was judgemental, wasn't she?" Jza quipped half-heartedly.

"Quite. Although the dreams ceased in frequency when I slept in the same room as you. I had expected the opposite."

"Do tell me you never watched me sleep. I would rescind my offer right here if you even hint of such tomfoolery," Jza asked a presiding question in her mind. After knowing the depth of his emotions she had begun to recall many of their interactions differently.

"Never. I could not inflict myself such torture. Why would one stare at something one could never have. I had thought you would be easy to seduce early on but I was wrong. Nothing I did made you remove the distance," Tarquin replied truthfully.

"And here you have me," The Princess gave an awkward sort of body gesture that seemed to give Tarquin much amusement.

"You changed your mind faster than I thought you would. I thought you have pity on me when I had one foot in the grave."

"I fought with myself for far longer than you think. If you've set me as some paragon virtue than cease that at once. I deserve no such platitudes. I never thought you were ugly," Jza explained hoping he understood she was just human.

"Yes, that explains all the staring," Tarquin teased.

"I am not the pervert you are so intent on making me," Jza blurted and removed her hand from his swiftly.

"You did proposition me while I am undressed," The Lord unconsciously took a stance that flattered his physique. The corded band of muscle was highlighted by the faint light coming from the windows.

"Get dressed then," Jza ordered redundently since he already had his attention on a rucksack hidden beneath a haystack. The man rummaged through it's sparse contents for dry clothing.

She turned away in a hurry. Knowing him he would start stripping while in her presence, not caring for her sensibilities, although now she wondered if this was one way he tried to seduce her. And besides who was she to censure him when she had all but attacked him with her lips moments ago. Maybe he thought she wanted to watch she thought with her face heating up.

"Why is Hyacinth such a dragon?" Tarquin's voice was muffled as he pulled his shirt over his head or so she imagined. The implications of the further slaps of wet material against flesh made her nervous. The infuriating man was taking off his trousers while she was in the room.

"She's always been like that. She never cared for having responsibility of a bastard child thrust upon her and made sure the entire world knew it," Jza fidgeted, trying to sound uncaring.

"They did not know of your father? They would not have dared to mistreat you if they were aware."

"My uncle never believed my mother. She told him about the young prince she met while he was hunting but they never knew if she was being truthful or not," Jza sat down next to the troughs and after carefully pulling off her boots started wetting the ruined ends of her dress, "He married her in a temple right at end of the town. I shall have to check the papers once I get a hand on them if it belongs to me or the neighbors."

"Your father never came back?" Tarquin asked, disapproval faintly lacing his voice.

"My uncle sent my mother away out of shame after she started showing signs of my existence. My father was trapped in the castle once his mother found out about his indiscretion. He was not let out until he became King. He sent servants to ask about her but no one but my uncle knew where he sent her. Father never could say my mother's name right. Perhaps that was his biggest impediment," Jza gave a bitter smile.

"Royal romances are often unnecessarily tragic. He should have tried harder. Fate is what you choose it to be not what drags you in like water," The amber eyed man was quietly furious at her father's weaknesses. Jza too had thought what would have happened had her father more of a backbone as a young man. Perhaps he would have fought harder if he had known he was going to be a father.

"Is that what you thought your fate would be? A Royal romance gone sour," Jza turned around and found Tarquin decent. He was looking into a piece of gagged edged mirror combing down his wet hair with his fingers. How the mighty had fallen just for love.

"Perhaps. I did not have hope you would relent..even now..." Tarquin placed the mirror away with an uncharacteristic fumble.

"Like I said I have thought about you for more days then I can count. My reasons for saying yes or no changed every day. Believe me when I say it was not as flippant as you imagine although today I did act most brazenly," Jza confided in him.

"I like it when you act impulsively," Tarquin gave her the most wretched grin she had ever seen although it dampened with his next words, "I can guess your father's acceptance was the biggest factor."

"No, not at all. It's the fact that you're willing to sit with me and help a heifer give birth. You could have captured me again and stole me back to your land but here you sit in my humble little farm waiting for me to say yes. I understand the honour bestowed upon me," The Princess finished her ablutions and put her boots back in place.

"I do not want to talk about honour. I wish to know what is in your heart," Tarquin aborted a step towards his goal.

"My heart is an open book but I do not let anyone in freely," Jza answered as truthfully as she could for she was still sorting through the thoughts in her head. She paused before asking a question that had been needling her, "I may be a Princess but at heart just a farm girl. Is that the life you want? Do you not want to be the master of your palace back home. Will you resent me for trapping you here?"

The brown haired girl implored more with her eyes than her words.

"I do want to see you covered in gold and silver but if you wish it I shall follow you to the ends of the earth. As a matter of fact let's find that farm boy and send him to Hyacinth. Then you show me your little kingdom. I will be honoured," Tarquin gave her his hand which she took without reservation. The days when she feared his touch were long gone.

"It is not sun up," Jza answered, "Not much to show in the dark."

"So transfixed by the sight of my unclothed body you've lost track of time?" Tarquin only half joked as he gestured to the rays of light entering the barn's window.

"I may be more like my sisters than I thought. Perhaps I lost my mind over your countenance," Jza replied feeling bold all over again, "Come on. Let us head out."

The couple opened the rusty barn door together and stumbled out into the courtyard. Outside slept the stable boy leaning against the well's stone wall. Jza felt pity but decided it would not do to leave the cow and Hyacinth without support. The girl tried to tap him awake but when that proved ineffective Tarquin gave the boy a short slap behind his head. The stable boy gasped awake.

"The deed is done. Hyacinth's waiting inside. Make yourself useful," Jza ordered and watched the boy stumble into the barn from the other entrance where the cow lay.

"What do you want to see?" She asked turning to her companion.

"Everything," Tarquin said with a brief look around the courtyard.

"You've seen the forest behind the barn and the orchards in the front. There is some land beyond the dry river that you might be interested in. The temple my parents got married in is situated there," Jza explained gesturing at all ends of her domain. She UT began to walk towards the left rambling about the history of the place while Tarquin followed behind silently.

Jza pulled up her skirts just enough to soak up her aching feet. They sat on the stream that meandered into the dry river from the opposite end of the bank. If they looked closely they could see the smoke puffing upwards from the farm's workings.

Tarquin suddenly burst out laughing from beside her. Jza was mesmerized by the rare sight.

"What?" She asked in a huff wondering if she had done something to entertain him.

"Ankles! I cannot believe I'm affected by a pair of ankles!" The man answered giving her an affectionate look which pleased Jza to no end. That feeling of being admired made her heart soar above the clouds dotting the sky.

"What do you mean? You must have viewed them so many times," The Princess answered while shoving her skirts down letting them soak up in the fresh water.

"Do you want me to tell you about how everything affects me? The way you laugh, the way you speak, the way you're pouting utterly offended by my words right now?"

"I am not pouting!" Was the girl's agitated reply.

"Very well, my bright sun," Tarquin uttered, mischief dripping from his expression. He let his hands into the cool water and took a sip.

"Is that what you used to say in your own language. Even then?" Jza asked shly.

"Of course. It was not as if I could express my true intentions without you scratching my face," The man answered with a shrug.

"You said I wasn't your type. I was relieved you could never want anything of that sort..." The brown eyed girl trailed off hoping he was not offended by her revelation.

"I distinctly remember telling you bruises weren't my preference. I relived that conversation often enough to remember it. I swallowed my instinct to rectify the situation afterwards. I just did not wish to frighten you," Tarquin explained showing how much thought he had given to their conversations.

"What would you have said instead?"

"It matters not. You would not have had me. You were afraid. Everyday when it was time to sleep I could see that fear in your eyes. I had no wish to be Ivan's image who enjoyed a woman's fright. His example should be shunned not followed," The Lord replied resolutely. Jza understood that his behaviour had less to do with his feelings for her and more to do with what he believed was right. Once again she was assured her decision was the correct one. He was not as morally deficient as her initial impression. She saw signs of his goodness everyday.

"I was cautious, yes, but I knew soon enough you were not going to force yourself upon me," Jza said, reassuring him she had deciphered his behaviour much earlier than he thought.

"And now? Are you still cautious? I understand it will take time to find a place in your heart," The man asked the pertinent question. She had accepted him mentally and acknowledged she was attracted to him. Would he have a chance to go further and be as important to her as she was to him.

"I could have left you here and gone back with my father but I couldn't," Jza answered with shake of her shoulders. She was frustrated how difficult it was to find words that conveyed what she felt.

"You told us your reasons. Your sisters, the court-"

"Of course, but I couldn't leave you here. It just didn't feel like the correct route to take. And I heard your words; your declaration. I wanted to give it a chance." Jza uttered with utmost conviction.

He took her fingers in his own in a delicate fashion. His thumb rubbed over the wrist. Showing ankles may be the fashion nowadays but having bony wrists was not which suddenly Jza rued. Tarquin's hands skimmed over a recent injury and he paused his ministrations.

"Stop hurting your self. It pains me," He ordered with a sigh. His wet hands were cool to the touch.

"Is that how the bond works?" Jza asked, curiously. He smirked at her assumption and shook his head in negation.

"Not at all."

Jza blushed prettily but was too stubborn to look away. They stared at each other before the girl announced her intention to take him to the temple close by.

The forest was denser around the temple although the path was clearly defined. Someone had at least taken the time to cut through any random shrubbery that blocked the path. They soon stood outside the temple which was a circular stone building with columns around it that came out of the woods without preamble.

"It's smaller than I remember," Jza uttered with a bitter smile. Everything was back at the farm. The courtyard that had seemed vast when she had first arrived after her mother's passing was insignificant in size now. She could cross it in s couple of footsteps when back then she had raced across it.

Inside there was no one to welcome them. The golden altar was empty and no flowers were laid out as was the norm. Only a dozen pews were laid out for the worshipers. The rest of the potential occupants either sat in the corners or stood on the rough stone floor.

The pair walked in together in hushed silence as if the deity was in the room judging their deeds as it would after they passed.

Jza watched Tarquin's pale features wash over with the light trickling through the large, glass windows. She pulled him close, her fingers clutching his threadbare clothes and raised her face expectantly. In the broad day light she had lost that fearless edge that had brought her lips to his at her own instigaton but she was still temped by his clever lips.

"The deity watches us. Hush!" Tarquin instead shook his head with a smile. Up close the girl could see his face was now dotted with a mild semblance of a beard. She had never seen him anything but bare faced and she could not decide what she preferred.

"I did not take you attached to a religion, particularly a foreign one," Jza tilted her head with curiosity.

"This is my religion too. The barbarians left it behind for the Goridians to appropriate."

"The badosh," Jza corrected, "Why don't we use the correct name of the Barbarians. I'm sure you know it as well as I. I did find the right book containing their true name before the ball occurred."

Tarquin nodded and walked towards the altar as if reliving terrible moments of his life. He placed his hand on the empty altar and let it slide over the marble.

"My mother was a religious woman. The only reason she tolerated her suffering was because she was waiting for the deity to save her. I grew weary of her waiting and decided to do something. The deity was too slow," The man explained with a bowed head hiding his features from her, "I have killed my own father in front of the deity. I cannot afford to make any more mistakes in a temple if for no other reason than my mother's beliefs. My weight of bad deeds overtakes the good which was not the man she raised me to be."

"The deity will understand, I vow it. You were saving your mother when you slayed your father," Jza tried to comfort him although she was not as well versed with their common religion as he was. Her uncle and Hyacinth had never saw fit to teach her anything beyond the basics. By the time she had gone to the castle her guardians had assumed she had been taught everything there was to learn.

"It does not excuse the blood I let after Ivan's demise. My- The Somerlian palace is made of pure white marble. The taint of red took so long to be scrubbed out. I could say I was a child but it excuses nothing especially not my overzealous takeover," The Lord said softly still not facing away from the empty altar.

"But you've repented. You can fill up your good deeds up to the brim and the deity will embrace you in his fold when it's your time," The girl was certain she was correct.

"At least there's a chance I will have a companion when I am judged," Tarquin turned around and gave her a thoughtful expression.

Jza suddenly remembered a key component of the vow and sat in the dusty pew with shock etched over her face. She had known the terms but she was hit by how real their predicament was. She had accepted her own existence was on borrowed time but she had still not accepted the truth was the other way around. The temple circled in her vision for a fleeting minute.

"If I die then you will be forced to follow me," The grief of the unfairness towards the man hit her profoundly. She did not wish for him to die just because her time was up.

"I shall never die abandoned and alone if you are by my side," Tarquin gave her his arm which she took, forgetting they were not back the castle with their contrived mannerisms but at the farm where no such formality was necessary. He held her as if he could bear her weight if she was to collapse which she did not mind at all.

- _ - _ - _ - _ -

They were back at the farm by noon, famished and exhausted. Jza and Tarquin had collected fruits from the orchard as they had meandered back in a leisurely pace. Jza had explained what she planned to do with the farm in the future while Tarquin had added his own suggestions.

They had walked into the courtyard surrounded by half the farm men loitering about almost as if waiting for them to make an appearance. Jza mentally sighed wondering what new problem she had to correct today. She approached Oliver who watching them nervously.

"Alright, what's the ruckus?" The Princess asked the man with an impatient look around. She was also desperate for a nap and did not care for the delay in her plans.

"Who is this Lord, your highness? The men are dreadfully concerned the identity of this man is being hidden from us," Oliver confided with a frantic expression.

"Lord?" Jza's eyebrows raised at the unexpected question. She knew a time would come where the truth would appear but she had hoped it was much further away.

"My Lady, it was James that revealed the strange Somerlian was a Lord."

Jza took a deep breath and decided it would be better to be truthful, "He is my betrothed. Father gave us his blessings."

"Of course, it makes sense the exalted King would never tie his daughter to a nobody," The bearded man persisted and the girl knew there was no way out.

"He looks it like he drinks very expensive wine," Someone called out from the crowd surrounding them which gave Jza much needed relief. The crowd was in a jovial mood. Their urgency was due to their overprotectiveness surrounding the Princess and less to do with hunting the man down.

"But a Somerlian Lord?" Oliver asked. He knew there was something not adding up. There was only one Lord they were aware off and surely the King hadn't embraced the enemy.

"He is exactly who you think he is. This is Lord Tarquin son of Altani the Bodosh Princess and the Somerlian Lord Ivan," Jza kept her voice strong and steady as she announced the man's identity to her small world. She expected more response than the defening silence. Tarquin walked up besides her gave the men his most placid look.

"I have ended the war at Princess Jza's behest and there shall be no more enemity between the two nations from now on," The man declared to the sea of shocked men who had been expecting many things but not this.

"The treaty between my father and Lord Tarquin shall be signed two months from now at our wedding which will be held at our local temple," Jza added to the statement and placed a hand over the man's shoulders.

"That's news to me," Tarquin hissed in her ear.

"For me too. What one must do to avoid a murderous crowd!"

The farm boys were still silent and beyond the light whispering among them it could not be deciphered what the reaction to the news was. Were they so incensed they intented to rip the pair apart in a fury it could not be guessed.

"Do not worry, your highness. I will talk down all dissent. No one will harm your Somerlian King. They will know the war ended because of him," Oliver looked apologetic for putting them in the spot.

"Yes, if it were not for his decision we would not be free," Dermot one of the original men who had elected to stay at the farm also added his support.

"We have seen Somerlian hospitality. It has not been an unforgettable experienceNow it's turn for us to show our guest Goridian hospitality. I will be pleased if we outdo ourself in our show of kindness. After all he must contend with me," The Princess' order was masked as a sweet request. She looked confident no would dare refuse her command.

"He doesn't look as blood thirsty as they said he was," Some comedian cried out once again making the crowd titter one response.

"He's not even fully Somerlian. His barbarian blood must be the reason he ended the war. The Bodosh are a fair nation," Another older man stated.

Tarquin looked baffled by the reactions. He had not realised the Goridians thought positively of his mother's nation. He had assumed like the Somerlians they reviled their existence and treated them like muck but he was proven wrong.

"He'll make a very handsome King when you become the queen," Rose whispered in Jza's ear finding courage to run through the crowd to give her the support.

"Oh, no! The only land I shall be ruling over is this land but he's rather handsome is he not," The Princess was feeling elated by the reception their future marriage had received.

"Now, what?" She sighed as she watched Oliver speak with the crowd. There were a few sour expressions that spoiled the mood.

"Now, we must decide what colour you're wearing at the wedding," Tarquin teased.

"I have a partiality for yellow," The girl answered.

"Gold it is!"

"What?"

Their compromise was a dress made of both gold and yellow her father had specially commissioned for his beloved daughter. The King had been liberal in dripping his wealth all over his daughter's outfits since he had not been allowed a free hand over anything else. Their temple had remained simply adorned and the farm decorated modestly leaving no room for her father to meddle. At least everyone at the farm ended up with new outfits

What had surprised them the most was that one of her sisters had also planned a wedding soon after. She had found the noble at the holding she had been exiled to irresistible and had planned a wedding a month earlier. But Jza had not attended the Royal wedding at the castle and had no interest in inviting anyone over to her farm for her own. She was uncertain if her father had even informed her sisters of her good luck.

The weather was chilly but the weight of the dress gave Jza the necessary warmth to combat the elements. She had signed all the necessary documents related to the wedding and the treaty in the rickety rocking chair in her small parlour. Even the half a dozen men witnessing the historical moment had made the room crowded.

Jza and her father had taken a newly built bridge over the dry river and walked solemnly over to the temple. They talked about the weather, the rain and the journey but never about their twelve famous beauties. It was unsaid how much Jza did not wish to acknowledge their existence.

Tarquin had stood at the alter waiting for his bride to make an appearance. He wore elegant navy finery that mimicked the outfits he used to wear when in power. Jza wondered if her father had returned all his belongings. Atop his head sat the crown he was wearing one last time. In the treaty he had signed away the right to wear it ever again.

The couple had beamed at each other brilliantly eclipsing all the others in the room. Jza had hurried over to her groom not caring what anyone thought because the only people in the room were her well-wishers although counting Hyacinth as one had been a stretch.

"Privet, moya lyubov," Jza whispered in his ear making Tarquin chortle had her sudden mastery of the Somerlian language. He had met his match and they would spent the rest of their lives vowed as one.

Epilogue

J za slept through the entire carriage ride and only awoke when she was gently tapped on the nose. The Princess blinked awake to the sight of the castle looming above the large carriage. She rubbed her face and gave Tarquin an exasperated look as if preparing herself for the nonsensical behaviour they were bound to encounter.

The girl gingerly stepped out of the golden carriage with her husband's support. She walked into the castle entrance remembering the last they had both been there. Her brown, intelligent eyes lingered over the changes made over the years.

"Y-your Highness," The young man assigned to them stammered. His gaze flipped back and forth over the pair who wore humble clothing but looked like they were merely play acting the part, "The King's private counsel has already started!"

"We were unfortunately diverted on the way here," Jza spoke with a reassuring smile. The younger man's eyes were fixed on her husband now. She hoped Tarquin was not glowering at him into submission. He had a tendency to be insufferable to anyone he deemed incompetent.

The younger man bowed again, nearly tripping over his feet, and frantically led them through the long corridors until they reached the King's study. Jza smiled at her husband recalling the time she had nearly killed a man within those walls.

They were announced into the room which was filled to the brim with people. Her father sat on his desk surrounded by papers and advisors while her stepmothers, sisters and their respective families sat on various chairs placed at the ends of the room. No one acknowledged their entering bow except the King who nodded with a pleased smile.

"My husband is brave and fair. His serfs all adore his presence. He deserves the throne!" Jza's third eldest sister, Jemima, proclaimed, heatedly, not pausing for the new arrivals.

"My husband will bring important connections. He is a northern noble. The most powerful of them all," Was Jasmine's stance. She had been the first out of her sisters to find herself a husband. Apparently this noble husband had many virtues including a stash of gold coins.

"What say you, Jza. What merits does your husband bring?" King Samuel asked indulgently. Suddenly all eyes were upon the couple who were dressed in modest outfits. Jza's own hands had sown the beloved pieces they wore but she knew in the smattering of gold, jewels and feathers they were not better dressed then any servant of the palace.

"Is that wise father? To have us in the running?" The girl asked with an unflinching stare. She had gained a certain confidence over the scant amount of years no one had thought possible.

"Why not?" Her father asked with a small smile gracing his features.

"Father," Jza returned his amused look, "You know of me quite well. I feel like I need not elaborate any further. I trust you will judge us fairly."

"Why won't you tell us what your husband has to offer," Rosalinda peered up from her perch on the sofa on their left. Her blue feather adorned dress matched her vibrant eyes. Beside her sat her mother who had same pinched look she always had when Jza was in the room.

"Our father knows I chose my husband with the deepest of affection. My recommendation should be enough," The thirteenth Princess answered with mirth dripping in her speech.

"You will not introduce him?" Gabrielle asked cautiously. She was young yet and unmarried. She wore a white lace cap to match her dress.

"Not in the slightest."

"Scared he might be wooed by the twelve famous beauties?" Jemima her most ardent foe said most acerbically. She clung to her husband like a vice. Her long fingers dug deep into the man's arm who looked uncomfortable as perspiration ran down his forehead.

"Twelve? I see only seven of your sisters," Tarquin addressed Jza completely ignoring his company. Besides the King, who was now engrossed in a discussion with his advisors, he had acknowledged no one. It was at times like this that she noticed his accent again. She realised her sisters had paused their chattering to gape at her husband.

"Father must have been busy narrowing down his choices," Jza tried to keep their conversation private but knew the silence in their corner was not his aim.

"I thought he must have excluded the ones entrapped in that scandal..." Tarquin paused faux apologetically, his voice loud and clear, "Oh, I apologize. I forget we must not speak of it."

Jza's older stepmother waved her fan with unbridled embarrassment while Rosalinda blanched at the mention. The rest of the room too shuddered at his words.

"Tar," Jza gave her husband an amused look. She knew the man had been itching to throw their reputations back at her sisters whom he disliked immensely. In her earlier days she had wondered whether her husband would be wooed by her sisters' beauty but now she was certain it would never happened.

"So, I forget which ones of your sisters participated in the tom-foolery?" Tarquin asked far too unsubtly.

"They are not here," Jza answered with a brief look around.

"Then my presumptions are correct. He has eliminated the treacherous ones from the running."

"Behave," She hissed in his ear, "You have your full form on advantage today."

"I wonder why their husbands are important?" The Lord turned farmer asked, as his eyes peered at the occupants of the room. Only five of the Princesses were married but the King had invited all seven. Cassandra had married an elderly viscount but her scheming before the war had rendered her ineligible so she was not present.

"They are to rule, are they not," Jza answered with a frown although she had reached the same conclusion. Her father was playing a game the rules they were not privy to.

"Are you certain? If that were the case then why are we here? Time may have passed but your father is never going to hand me his throne," Tarquin murmured barely moving his lips, showing how perfectly capable he was of a private conversation in a room full of people.

"Is he Somerlian?" Lucita's timid voice asked no one in particular.

"No, you little fool. Does he look so? They have round eyes and fair colouring," Her stern looking husband sneered at his wife contemptuously.

Jza gave Lucita's odious husband such a pointed glare the man had to look away in defeat. Her jaw clenched as if swallowing back her anger. Her toleration for ninnies had grown considerably smaller as the years had passed.

"What is it that you do? We have not heard of you for so long?" Jza's other stepmother asked with overpowering curiosity. It must have been a devastating blow to her gossip vine to have no information about Jza who never visited the castle after the war ended.

"I was tending to my uncle's farm. He was unable to return to it," Jza replied curtly.

The women in the room tittered at the explanation behind their fans, which was a new fashion in Goridon. At least the other princesses had been exiled in relative luxury. The holdings may have been smaller then anything they had lived in before but as the only Princess in the vicinity they had enjoyed the attention on them. None had fallen so far to have been forced into working on a farm.

"You have missed much, especially the fashions," Jacqueline gave her sister's unadorned green outfit a disgusted look. Her own was sparkling like sun had fallen down to earth.

"I believe I have not missed anything at all," The thirteenth Princess replied with a mirtless show of teeth.

"No, my millay moy you have not. The Gordians have never been particularly fashion forward and I can see the evidence in this very room," Tarquin's censure was palpable despite the smirk.

"See! I told you. I am not completely lacking in sense. He is Somerlian," Lucita exclaimed. Her voice caught the attention of most of the occupants in the room.

"You married a Somerlian?" Jasmine gasped clutching her fan to her chest dramatically. Three of the Princesses scooted their chairs closer to give Jza's husband a rigorous look. They were disheartened to see that beyond his plain clothing they could not find fault.

"Yes," Jza shrugged, not caring what they thought of this pertinent bit of information.

"Father would not let your husband on the throne," Jacqueline unknowingly repeated Tarquin's assertion, "I wonder why he even bothered calling you here. Is that what you did to be banished to a disgusting farm. Run away with some Somerlian soldier?"

"Look closely," Jza sheer amusement dripping over her brittle smile. When she had accepted her father's invitation she had informed him she had no intention of hiding her husband's identity. There were people who knew what he looked like and it was just foolish to not expect them to talk, "I know you've seen him before. There was once a painting being bandied about of a certain Somerlian King that caused Cassandra and our other sisters to lose their heads. Is he as handsome as the image you saw of him?"

"You did not!" Rosalinda shrieked alarmingly loud. Even her father and his advisors who were quite removed from the conversation looked up in alarm.

"They're not very bright are they," Tarquin completely ignored the women craning their necks to get a good look.

"Ah, yes," Jza's father interjected, cutting off whatever his daughters had to say, "Lord Tarquin joined our family as did all of your husband's."

"Father, he is the enemy!" Rosalinda protested, "How could you allow her to be so odious."

"He was but he laid down his arms and signed a treaty indicating so. It was signed and approved by me not long after the war ended," The King explained and pointed at the framed treaty on the wall none of the occupants had noticed besides those that had signed it. The sisters closest to the wall peered at the treaty, hoping to get a closer look.

"And you would have him in running for the throne. Just because he is royalty unlike my husband," Jasmine was most put out by the fact that her husband was no longer the highest ranking in the competition.

"He is not under running and neither were your husbands," King Samuel placed his hands on the desk in a commanding fashion, "But all of my daughters were, especially Jza. I have reversed the law of Primogeniture. A male heir is no longer required to be sat on the throne. We voted in the law last month. I have chosen my heir."

"You would have a farm runner sit on the throne," Rosalinda was scandalised to have Jza's name be placed in the forefront not knowing they were not even in the competition despite her father's claims. He only spoke as such to soothe their fragile egos.

"You do not know how she led us to victory during the war. Jza broke out of the castle and rescued the captured Goridian men. She also took Lord Tarquin prisoner. I assure you the fall of the Somerlians had nothing to do with me," King Samuel explained with a grave expression. His temper was starting to flare at their insolence.

"If she took him prisoner then how come they are married?" Jacqueline was the only one who dared to inflame her father's ire. She could not believe the improbable tale her father was uttering.

"A strong women can fell any man's heart. Jza's mother nearly gave me a black eye when we met and yet I married her," The King uttered with bark of a laugh at the end.

"Father you must reconsider," Jza walked to the her father's side barging through the army of advisors that were on all sides. She knew very well what her father had planned for her.

"Why? The throne must go to one of my heirs. Why not you?" The King shrugged as if the matter was out of his hands which was not even remotely the truth. He was the only one with the power to choose.

"The people will revolt if they knew who my husband is!" The girl tried to reason with her stubborn father.

"They will accept you when they find out you are the sole reason the war ended. Everyone will know of your bravery. And people love a good romance, do they not? A war that began with hate ended for love. What a tale for the generations!" The older man laughed as he imagined the glory that was to follow. He was already planning to find the best poets to create pretty poems for the bards to spread. If his daughters' beauty could have a multitude of famous poetry then why not his daughter's bravery.

"I must think. Father, I have my farm, my cows, my family," Jza said. She inadvertently looked down at her belly that had yet to show any sign of the impending good news.

"Darling, I am young still. I do not intend to pass on the throne so soon. You will have time to run your farm, to raise a brood, the cattles and your own," Her father reassured her knowingly. Tarquin had already written to him about the arrival of a new grandchild.

"I must think upon this matter," Jza announced and with her father's dismissal she left the study with her husband trailing behind. Before the door could close behind them they could hear the room errupt in a cacophony of sounds. Her attendant was alarmed to find them out of the room so soon but found his composure and started to lead them to their rooms.

"I do not believe I can do this," Jza exclaimed in the privacy of the corridor as her feet stilled of their own accord. Their accompanying attendant was keeping a safe distance from them as he led the way.

Tarquin laughed at her uncertainty and pulled her close to him. His nimble fingers tilted her face up.

"My brightly lit sun. If there is anyone who can do it, it is you. I will always remember the fire in your eyes when you told me you would not bow to a false king. That fire will make people follow you to the ends of the earth. You are more than capable I vow it," The man whispered so close his breath gently flowed over her face. It gave her much joy when he unconsciously exhibited Goridian mannerisms and speech because of her influence.

"You are not sad you gave up your throne but here I am gaining mine," She asked, as she started moving again.

"I am proud you gain it on your own merits then having to snatch it," Tarquin answered truthfully. His wife rested her head on his shoulder as a wave of nausea hit her.

"Their perfumes were obnoxious," The Princess said with a growl.

The rooms they were given made the pair laugh out loud alarming their attendant even further. The man gave them a tour which was far from necessary. They could navigate the room blindfolded.

"It's our room," Jza hissed with a wave of the hand.

"The room of the future heir," Tarquin remarked understanding the meaning behind the King's gesture.

"Father must have decided before we arrived if he had given us this room. Only the future heir can stay in these rooms."

The room was remarkably different from the time they had spent on it. The wall coverings, the bed, the paintings were new. Even the extensive wardrobes from the previous time had been changed.

The King had left many gifts for them to explore at their leisure along with delicacies from all over the kingdom. Their outfits for the upcoming ball were laid out on the new seating area as a gift from the King. Tarquin's clothing gave them pause. His clothing was the exact replica of his Somerlian military outfit with sash and medals laid out in their boxes. The largest jewelry box contained his crown.

"Tarquin!" Jza shook the silent man. The sight of his outfit had rendered him speechless.

"He truly intends for me to retain my identity," The man answered with disbelief still lacing his tone of voice.

"I wouldn't let him hide you," The Princess was adamant.

"I know," The Lord answered with a saccharine sweet smile. He turned around and his easy grin turned wicked, "At least we can now share a bed."

"Hush! Or you shall have the floor for once."

+++++++++++++

Their entry in the ball caused a small commotion with all heads turned towards their arrival. Perhaps the attention was gained because of Jza's radiant silver dress that reflected in the mirrors all over the wall or perhaps it was Tarquin's foreign military attire. He certainly looked the part of a Royal if he had not before.

After being announced by the herald and bowing in front of the King they took to a sparsely crowded corner to avoid the stares being sent their way. Jza was looking at the young children also present as custom of the Goridians when she realised the nanny caring for a small child was familiar.

"That's Sofiya!" Jza nearly pointed but remembered to keep her voice discreet. Tarquin looked away instead of facing the direction Jza was gaping at.

"Do not bring attention to her," The man muttered before being handed his drink. He sipped slightly and with hooded eyes gave Sofiya a glance which the woman returned.

"I wondered where they went," Jza said, mimicking her husband in discreteness.

"The harem always land on their feet," The Lord answered with a smirk. His back was now towards his old friend. They would pretend they were strangers from now on.

"A nanny to a child is not a glamorous task," Jza said, although she wondered if Tarquin counted himself as one of the harem members.

"It is still close to as much luxury as possible in this political climate. I just worry the next time we meet she isn't the wife of the Lord's baby she is holding. At least she shall not have to kill the wife. Multiple wives are allowed here after all," The amber eyed man speculated leaving his wife speechless. She merely snorted into her glass of water.

"I would warn them but I do not wish to unseat Sofiya's position especially if she has no insidious plans," The Princess thought out aloud.

"Let them learn the harsh lessons. If the man is stupid enough to be seduced away from his wife and child by a governess then he deserves the loss of fortune he will soon have at her feet," Tarquin said with disgust. He could not abide by weak people who showed no loyalty to the ones they loved.

Their conversation was interrupted by the herald's announcement for silence. The King was about to make his speech.

"Tonight we are here for a momentous event. I wish to declare to the world my heir. She is beautiful because she looks like me but beyond that she has all the qualities that are required to rule the nation. She is quick thinking, smart, brave and determined. She is the reason we ended this war on a peace treaty instead of further bloodshed. She is my daughter Jza who carries a fragment of my heart!" The King announced at his throne and gestured towards his child. A servant revealed a gold crown far grander and intricate than her usual tiara.

"I suppose that's why I did not have my crown with my outfit," Jza's face was steely as if she had a battle to contend to. Tarquin gave her a lingering kiss on her cheek and his smiling face was the last thing she noticed before heading through a sea of faces to her father's side.